First Thunder

First Thunder
An Adventure of Discovery

By
MAHARISHI SADASIVA ISHAM
MSI

THE *Ishaya* FOUNDATION *Publishing Company*

1-888-474-2921
www.theishayafoundationpublishing.org

ISBN #978-0-9843233-8-8

Dedicated to

the Ishayas of the past, present and future

"And I saw another mighty angel come down from heaven, clothed with a cloud: and a rainbow was upon his head, and his face was as it were the sun, and his feet as pillars of fire:

"And he had in his hand a little book open: and he set his right foot upon the sea, and his left foot on the earth,

"And cried with a loud voice, as when a lion roareth: and when he had cried, seven thunders uttered their voices.

"And when the seven thunders had uttered their voices, I was about to write; and I heard a voice from heaven saying unto me, Seal up those things which the seven thunders uttered, and write them not."

-- The REVELATION of Saint John the Divine

CONTENTS

Part I: *Seattle*

Part II: *Greece*

Part III: *India*

Part 1
Seattle

*"Vitam Impendre Vero --
Consecrate Life to Truth."*

-- Juvenal

1

Spring Crocuses

My old Chevy truck, last with me as it had been the first, carried me to Seattle, burning only slightly over a quart of oil every two hundred miles. Mother welcomed me, but I knew her too well to miss her disappointment. The daughter of a devout Presbyterian and the sister of a Missionary, she felt violated by my life. None of her core beliefs about divorce, employment, responsibility, family or honor were unshaken by my fall.

My plans pleased her even less. During the long drive home from Missouri, I realized that above all I needed time to nurture and heal. I wanted to understand why my life had run aground on the reefs of outrageous fortune, why my business and marriage had been ripped apart by the hurricane of despair; I desperately sought a new course for the foundering ship of my being. Why was the Universe so callous, so hateful? I had only wished to be a good person. Why was the desire to be an honorable citizen, husband and father not enough?

I recognized now that even during the best times in Missouri, I had felt an emptiness inside, a strange and painful hollowness no amount of prosperity had ever filled. My new cars, my limestone castle, my family, the honor of friends and community -- nothing satisfied the undercurrent of discontent moving just beneath the calm surface. The tragic lie of false peace!

I still hoped there must be answers somewhere; but I was sure no one I knew had any -- scrape away the veneer of their belief in God, Science, family or wealth, the same emptiness was growing in them, a destructive mocking authority that found joy only in pain. No, everyone on Earth was as lost and confused as I: everyone believed in struggle, in suffering, in sickness, in death. I did not feel life should be so, but I had no alternatives to the imperious demands of my melancholy. The answers from religion, science, philosophy were incomplete, incapable of offering more than a sugar-coating of belief over the raging cancer of inevitable ruin.

So began my withdrawal from the world. I could find nothing of interest to do. I no longer ran, I no longer read, I called no one, I saw no one except my mother who gradually lost all hope in me but at least housed me and fed me and talked to me -- from time-to-time.

I don't know how long this soul sickness would have lasted as I descended from thoughts of self-violence to immersion in a dull apathy that left me staring at the walls of my room, praying for sleep so I could stop regretting the past; nor do I know how it might have ended in a final cataclysm of despair or rage had nothing different happened. (I do know this, however: never again will I harshly judge those who end their own lives or surrender control of themselves to jailers of the body or the mind.)

But finally something different *did* happen -- at last the winter of my life ended with the first buds of spring. The Universe moved on, God or an angel was moved to compassion, some good karma returned from a previous existence -- for whatever obscure reason, a new theme ascended through the frozen wasteland of my heart.

This new movement began simply enough -- a former high school friend called late one Friday evening. His name was Ollie Swenson, he had just returned from the Greek island of Patmos off the coast of Turkey, he had something he wanted to share with me, could I ferry over to Bainbridge to see him?

I remembered Ollie best as the linebacker on our varsity team who negated my single touchdown interception by clipping the quarterback, but he had through much of high school been my best friend. We lost touch when he went to Washington State

University in Pullman to master agriculture; I had gone to the University of Washington in Seattle to become a research physicist. I didn't know if he had changed his desire or not, but mine transmuted drastically by graduation, due in part to my terminal romance with a Missouri farmer's daughter.

What would he be like, my old high school buddy, Ollie? I remembered he married his teenage sweetheart, a pleasant girl who grew up near his grandparents' home on Bainbridge Island; I also vaguely recalled hearing he was divorced. What had carried him to Greece? And why an island?

Fearing he wanted to sell me insurance or interest me in some new pyramid scheme, I nevertheless agreed to come to Bainbridge on Saturday.

When I walked off the ferry and met Ollie, at first I did not recognize him: he looked about as different as I could imagine. I remembered him with a crew cut, bulging out T-shirts at 240 pounds. Now he was quite slim, maybe 170 -- trim, not malnourished -- and his hair had grown long and was flowing in dark waves all around his tan silk collar. He was beardless, but something about his brown eyes reminded me of a feral animal -- free, wild, unpredictable.

There was more to him than this, a feeling I couldn't pinpoint or readily describe. He was calm beneath the wildness; there was an aura of wisdom about him. This did not come from his appearance, nor from his greeting (he hugged me warmly, then kept his hand lightly on my arm as he escorted me to his Honda), nor even from his words; this deep serenity and knowingness radiated from his presence itself. I did not understand it, yet it resonated with *something* deep inside me. I did not know it, and yet I also felt I knew it well, as if it were speaking to an integral part of me, a part with which I was hardly familiar and yet was my fundamental reality.

His peace resonated within me; at the time I did not have the words nor even the thoughts to understand this, but I did recognize

I felt extremely comfortable in my old friend Ollie Swenson's presence. Why?

Someone was waiting for us in his Civic. Someone wearing a bright red blouse and gorgeous golden curls. Ollie opened her door; she stepped out gracefully. The curls flowed in glorious profusion around a flawless face. Her azure eyes were deep yet warm. I felt myself blushing. Stunning beauty always makes me feel like a school child standing before the principal.

"I'd like you to meet Sharon Alice Stone," introduced Ollie. "She is the most exceptional woman I've ever known."

"Sharon Stone? The movie star?" I asked, attempting weak humor, entirely missing Ollie's point.

Sharon smiled at me genuinely, oblivious to Ollie's praise, unoffended by my poor joke (doubtless far beyond stale to her, I realized with growing chagrin), and embraced me warmly. I hugged her awkwardly as Ollie finished his introduction of me, "...The best defensive end Shoreline ever had," which did nothing to lessen my embarrassment.

"Come on," said Ollie, "we can talk back at the house. Sharon's made us some lunch." I squeezed into the back of his Civic, Sharon settled like a feather into the front passenger seat, then turned to talk to us. Neither of them fastened their seat belts. I reached for mine but soon gave up, realizing it had been swallowed by the seat. *When in Rome,* I thought, mostly listening to Sharon chatting about her childhood in Oklahoma.

"Why did you leave the Midwest?" I asked, briefly reliving the horror of my past few months there. "Tired of the cold?"

"Following my heart," she laughed gaily. "Seeking larger meaning than I was finding in Tulsa."

"But why Seattle?" I persisted, her easy manner causing me to feel more relaxed. "Three hundred days of rain a year makes all Seattle-ites gloomy and introspective, didn't you know?" My past month of an Eeyore-like existence was not easy to drop on instant demand -- even in the presence of Ollie's transcendent peace and

Sharon's joyful beauty. *Even Pooh and Piglet can't reach me, eh?* I thought, judging myself again.

But they both laughed generously and brightly as Ollie replied, "That's three hundred days of *clouds*, old friend; it doesn't rain so much, only forty inches or so a year -- hardly ever on Bainbridge, as a matter of fact. Part of the rain shadow, you know. A real banana belt. Plus these days, espresso grows on every street corner. Starbuck's coffee capital of the world, that's our Emerald City. People are much too hyper to be depressed here."

Sharon added earnestly, "For the first six weeks, I had no idea why I was here. I had begun to think maybe I was insane, as my former boyfriend tried to convince me. But then I met Ollie three days ago; now I *know* why I came to Seattle." She looked at him and smiled with radiant warmth.

Will anyone with such gorgeous lips ever look at me like that again? I thought. My heart longed to ask her what she meant -- Why had she come to Seattle? What had she found? -- but something inside me was afraid of what she might say. I didn't want my life to become more complicated. Even though it was killing me, it was all I had of security in a painful world.

So instead, I asked the vastly easier, "How did you two meet?" What were they? An instant romance? They didn't seem to be affectionately touching. *Certainly not like I would be if she were my girlfriend,* I thought, then felt embarrassed again. This time my feeling was embellished by contempt for my arrogance and self-loathing for my stupidity. What could I offer any female these days? Poverty and failure? My life was ashes; I was the original fool.

Ollie was staring at me in the rear view mirror. His brown eyes were dancing with mirth! It was not a judgmental laughter mocking me; it was a pure and simple happiness singing there. It felt as if he were looking right through me. How much had he intuited of my thoughts?

He smiled warmly at me and said, "I had a feeling I should walk over on the ferry last Thursday. Sharon was sitting alone on the Observation deck, crying as if her heart were breaking. That was just too sad: it was a gorgeous Seattle day -- the Olympics *and* Cascades were out; Mt. Rainier was floating like a vision of dream heaven over the city; even Mt. Baker was visible in the distant North. When the sun shines in Seattle, it's like nowhere else on Earth. The sky was a fabulous royal blue, the Sound a deep, royal aquamarine, the forests a dark, fathomless green, the sunlight glittering over the water a royal pathway to the gods. I felt as if I were in the Wizard of Oz, Seattle truly deserved its nickname of the Emerald City -- and there was poor Dorothy, completely missing this glorious Pacific Northwest moment, crying her eyes out on the Observation deck, oblivious to all the wonder and joy. I realized I had to talk to her, to offer her an alternative to life as she knew it... Here we are."

He pulled into his driveway, lined with old Douglas fir -- not first growth (there are precious few left of those primeval trees anywhere -- a logging tragedy inherited from our careless ancestors and continued by our own thoughtless generation) but some ancient second growth. *Bainbridge was probably logged fairly early in Washington State history,* I thought, impressed by the size of the hundred year old trees. I remembered suddenly I had been here before -- this was once his grandparents' farmhouse. It dated from the turn of the century, by its appearance; apparently several acres still went with it: no new homes were encroaching.

The yard was unkempt, but someone not too many years before had sculpted it to perfection. The weeping cherries and flowering crabs and plums had already strewn the ground with their blossoms and were fading, but the azaleas were bursting in glorious crimson, violet and gold profusion and the rhododendrons were counting down to their annual explosion with thousands of mature buds. It all appeared a little slice of paradise.

Ollie took us around his grounds before we entered the house. In the back, he had built a huge Japanese garden complete with weeping cedar and hemlock and an enormous koi pond with waterfalls and stream beds. "Take me a while to get it back in shape," he said, a touch of melancholy kissing his tones. "I hated to leave this for Patmos. But it turned out to be the smartest thing I ever did."

"How long were you in Greece?" I asked, mostly to be polite -- my attention was captivated by the size of some of his bonsais -- I had never seen larger or more beautiful specimens. Even in neglect, Ollie's garden was magnificent.

He noticed my true interest; instead of answering me, he said, "That one is nearly three hundred years old. Mo Takata gave it to me when I graduated from Pullman. His great grandfather brought it over from Japan. Interesting it should be so attracted to you. It doesn't often respond to many. Too old, I suppose. See how it sparkles, Sharon?"

She smiled at him and said uncertainly, "I think I'm beginning to, a little."

"What are you two talking about?" I asked, impatient with what seemed mystical nonsense.

"It doesn't matter," Ollie chuckled good-naturedly. "Come on in, let's have lunch. I told you Sharon made a *great* fruit salad, didn't I?"

Something about his manner soothed me instantly. We entered the kitchen and sat on wooden chairs that looked as old as the house. There was a bright blue plastic cover on the table; the walls were a pretty yellow; a skylight above let in ample light; all-in-all, Ollie's kitchen was airy, very pleasant and well equipped. Sharon dished up three enormous plates of her fruit salad. The porcelain serving bowl was so full it looked as if they were expecting about half a dozen others.

"Your mom about?" I asked past a bite of fresh strawberries and watermelon. I remembered her warmly. Ollie's father had been a full-blooded Norwegian, a builder by trade; he was killed when Ollie was young; she'd raised their five children alone. Her name was Gladys, but we always called her, "Happy Bottom" -- which she always took in the best of humor.

"She died two weeks ago," Ollie said without any discernible sadness. "That's why I'm here and not still on Patmos with Lance and the others."

"Oh! I'm sorry," I said sincerely. I'd liked her a lot. She'd always seemed an ideal mom.

"There's no need," he replied warmly. "She lived a full life and died peacefully. I don't think she'd have accomplished much more, even if she'd lived another twenty years. My only regret is I didn't have the chance to share what I learned in Greece with her. She'd have loved it."

"Tell me why you were there," I said, putting down my fork. I liked the fruit, but would have been happier with something a little denser. A Big Mac, in fact, would have suited me just fine.

Ollie, perhaps simply desiring to be a good host, followed my lead, put down his fork and pushed back from the table. He studied my face intently for a moment, then said, "Do you remember Alan Lance?"

"No -- oh, you mean the All-State fullback over at West Seattle? Vaguely. We partied together after games a few times. A really nice guy. Why?"

"We became good friends at W. S. U., but I lost sight of him after we graduated -- I went into the landscaping business, you know, with Mo Takata and his sons; he moved out to Sedro Wooley to work his uncle's dairy farm. I pretty much forgot about him, but three years ago, he called me up; I went to see him. He looked completely transformed; I liked what he said and decided to return to Greece with him. He's still there, on the little island of Patmos, with a dozen or so others."

"What are they doing?" I asked, wondering if that was the very question that would begin what I was afraid was going to be a sales pitch.

"Studying, mostly," he replied with a far-away look in his eyes, "but not in the sense you are likely to think. Most of their work is done in Silence, seeking to understand the inner Self."

"They meditate many hours every day?" asked Sharon, looking up at him as she popped an enormous cantaloupe ball into her mouth. She was obviously enjoying the sweet fruit very much -- she had already made a big dent in the large bowl.

Meditating, I thought. *I have entered the Land of the Weird.* I wondered how long before I could gracefully leave. Did I even care if it was graceful? I had no fondness for cults or anti-Christian practices, no desire to get involved.

Ollie seemed aware of my discomfort. He smiled at me, then answered Sharon, "Well, they *Ascend* eight to twelve hours every day, normally. But it's not exactly meditation, it's not some strange Eastern or 'New Age' kind of thing. It's more like prayer -- but even that word doesn't convey what Ascension *is*." He looked affectionately at me. He didn't seem to be frothing at the mouth, just sincere. And earnest. "Both words lead to misunderstandings, based on previous and common uses of them. Most people think of concentration or mysticism when they hear of meditation; Ascension is effortless and systematic. Or they think of religion when they hear of prayer; Ascension requires no beliefs of any kind. That's why we call it something new, we call it Ascension. They -- and I -- practice Ascension, which comes from an ancient Teaching, never before widely available in the world. It is a type of silent inner prayer or meditation that everyone there believes came from the Apostle John."

"Patmos!" I exclaimed as an old college memory collided with the present. "Isn't that where St. John wrote his Apocalypse, the Book of Revelation?" I had once thought of visiting there -- when I was in the midst of a short-lived burst of "Born-againism." My fundamentalism lasted until I realized I couldn't resolve my root belief in a loving, caring God with a God who could condemn 99.99% of humanity to eternal damnation.

"Exactly," answered Sharon, smiling approvingly at me. "Ollie has been studying and Ascending with a group of monks who believe they are following the true but hidden teachings of John -- and of Christ."

"Oh now, come on," I said, my temporary enthusiasm transmuting to a repulsion born of fear. "Every sect of Christianity, every cult on the Earth from Waco to Guyana says, 'Our way only! All else are doomed to hell. Why, we won't even be buried with those miserable sinners -- we'll have our own private graveyard so we'll be easy to find during the Second Coming.' I don't need this." I pushed my chair back and stood to leave.

Ollie did not stand, but looked at me with eyes filled with fire. It was not anger, I sensed -- it was intensity of commitment.

"Patience, number 70. Let me explain before you storm out."

Hearing my old football number triggered a flood of past memories of my friend. I had been very close to him. Could it be so bad, just to listen for a little while? After all, he hadn't asked me to *do* anything, nor even to *believe* anything -- at least, not yet. And I *had* asked him what he was doing in Greece -- and, to be fully honest, who could say? Maybe if I could cut through all the silliness, he might know *something* which would help me -- my life wasn't working as it was going, that much was certain.

"Well, all right," I said gruffly, sitting down again. I was still flushed and not sure that I was making the correct choice, but perhaps I owed my friend this much. "Just keep it short, OK? I've got a lot to do today." A bald lie which fell flat even to my ears.

Ollie didn't say anything, instead slid his chair up and leisurely ate his fruit. Meanwhile Sharon, to all appearances oblivious to my rage and discomfort, emptied the rest of the bowl onto her plate and set herself the task of finishing it. *Fruit must be all she eats,* I thought, observing that the quantities she was consuming would give terminal gas to many others -- myself included. I poked at my mostly full plate but ate little more.

Ollie finished his lunch, sat back again and said to me, "You remember my true love was baseball?"

"Sure, you bet!" I exclaimed, grateful the subject had turned to something less threatening. "In fact, weren't you scouted during the playoffs, our senior year?"

"I was. Two agents came. I knew they were there, so before the game, I went up to the umpire as they were talking with him and said, 'Hey, if I hit the ball over that fence, is it an automatic home run?' He kind of sneered at me and replied, 'Sure, kid, but don't worry, it's never been done, by much better hitters than you.' I could tell he was thinking I was some kind of case. But when I saw that pitch coming in the seventh, I *knew* I would hit it over the fence; after I did, both the Cubs and the Red Sox said they wanted me in their training camp."

"But you didn't go," said Sharon simply, wistfully eyeing the empty bowl and my nearly full plate.

I pushed it over to her; she gave a little gasp of surprise or joy and leapt at it as Ollie answered, "No, I wanted to be educated. And I wanted to master agriculture. So I chose what I *really* wanted."

"Riches and fame or happiness?" I asked sarcastically.

Ollie ignored the tone and answered earnestly, "I chose what I thought would bring me the most happiness, yes. The most growth. And the choice worked well for me; I was successful materially and enjoyed my job. I love working the earth, sculpting beauty in three dimensions. But when I saw Alan Lance again after all those years, I realized he had something more than I, something for which I longed but thought I would never find. I couldn't quite identify it, but he was radiating a kind of peace or understanding I did not know."

"Born again?" I said, but the sarcastic tone was gone -- his description exactly matched what I'd been feeling in him -- a serenity and wisdom I longed to share.

"Not at all. Or not in the sense that you mean it. But that is exactly what I asked him three years ago. Lance laughed and explained he had learned a series of techniques called 'Ascension Attitudes' that were transforming him. He told me his life was changing on the basis of new experience, not new belief, and said I would discover the same thing if I could be bold enough to try it. He said there were twenty-seven techniques in all, divided into seven 'Spheres' of Attitudes, each Sphere consisting of about four techniques, each Sphere more subtle and more powerful than the one before. He said that humanity as a whole was going to learn to Ascend, and commented this was all prophesied by St. John nearly two thousand years ago and also by every other great culture on the Earth at one time or another, including the Egyptians, Mayans, Hopi, Chinese and West and East Indians; but most if not all of these prophecies had been distorted or misinterpreted or lost."

"How could Alan have discovered those techniques?" I asked with little interest, believing nothing.

"He met a monk in an orchard on Samos, one of the Greek Islands. This monk said he was one of a hidden order that had retained the full Teachings of Christ through John; for the first time in history, they were desiring to share these with the world. Think of it! The original Teachings! Unadulterated by centuries of distortion, poor translation and selfish revision." He stopped and looked at me as though he expected me to comment.

"This all sounds too fantastic, Ollie. Alan Lance, star fullback turned dairy farmer, stumbles across the authentic teachings of Christ? Come on, you can't believe this, you're sounding like a psycho." I had never stopped wondering how I might leave without violating the bond of friendship; the desire was at times intense, at others subdued, but always there, gnawing at me. This whole escapade was ludicrous. I wanted to get out of there, to go back home to my room.

"You may go back home to your room anytime you wish," said Ollie with perfect sincerity.

My jaw dropped slightly -- was my thought so transparent? "I - - I don't care to leave," I stammered. "At least, not yet."

"I have no desire to convince you," Ollie continued, again smiling at me. "I don't want to browbeat you or convert you or anything like that. I'm only telling you that Ascension is available. Either you will resonate with this opportunity -- or not. I don't care if you believe it came from Christ or from Joe the Hot Dog man down on Pier 59. Nor does it matter in the practice of Ascension if you believe in it or not. Belief is not required, it is absolutely not required.

"I called you because I heard you lost your business and family and were in Seattle at your mother's, seeing no one, withdrawing from the world. I *know* what I have can help you, but you are not expected to know this. All I ask is for you to suspend your disbelief just long enough to give the First Attitude a fair chance. If you can do this, it will transform your life. The self-destructive internal programs you've picked up from childhood will melt away as you experience the Silence within; your constantly running habits of judgment will be replaced by a constant appreciation of the wonder and beauty of the world. No stress, however large or small, can withstand the power of this Teaching. Ascension has cured me of my childhood traumas; it has led me to an under-standing of the world I often dreamed about but never thought possible to live.

"Every word I have told you today is true. This is not my belief, it is my *experience*. Each of the twelve Ascension Attitudes I have been given -- each of the three Spheres I have been fortunate enough to learn -- is magical, transforming, unequaled in my personal history. I do believe this Teaching came from the Christ -- it is that good. But again, don't take my word for it! If you wish to learn even the First Ascension Attitude, if you can be that bold, come back here tomorrow again at noon.

"This much more I can tell you -- you have nothing to lose and everything to gain. You only have to be willing to take a stand for Life -- you need only to be willing to say to the hurt and crying self inside that the guidance of your ego has led you nowhere but to destruction. Your ego wishes to kill you; it is making you very uncomfortable right now, because deep in your heart you *know* what I'm telling you makes perfect sense and is consistent with what the best part of you knows to be true. That part longs to be innocent again, to be free, to believe it is possible to find meaning in this harsh world, to remember that life is filled with magic, with wonder, with joy, with Love, with Truth, with Beauty -- and another part of you wants to keep you locked in your mother's house, staring at the walls, waiting for death to free you. Part of you feels you deserve to suffer, that anything that happens to you that is bad is not only warranted, it is probably not even enough. You have to decide which voice you wish to hear!

"The fact is, I'm here now; you're here now; something inside you must be ready to learn the highest Teaching or you wouldn't be here. Your time and your world is ripe. The simple truth is: no one can even read about Ascension without being ready to read about it. Your challenge is to recognize the part of you that is responding to my words and realize that it stands for your lost dreams and true hopes. You need to acknowledge the way you've been living your life is not only pointless, it is leading you nowhere you want to go. Partly you need to see that *you* are worthy of miracles in your life. You are a child of God, a creation of omnipresent Love and Power, therefore worthy of all success and happiness. Truly now, truly! Do you think you *deserve* to suffer?"

Ollie ended his monologue and sat back further, watching me, waiting for my reply, wondering, perhaps, about the effect of his words. I glanced at Sharon; she had stopped eating to stare at him, my unfinished fruit still before her, a watermelon ball stuck on her fork, her hand part way to her mouth, her arm frozen in space. Had she never heard him talk this way? Did he have a different approach for everyone he felt drawn to contact?

Finally I swallowed hard then confessed softly, "Sometimes I think I must. I don't understand why God let my life get so messed up. I don't know if you can help me; I guess I would like it if you could." What did I have to lose, after all? Sitting in this bright kitchen with Ollie and Sharon was like a vision of paradise. With a shudder I remembered my dark room in my mother's gloomy forest. Even as my mind had rebelled at the thought of trying anything new, my heart had been opening to the presence of peace I felt in Ollie. "What do I have to do?" I asked, with almost complete sincerity. Was I really ready to move ahead?

"Not much. Come back tomorrow at noon -- I want you to think about it overnight, see if you're really ready to move ahead, if you're willing to try anything new." A thrill shot up my spine as I realized he again used the words I was thinking. Ollie grinned at me, apparently noticing and understanding my surprise. This did nothing to lessen my confusion. Who was this guy? An empath? A walk-in from the Pleiades, replacing the Ollie I had once known?

"So, if you're willing, come tomorrow; I'll teach you the First Attitude. If you take to it (as I'm sure you will!) I'm qualified to share the first twelve with you over the next few months -- I can teach each of the first three Spheres. Try it and see. As Lance's Teacher told him, 'If you want a different fruit, plant a different tree.' Plant the tree of Ascension in your garden, water it well, tend it and see if it matures into the Tree of Life for you -- see if its fruits of Peace and Joy and Health don't suit you better than the painful fruits of fearful ups and sorrowful downs you're harvesting now."

The phone rang from the living room, Ollie said, "Excuse me a moment," and went to answer it. It was perched high atop a mountain of sheet music on the Baldwin Grand that filled most of that room -- I remembered Gladys had once been a concert pianist; it was her music lessons alone that enabled her to support her children after her husband died.

"Hello?" he said. "Yes, oh, it's you! Nice of you to call again. Yes, tomorrow will be all right. No. No..."

I glanced at Sharon; she had resumed eating, was just now stabbing the last of the strawberries. Apparently she felt my eyes, for she looked up at me and smiled.

"Never heard him talk that way?" I asked.

She shook her head and answered, "I guess you needed him to be that forceful. If you have mountains of stress, it might take dynamite to remove them."

I replied it was probable I had mountain *ranges* of stress, but suddenly Ollie was shouting into the phone, "No! That is completely wrong! The world needs this Teaching! It has to be released! John never intended this to remain a secret tradition for monks only! No one has the right to keep it from the world! I tell you, this has to come out, and it has to be now... No, I don't care what you do... No... No, I don't believe what he says. I tell you, you have it completely wrong... Fine. Tomorrow then." He slammed down the phone and leaned into the piano, breathing deeply to regain calmness. Finally he shuddered, straightened slowly, turned back toward us with a forced smile and came back into the kitchen. He looked grim and pale.

"Sharon," he said softly, "could you take him back to the ferry? I just realized I've got something I must do, something that should wait no longer. If you hurry, you'll just make the 3:50."

She stood at once. He hugged her then added to me, "You're wise enough not to let your prejudices blind you. Give this a chance; you have nothing to lose and everything to gain." Without waiting for a reply, he vanished into a back bedroom.

I recognized his look -- I had once seen it on my aunt's face when she learned her cancer was pancreatic and terminal. Or was my friend's grimness from another cause? Was I such a hopeless case? I hoped not and resolved to return. After all, what *did* I have to lose?

2

Unrequested Journeys

I did not speak much to Sharon on the way back to the ferry. She seemed somber, darkly thoughtful, almost glum. Was she so attached to Ollie that his slightest mood swings affected her? Visions of cults danced through my head; my ego squirmed in me, telling me to leave and never return.

When Sharon dropped me off and asked, "I'll see you tomorrow?" I replied lightly that of course she would -- but I no longer felt it.

The day had begun gloomily, dismal and threatening, but now the clouds were broken and tattered; cathedral-like rays of sun shone through in many places; the water sparkled with golden brilliance; the verdant forests seemed magical and alive. *It really is the Emerald City,* I thought, remembering Ollie's tale of meeting Sharon. But the beauty did not move far in me: I was more certain with each mile Bainbridge had been a waste of time. "'Omnipresent Power and Love' indeed," I sneered. "Garbage. I've lost a whole day for nothing." I decided to file the whole episode under, "Friends, Past, Insane."

I bought a Times and read the Sports section, then decided to go to the Tractor tavern in Ballard to listen to "Point No Point," a four man band with electric violin, guitar, bass and drums. Maybe their sweet sounds and a pitcher of dark beer would help me forget my day. Of one thing I was sure: I was *not* returning to Bainbridge.

But Sunday found me, only slightly hungover, racing down I-5 to catch the 11:20 ferry. I didn't know why I was doing this, but I did know nothing else had worked for me for a long time and *any* door was better than no door at all. Besides, I *had* felt something from Ollie -- and then there was the *unusual* Sharon Alice Stone, lovely enigma. Another day with them seemed preferable to staring at the lime green walls of my childhood bedroom. After all, I told myself, if I didn't like their so-called Ascension, I certainly didn't have to keep on with it, did I? *Probably some quirky Hindu mantra or something,* I thought as I drove onto the ferry, last in line for the crossing.

I didn't bother to leave my truck during the ride -- I had no desire to mingle with unknown humans. Besides, it was a gray, heavily overcast, drizzly day; Puget Sound at her depressing worst. So I sat in my cab and ate the cheese sandwich my mother insisted I bring and felt bored and stupid.

Ollie's Honda was not at his house; instead a late model and bright red Acura was parked in the driveway. I pulled up next to it and hoped Sharon would think the Acura was mine. *Unless it's hers,* I thought, irritated at my poverty and chain of failures. *At least I can look forward to a pleasant and quiet afternoon. Maybe I'll even learn how to relax, how to suspend my "Type A" behavior. That would be worth the cost of the ferry.*

As soon as I opened the screen door into the kitchen, I learned my hopes about this Sunday had gone seriously awry. The inside of the house was a shambles. *Everything* was upside down, broken, torn open, smashed, ruined, strewn about. I stood aghast in the kitchen doorway. It looked as if a tornado combined with an earthquake and a gang war had overwhelmed the Swenson home since yesterday.

I realized with a nasty shock someone was standing in the doorway to the living room, staring at me. His hair was short, black and tightly curled; he looked as if he might be of Italian or Greek descent; he was dressed in expensive and collar-less black silk shirt and pants. As these perceptions flashed through me, my viscera tightened into a knot and my heart screamed, "Get out of here! Now!"

"Who the hell are you?" he asked harshly.

"None of your business!" I replied. "What's going on? Where's Ollie? Who are you?"

The stranger came toward me warily, moving as if he were not only a trained athlete but a lethal master of his body. I stepped back out of the doorway; the screen slammed shut. That startled us both; he stopped advancing toward me, smiled coldly and began again, "Sorry. I'm Mark Edg. That's E, D, G, Edg. I answer to both but prefer Edg. Ollie told me to meet him here today at noon. I don't know where he is. I found the place like this when I arrived; I don't know what happened. I didn't mean to frighten you. Come back in; we can look around together; you can tell me what you know about this."

He finished crossing the kitchen, opened the screen door and held out his hand. The feeling in my gut had not abated, but I could find no reason to doubt him. Hesitantly, I took his hand, saying, "Ah, you didn't scare me. I was just startled to see the kitchen, that's all." His grip was powerful; his skin cold. I wondered if I had frightened him as much as he me. The weeks of idleness had flabbed me somewhat, but I was still strong -- and the scant attention I'd been paying my appearance lately hadn't helped much. I'd dressed up slightly because I expected to see Sharon again, but my hair was completely unruly lately; my week-old beard probably wasn't serving me well either. This Mark Edg had probably concluded I'd trashed the Swenson's.

The house was a wreck. Every cushion was torn open, every pillow and mattress slit, every picture pulled off the walls and ripped, every drawer open, emptied, broken.

"Why would anyone do this?" I asked, expecting no answer.

"Looking for something, of course," said Edg coldly. "Something small -- a computer disc, perhaps, or some papers. Whatever it was, they must have assumed it well hidden. I've never seen a house so thoroughly dismantled. Even when I was with the blues, we never did *this* much damage to a place."

"You're a cop?" I asked, wondering how straight this Edg guy was being with me.

"Not anymore. Years ago, actually. Undercover mostly." He spoke abstractedly, as if he were hardly listening to himself. His eyes, however, darted everywhere, searching, searching -- he reminded me of a wolf, relentlessly hunting. "Well, maybe Ollie will tell us what they were after. I hear a car coming -- *this* time, I suppose it will be him."

Had we been looking around for an hour already? We walked through the mess back to the kitchen door. It was Ollie's Civic, but Sharon was at the wheel; she was alone.

She looked terrible -- dirt and tears had turned her face into a crumpled pastry of chaos; her crimson blouse was torn; a nasty cut on her leg was only beginning to scab over; her other leg was bruised down its entire length past her shorts. She saw me first and started to smile -- with effort -- but then saw Edg; she blanched and gasped in fear. "Who -- who are you?" she said shakily, as if speech were hard.

"Sharon!" I exclaimed. "This is a friend of Ollie's -- Mark Edg, E, D, G, Edg. He came here to meet Ollie at noon too -- but *what's* happened to you? Forgive me, you look *awful.*" I walked to her and put an arm around her. She sagged into me; she seemed so weak she could hardly stand.

"I -- we -- oh, God! How can I tell you! It's too awful! Here, help me inside, I want to sit down, have some tea; I'll make it, take no time, be just a second." She shrugged off my arm and pushed past Edg. As soon as she opened the door, she screamed. "Oh! Oh! No! Oh, what's happening today!" She started wildly sobbing. I held her again, more tightly this time -- she was shaking all over; her heart was hammering at her chest. Edg walked in past us, righted the table and three chairs, motioned for me to guide Sharon to one, found a pot, filled it, lighted the stove.

The hot tea calmed her. Gradually she shared her story: she'd met Ollie early on the Seattle side -- he came over on the 7:10 to visit an old friend, an herbalist in Chinatown. They never made it. As they were walking up Yesler from the waterfront, a black limo jumped the curb and killed Ollie instantly. "He only had time to push me aside," she sobbed, shaking again. "They didn't even stop! Just raced on down the hill."

"Where's Ollie now?" Edg asked grimly.

"I don't know. I guess they took him to Harborview. That's where the ambulance came from. But he was dead! What difference does it make?"

"You're *sure?*" he persisted, unsmiling, the incarnation of intensity.

"Yes!" she cried.

"I'm sorry," Edg said mechanically, smiling now, but without the slightest warmth. "This is so strange, a horrible tragedy. I don't know what to do. What a nightmare... He didn't by chance leave you anything, did he? Any instructions, any messages? Here or perhaps in his car? Anything about this Ascension he was always talking about? I'm quite curious about it, you know."

Sharon looked at him through her flooding eyes and answered, "I only learned the First Attitude. That's all he had time to teach me. He said today would be a special day, today I would get the Second. I love the First! It works like magic. But he didn't give me anything else. I already looked through his car. There was nothing there. Why? What are you expecting?"

"I don't know. Nothing. Something. Anything. This is all so senseless. He's hardly in Seattle a week and some drunk or druggie kills him. I can't figure this out... Guess I'll go catch the 2:10. See you guys around." He stood abruptly and, giving a half-bow, exited.

I stood up and walked behind him to watch him leave. He did not go straight to his car, but slowly circled the Civic, examining it intently. Apparently finding nothing, he walked over to his Acura and got in, started the engine, powered down his window, looked up at me and called, "Tell your girl friend she's picked up a nail. See ya." Then he backed up and roared away, sending gravel flying all over the lawn.

"What did he say?" moaned Sharon from behind me.

"He said you've got a flat," I answered, editing the words slightly. "He seemed quite interested in the Civic. Damn suspicious fellow. I don't trust him."

"Neither do I," she said slowly, "Which is why I didn't tell him Ollie made us a video. I think he knew something was going to happen."

"No kidding! Ollie *knew* he was going to die?" The hairs started prickling on my neck.

"No, I don't know, maybe. I don't know if it's related or not, but he said there's a group trying to stop the teaching of Ascension. He said they wanted to keep it a secret for monks only; they believe it's too good for average people and belongs only to those who give up all worldly desires and dedicate their lives completely to God."

"Why? It's just a bunch of techniques for meditating, isn't it?"

"Yes -- and no. I don't know much about it, of course, I've only just barely begun with the First Sphere, I've only got the First Attitude and there are twenty-six more. But from what I've experienced so far, Ascension is amazing. I've never experienced anything like it. If it's really true each Sphere is more subtle and powerful than the one before, I can imagine this Teaching is priceless -- *and* it wouldn't be too much of a stretch to imagine some shortsighted and selfish people might want to control it, keep it for their own ends."

"But if it only helps people be better, why would anyone be against that?" I asked, confused.

"Boy, you *are* naive!" She actually smiled a little. "I don't think the world is quite so nice a place as you believe."

"Maybe I have lived in Missouri too long," I answered, half smiling myself. "I guess I believe in the innate goodness of humanity."

"Underneath all the stress and twisted beliefs, maybe," she replied, almost crying again.

"Wait," I said quickly to forestall her, "Ollie made us a video? Where is it?"

"Don't know. Here somewhere, I guess. Let's find it."

We searched through the chaos for two hours but found nothing. If the tape was ever there, apparently someone else beat us to it. Frustrated, I said, "Sharon. Let's give it up. It will be getting dark before long. I'll change the tire on the Civic, then we can decide what to do next."

"OK," she said sadly. "I guess I'll have some fruit. I'm starting to feel hungry again. Didn't think I ever would. This search helped, I guess."

"That's a good sign... I'll be right back."

I returned a lot sooner than I thought I would: as soon as I opened the spare tire compartment in the hatchback, I found Ollie's video camera with a tape in it!

We set up the VCR and TV and were surprised to find both still worked. Sitting on the shredded couch in the disaster that had recently been a well-ordered home, Sharon ate some dates and figs and grapes as I gulped down some cheese and crackers and we played the video.

Ollie was wearing the same tan silk shirt he had on yesterday. The date and time flashed briefly -- it *was* yesterday, and right after I left. Sharon sobbed a little to see him. "He must have taped this when I took you to the ferry," she breathed.

Ollie was sitting on the same couch as we were now. He was smiling, but grimly -- it was the expression he left me with yesterday.

He didn't speak for awhile; at first I felt he was thinking about what to say, but then realized he was trying to master his feelings. He sighed, then began in a low, mournful voice, "My friends. Well, since you're watching this, I guess I'm not crazy -- it must be a valid intuition and now... Now, I'm gone. Strange world, hey?

"But really, this isn't surprising, you know? My father died violently, as did his before him. Youngest son of a youngest son of a youngest son. We were fishing the Campbell River up on Vancouver Island, dad and my brother and mom and me. I was eleven. Roger -- my brother -- didn't go out that morning; said he was too tired. We were trolling out from the shore -- a boat ran over us. The kid was driving, neither he nor his father was watching where they were going. Neither were we -- Dad had just leaned forward to bait the hooks. Mom and I were in the bow. It was quite early, fortunately Roger slept in. Mom sat in the middle, but I was cold and scared and I asked her to come up beside me. Good thing, the other boat would have killed her too...

"I saw it, you know, at the last instant before it hit us -- I had time to shout, 'My God, no!' The boat was coming straight at *me,* you see. I was sure I was dead -- my whole life flashed before my eyes. Yes -- it does do that. Quite short and fast. And an enormous light that is more than light at the end. I remember being confused: I didn't think it was supposed to be my time yet.

"It wasn't. Because we were moving out from the shore, the boat missed me and took my father. Didn't touch me or mom at all. Right over us it went, gouging out the side of our boat. Mom flew to the back, crying, 'Jack! Jack! My God, Jack!' She held him, but his head was smashed and ruined; he didn't live long.

"When she moved, the water started pouring in. I had to shift sides so we didn't flood. Took a picture of the gash in the boat after they towed it back to shore. Still have it somewhere. It's hard to believe they didn't sink us. For years afterward, I had visions of that boat coming at me; every night when I went to sleep, every time I closed my eyes. It burned that deeply into my soul.

"Violent karma in our family. Former Vikings, you know. Killed many in war. Fierce, vicious, violent. Might have been cursed, I guess.

"No, this doesn't surprise me. A palm reader told me I'd never see thirty-five -- abrupt end to my life line. I outlived that! But I always kind of believed her, she said this other break here meant I had nearly died at eleven, had been as if reborn at that time. So she must have been pretty good, huh? To hit the boating accident so well?"

Ollie stopped speaking and stared down at his hand. He looked up after a moment, tears welling in his eyes. "I've actually been lucky. One Vedic astrologer in India, studying my birthchart, exclaimed, 'Mars, so unhappy in the Eighth, the House of Life! Amazing you haven't died yet. Violent death probable.' Beat that too. So far."

He put his head in his hands and said nothing more for a long while. Then he shook himself all over, looked up, chuckled a little, smiled with an echo of exuberance and continued almost cheerfully, "Hey, none of this matters! I'm probably just making all this up. No one will ever hear this tape. And even if I'm not, so what? Life in a body and death of a body are two sides of the same coin. What endures forever is the One Unchanging. I don't think many people on Earth even have a clue about the Ascendant. It is all that was, is or ever will be. This existence in a body is meaningless.

"What *does* have meaning here is the helping of others. Our world stands poised on the brink of destruction -- you know that, of course. I have been fortunate to discover an ancient series of techniques, a Teaching founded by Christ and his beloved Disciple John, a precious knowledge with enough power to transform this Earth within a single generation. I believe the Seven Spheres of this Teaching have to go out from the single monastery where they have been preserved for the past two thousand years. There are some who agree and inspired this way of thinking in me; there are some who disagree for various reasons; there may be a few radical ones who are violently opposed to Ascension entering the world.

"I don't expect either of you to understand this fully, not yet, for neither of you knows much about this Teaching. Nevertheless, I'm asking you to do this. I want you to go to Alan Lance in Patmos and tell him he was right, the Opposition will stop at nothing to keep Ascension from the world. You could call him, but I feel it imperative you go there. I believe you both have something great to contribute to the world; you *need* the full power of Ascension to bring out your own special gifts.

"I'm not saying you *have* to go to Greece. I'm *asking* you. If ever you have loved me, if ever we have shared anything of Truth or Beauty in this world, if ever you have respected me or wished me well, do this for me. I have a little over $20,000 left; I've written you a check; it's in the video camera case side pocket. You'll need to cash it as soon as you can: they'll probably freeze my account once they know I'm -- once they hear the news.

"I want you to fly to Athens -- no, wait a moment..." He cocked his head to one side and stared off into space as if he were listening to someone we couldn't see or hear. "No. No, first, I want you to contact my friend Dave Tucker. Tell him what happened, explain Ascension to him, invite him to go with you. He was the next person I was going to call... He's a doctor who lives on Clyde Hill in Bellevue. Yes, it's worth looking him up. Then after you ask him, if he agrees or not, on to Athens. Catch the first boat to the Dodecanese Islands. Alan Lance has a villa near the monastery of St. John. He'll tell you what to do -- *and* teach you more of Ascension.

"You must be thinking this is all too bizarre; in one sense, you're right, it is. This Teaching should be available to all as our birthright. It can be and must be a vital force for good, to uplift the world from the destructive dominance of the 'Me-first' ego. Really, I don't see any other hope for the world. If my life is given to further this Teaching, my death will not be pointless.

"I want to inspire you! If I can just make you understand: this Teaching of Ascension *is absolutely real*, if you can just *see* that, you will join us in this quest. You will practice it yourself, you will discover it is as natural as life itself, you will help others learn; the entire Earth will rise in glory, in a crescendo of Praise and Gratitude and Love; the Golden Age will return and stay for all time. This, I believe, is the collective destiny of humanity. Not to suffer along more and more painfully and eventually fail, but to rise to perfection as a fully evolved human race. This is the future Ascension freely offers the Earth.

"I love you guys. Sharon, I -- I hear the Civic returning. I'm sure we'll have a nice evening together. I'll mention nothing of this to you until tomorrow. I love you!" He stood up and walked toward the video camera; the picture clicked off.

Sharon was silently weeping, her fruit largely untouched. I put my arm around her and said, "Guess we better call this Lance guy, huh?"

She pulled away and almost spat at me, "Call him! I'm going to Greece! Didn't you hear him? What he said? Are you a coward?"

"Well, I might be," I said, looking for and finding the check. It was made out to no one, but it was for $20,320 and was perfectly signed. "This sure would be useful right now, though. I'm behind two months on child support, I need a new car -- this could be the break I've been praying for. A chance to start over."

"That is for my trip!" she said icily, her eyes daggers. "If you cash it, I'll tell the police you stole it."

I sighed and said, "Oh, I wouldn't use it. I'm too honest for my own good. I was just playing with the idea. An idle fantasy. Here, take it, it's yours... You're serious about Patmos?" It was mad. Two days ago, Ollie Swenson was a pleasant childhood memory. Then he shows up in my life, speaking impossible dreams, is killed by some drunk, leaves me a video saying he expected to die and asks me to go to Greece to further his vision.

Why would I want to go to Greece? Images of the Aegean Sea flashed through me -- whitewashed buildings, deep blue waters -- I *had* desired to go there once, but had never made it farther than Italy. I realized my passport was still good for another couple of years, but had no desire to leave the USA. I could hardly get out of the bed in the morning! Travel to Greece! What a nutty idea. How could Sharon be committed to it?

"Of course I am. You haven't Ascended, but I have. If this technique is only the beginning of the First Sphere and each Sphere is more than the previous, I *know* I want them all."

"Well, I haven't experienced it. Can you teach me? That might help me understand."

"No, I haven't been trained. I promised Ollie not to teach others until I learned how. That surprised me a little, the First Technique is so natural and simple. He told me people might misunderstand it if it were not properly explained; he also felt they might not value it unless they worked at least a little at it to get it. He said he might charge $100 or $150 for each technique, simply so people would feel it was worth practicing for awhile, give it a chance. We are such an 'instantaneous gratification' society -- if it were free, people might not give it a fair trial. Many people want change immediately without being willing to go through the inward work that makes growth real and permanent."

"I can see that," I agreed, thinking with embarrassment of the hasty choices I had often made in my life. "People want everything on a silver platter -- and they don't value anything that is free. No one wants to work for anything anymore, it seems."

"So, I can't teach you. I mean I could, but I won't. He may have had other reasons as well, I don't know; but the bottom line is: I promised him. The only way you're going to learn is by dropping your doubt and cynicism long enough to be bold and come with me. Think of it as a great adventure -- after all, what are you doing with your life now?"

Not much, she had me there. But traveling half way around the world? Was I that nuts? "I tell you what. Let's get out of here. My truck isn't much, but it will take us back to Seattle. Let's get you cleaned up, go out to dinner somewhere really nice -- up on the Space Needle, maybe -- the dinner deck revolves, did you know? See the whole skyline by the time dessert is over. Once I get this all in perspective, I might see my way clear to join you. Where are you staying?"

"With my aunt -- she lives near Green Lake in a duplex. Mary's nice and supportive but hasn't shown any interest in learning to Ascend. She thinks it's just another fad."

"Well, maybe it is. But Truth is True. If this Ascension works as you say, sooner or later everyone everywhere will be doing it. Everything has to start somewhere, sometime. Even the belief that the Earth is round was once cause to be burned at the stake. The flexible change and grow and enter into a new world. The inflexible can't change, they don't continue growing, they fail to make the transition and they die... Come on, let's catch the next ferry. I don't think there's anything else here for us."

"Well... there might be one more thing. I saw some pretty dresses in one of the closets. I don't suppose Ollie or his mother would begrudge me one. If any of them fits... Make us some reservations, I'll be just a minute."

She hurried into the other bedroom and shut the door. As I heard the shower start, I smiled, oddly feeling better than I had in many days, then looked for the phone to call the Space Needle.

3

Dinner on the Needle

Sharon emerged from the bedroom, ravishing in a floor length, low-cut ball gown of silver and black. "Wow!" I exclaimed. "You look great!"

"Don't look too bad yourself," she smiled back at me. I had taken her lead and found a white tux that fit me surprisingly well -- Ollie must have last worn it when he was still larger. I glanced in a frying pan hanging by the stove and had to admit I did look pretty good. I chuckled to think how such elegance would appear in my nasty old truck. There was no way to take the Honda -- the spare was not in the trunk.

We drove in silence to the ferry. Even my mind felt numb. I don't recall thinking about anything. But after we'd parked and were waiting for the ferry to empty, I told Sharon I'd gotten hold of Dr. Tucker; he'd agreed to meet us at the Needle.

"Great!" she exclaimed. "Receptive?"

"Hard to say. He didn't know why Ollie included him in his message, but his curiosity was piqued. I didn't mention Greece or Ascension, thought I'd leave that for the expert." I grinned at her.

"I'm hardly that," she smiled back at me. "But I know the First Technique must work for me. I never could have been this calm after a day like today ever before. All the stress just washes over me; I feel a deep peace that says, 'It's all right. In spite of all appearances, it's OK. Don't worry, everything *will* work out.' I don't know, I've never felt like this before."

"I feel that calmness in you. If Ascension can do that for everybody, it will sweep the world."

Our line of cars started inching forward, entering the ferry. "Such wonderful creations our civilization makes," I mused as we drove aboard -- the size and power of the huge boats always deeply impresses me.

A sack of garbage was broken open on the beach beside the dock; three black crows were picking at it; a dozen seagulls flew around them, cawing angrily. "And yet, our stewardship of the Earth is so imbalanced. Look at that trash! How could anyone be so careless? What value our technological marvels if we kill our planet?"

"I think if people became more conscious, they'd act better. There wouldn't be so much short-sighted violence if we understood how our thoughts and actions influence everything around us."

"Maybe. But we have a horrible habit of spoiling our garden. I can't help wondering if there is a devil working to mess everything up."

"Don't know! But I think we need to do the best we can, regardless what other powers may act behind the scenes."

I stopped the truck behind a new gray van and asked, "Shall we go up?"

"No -- I want to Ascend. Go up if you like. Or stay. But I want to do this for awhile." She shut her eyes.

"My being here wouldn't bother you?"

"Not at all," she answered dreamily. Her breathing had already slowed, become shallow; her face looked more peaceful than it had all day. She seemed to shine with an internal radiance.

Quite curious, this Sharon Alice Stone, I thought. *What a bizarre day. How could Ollie have known he was going to be the victim of a freak accident? Well, what if it wasn't an accident? Why was his home ransacked? What if it was murder!* A chill shot up my spine; a cold sweat broke out on my face. I gripped the steering wheel to give me some stability, but it didn't help much.

Calm down. Relax. Think this out. Ollie wants us to tell his friend Lance that 'the Opposition' is real. What does that mean? Were some of those Opposite people here, in Seattle? I recalled what I had heard of his phone call yesterday and shuddered. My heart started pounding at my chest. *Why did someone trash Ollie's house? What were they after? His notes about Ascension?*

I wanted to ask Sharon what she thought and glanced at her. Her radiance had increased: she was glowing, bright as a light bulb. I stared at her in amazement: golden light was flooding out through her skin. She looked as if she were about to Ascend permanently.

I was calmed to see her, but then I remembered a third time the way Ollie's house looked today; my heart thudded harder, feeling as if it were trying to burst out of my chest. I gripped the steering wheel so tightly my knuckles turned white; I willed the ferry to race across the Sound so I could drive again, be active, do something! Anything not to continue thinking.

What was I dreaming of? Greece? I must be mad! The idea seemed like lunacy, born of a deluded mind, frustrated by my recent string of failures. *What if it's true Ollie was murdered? Will they come after me? Are they so determined to stamp out Ascension in the world? Who could say? They might be watching me right now!* I looked around furtively, terrified. *That gray van in front! Why were its windows so dark? Was there someone inside?* I tried to remember whether anyone had gotten out of it when we parked.

Sharon touched my arm lightly and said, "Are you all right?"

I jumped and hit the top of my head on the roof. "Don't do that!" I cried, rubbing my skull. Realizing I was being unreasonable, I continued, "Sorry. You startled me. You have unbelievably blue eyes, you know? I've never seen anything like them. Not ever."

"I don't know if that's exactly what you were thinking, but thank you... You were shaking the whole truck, sighing, groaning. What's going on?"

I looked at her sheepishly and answered with a question, "You don't think we're in danger, do you?"

"Is the ferry about to sink?" she asked with mock concern. "No, I don't think so. Not at the present time. Why should we be?"

"I don't know; I was just putting everything together: Ollie's death, his trashed house, his saying someone didn't want him teaching Ascension, that Mark Edg fellow, Greece. I don't know. I just started feeling something awful was about to happen. I guess I'm paranoid, huh?" Talking had composed me: I was embarrassed for disturbing her Ascension.

"I think Ollie's death was an accident. And simply a coincidence some crazy kids vandalized his home. I don't think anyone would care *that* much about stopping Ascension. I think his time here was just over, you know? But, hey, even if I'm wrong, you and I don't know much. Next to nothing. Not worth anyone's time."

"*We* know that. But do *they*?"

"Assuming 'they' exist, who knows? But we're leaving for Greece anyway. Or at least, I am; I hope you'll join me... Feeling better? We've still got twenty minutes or so, I'd like to Ascend a while longer, I am (or was) having a *great* time."

"Sure," I said, even more embarrassed. "Sorry. Kind of lost it there for a moment." I closed my eyes as she did. The steady throbbing of the ferry's huge engines was soothing, relaxing; I felt myself drifting into silence...

The next thing I remember was Sharon shaking me and saying, "Hey, wake up! The cars are moving." In a daze, I started the Chevy; we drove off. It was low tide, the ramp was steep. The Washington State ferry attendant raised his eyebrows when he saw how much smoke I was polluting his blessed Emerald City with.

"Wonder if Ascension could fix my rings," I muttered, blushing.

Sharon laughed and replied, "Maybe if you'd stop beating yourself up, your life would start coming together."

I looked at her with respect and said, "You know, that's good. I didn't know I was so easily Seen. I thought I was hiding pretty well."

"I seem to be becoming clearer," she said without pride or false modesty. "I don't think I would have known so much before Ascension. Mostly my life was boring if not downright awful -- my last boyfriend was a disaster of abuse; I was lucky to get away before he killed me. I think, no -- I *am!* going to make an executive level decision to stop dwelling on what's gone wrong today and look instead at what's going right.

"Ollie said all Power and Healing is in the present moment -- in the pure joy of Here and Now. 'The past is over, better to forget it,' he said; 'the future never comes, better not to worry about it.' I think I know what he meant. Regret for the past and fear for the future are the twin nets the ego uses to keep us bound to its petty demands and faulty counsel... I think this is why Ascension is practiced not only with the eyes closed. Ollie said all the First Sphere Techniques are also done with the eyes open, whenever we happen to think of them. Not by straining or forcing but by simply choosing, we Ascend consciously. I'm doing this right now, for example. And in this way, my mind is being restructured from fear to peace and harmony and love."

"That's beautiful. I wonder if it's possible for that to happen all the time?"

"Don't know. But it sure feels better than the old way of using my mind."

We pulled into the parking lot at the Space Needle. A holdover from the Seattle's World Fair of 1962, it rises in strangely steeled beauty more than 600 feet; it is the one structure that makes

Seattle's skyline absolutely unique. I was feeling considerably better -- so fine, in fact, that I let the valet park my truck, rather than look for a parking place. I perversely enjoyed his look of dismay when he saw me turn into his lane. *Afraid his pretty outfit will get dirty,* I thought. *What a shame.* But I told him, "Take good care of it. They don't make them like this any more."

"Boy, is that the truth," murmured Sharon. I grinned at her as we walked to the line for the elevator.

Dr. David Tucker was already seated, staring over Elliott Bay. He was about our age, tan, muscular with close-cropped blond hair and a handsome face. I felt a twinge of jealousy. The good doctor was languidly stirring a green olive in his martini and was slouched forward, indicating, I thought, he was ever so slightly bored -- he was too important for this kind of thing, perhaps, or maybe he was simply weary of a life of wealth and prestige. I wondered how well this meeting might go. But he straightened when he saw us and flashed us a smile that seemed sincere.

The doctor made no joke about Sharon's name; my face colored, remembering yesterday. *He's probably too busy to watch movies,* I told myself to defend my ego. It was all small talk for a few minutes as we settled in and ordered our dinners. Sharon declined a cocktail; I ordered a glass of chardonnay and told the waiter to bring it with the meal.

As soon as the waiter left, Doctor Tucker leaned toward us and said earnestly, "Tell me what happened to Ollie."

Sharon described the accident at some length. She remained much calmer this time and added the detail, new to me, that the limousine swerved all over Yesler before and after it hit Ollie.

Was that so? I wondered silently. *Or is she trying to convince the doctor it was just a drunk? Definitely an accident? Is distorting information wise?*

But I held my tongue and did not ask for clarification. After all, I had not said I would accompany her. Doctor Dave was doubtlessly well off. And was tall, tan and good looking. To be tan in Seattle's spring almost certainly bespoke of wealth. Could I blame her for seeking another companion on her trip to Greece? Especially one sanctioned by her recently departed mentor? Had she ever been abroad before? Here she was, ready to plunge boldly into the unknown, and I was too afraid to say I would go with her.

"So, why was I mentioned on the video?" Dr. Tucker asked as she finished. "What did he want to tell me? I didn't know him that well. Met him in church a few times, shared a couple of salmon barbecues, that sort of thing. Hadn't seen him at all in what? Two or three years? I'd almost forgotten him."

"Ollie just returned from Patmos, where he --" I began, but he interrupted me.

"Patmos! Where St. John had his Revelation and wrote the Apocalypse? You're kidding! I've always wanted to visit Greek's Holy Island! Tell me more about this!"

Sharon and I exchanged surprised glances; I continued by visual agreement, "Ollie said he had just returned after three years there, studying with a group of unusual monks. He was learning a series of techniques called 'Ascension.' Everyone there, he said, believes the Seven Spheres of these techniques came from the Apostle John."

"Ascension? The White Brotherhood, the Ascended Masters, that sort of thing?"

"I don't think so, no. No, not at all. Something from Christ."

"What then?"

"A series of techniques to Ascend, or rise beyond, the chatter in the mind and experience silence," answered Sharon, for I had run out of words. "The mind is normally quite noisy, you know, thinking useless and self-contradictory things all the time."

"It certainly is," agreed the doctor. "I have a friend at Stanford Research Institute who says the average adult thinks some fifty thousand thoughts *every day*."

"Right," I continued, having discovered something else I thought worthwhile, "and how many of those serve anyone? Most of them are about the past or the future or the distant -- about things that aren't Here and Now. Ascension changes that by stilling the pointless noise in the mind."

"To what end?" he asked quietly, almost too quietly. Were we losing him?

Sharon beamed at me in obvious approval and answered confidently, "When the mind is still, the body works less hard. The mind and body are one -- two expressions of one reality. When the mind settles into silence, the body stills. Deeper rest than sleep results; this allows stress to be thrown off, improving the healing process. This silence also rewrites the old internal programs. Beliefs based on limited and painful experience are replaced with a new sense of wonder, joy and peace as one learns to remain in the Ascendant."

"The Ascendant? What's that?" The doctor's eyes had glazed over; he looked like a case of information overload. Or maybe he was reacting as I had yesterday; fear was closing his mind.

Sharon answered, "The Ascendant is the One Source of everything," but just then our waiter returned, bearing our four dinners -- lobsters for the doctor and me, a fruit salad *and* a dinner salad for Ms. Stone.

"Hearty appetite!" exclaimed Dr. Tucker, looking more amused than critical.

We ate without speaking much as we gazed from time-to-time at the panorama of Seattle turning slowly below. The clouds had scattered and largely ended; stars were peeking out beyond the glare of the city lights.

Finally the doctor put down his fork and said, "Your Ascension sounds like a panacea. Too good to be true. It's like a medicine man's snake oil for every problem. It irritates me Swenson was involved. I always thought of him as intelligent. I don't know you two, but you seem pretty sharp yourselves. So what are you doing, getting into this? Sounds pretty far out."

"I've found it does wonders in calming the mind," began Sharon, but Tucker interrupted --

"So does Zanax. But I don't think everyone should take it."

"The difference is that any drug has side effects. Ascension is completely natural. It's the best thing I've ever done. I don't pretend to be an expert on it, I've only just begun, but I'm going to Patmos to study it. And Ollie asked us to invite you. You seem successful in your work. I don't know why he wanted us to talk to you, nor do I know what he would say if he were here. Perhaps he would simply ask you, 'Are you happy, Dr. David Tucker? Are you content with your life and your world?' Only you can answer that, but I'm pretty sure Ascension holds gifts for you too."

I expected the doctor would be offended and answer self-righteously, "Of course I'm happy! Who are you to ask!" Or else simply get up and leave, but instead he stared down at his nearly finished lobster and said softly, as if to himself, "Everyone expects doctors to be gods, to have all the answers about everything, all the time. I haven't had a real friend in years. The truth is, I don't know anything, anything at all. I don't think anyone does. I make over two hundred K a year and live in a seven thousand square foot home in one of Bellevue's nicest neighborhoods and you know what? I'm miserable! And so *bored.*

"I can't believe I'm saying this. I never talk like this to anyone. I can't believe I'm considering this. But I am!" He looked up at Sharon and stared her squarely in the eyes as he continued, "No, I'm not just considering it, I'm going to come! Yes! Yes, I will drop everything of my life and run off to Greece with the two of you!

"God knows, maybe I'm having a breakdown and you two with your mystical talk are just dreams, flitting through my padded cell at Overlake General -- but then, I don't care! I've never been to Greece, and you know what? I always wanted to. Almost majored in Grecian studies. Loved the *Iliad* and the *Odyssey*. Dreamed I would wander all through the Greek peninsulas and islands, writing novels about my experiences, traveling from Thrace to Rhodes to the Peloponesos to Attica to Syracuse...

"But then this confounded doctoring with its dull grind buried it all and here I am, years later, living a phony life of false power. No, I've nothing to lose. And who knows? Maybe everything to gain. At the least, it will be better than this. So, what the hell? Sign me up. When are we leaving?"

The restaurant had turned as we talked; now we were facing East, toward the Cascades. An enormous, slightly past full Moon rose over the peaks, bathing all of Seattle in a magical, silvery light. "Tomorrow," I replied, grinning hugely at them. "There's a TWA flight to Athens via Cincinnati and Frankfurt, leaving here at 1 PM... Well, I never said I wouldn't *check*," I added to Sharon, seeing her mystified smile.

4

Dancing in the Moonlight

Monday morning was a whirlwind as we packed, cashed the check, secured our tickets, bade hasty farewells and hurried to Sea-Tac. Sitting in row three of the giant 747, shaking our heads in disbelief, we found ourselves taxiing down the runway at 1:15.

I had thought first class extravagant, but my companions reminded me what our legs and backs would feel like tomorrow if we were cramped in coach; their arguments, Tucker's casual use of wealth plus the heady feeling of having ten thousand dollars cash in my pocket all combined to persuade me.

Sharon and I were on one side of the aisle; the good doctor on the other: he opted for the extra seat, in case the flight was not full. His fortune was good -- no one sat beside him. Settling back with a sigh of contentment, he closed his eyes as we moved to the takeoff lane.

I was in a minor state of shock I was here at all. I was half-praying I wasn't being a fool, my sanity burning up in the fires of jealousy. Seeing Doctor Dave's Porsche as we exited the Space Needle last evening hadn't exactly put out the flames. Once I saw his car, I decided to wait for my truck; instead I asked Sharon to walk with me through the Seattle Center, enjoy the moonlight, watch the dance of the International Fountain. A host of bittersweet memories flowed through me (my father died there when I was fourteen, victim of his second heart attack); I rationalized my desire to walk with Sharon and did not attribute it to jealousy.

Regardless of my initial motives, Sharon was a wonderful companion. I'd never felt more relaxed with anyone -- she was light, charming, even joyous, the more remarkable considering the harshness of the day.

Afterwards she agreed to accompany me to the old stone water tower in Volunteer Park on Capital Hill -- climbing that and staring over the city was an experience from high school and college I had enjoyed with many. But time changes all. The tower's gate was chained and locked -- a small sign said it was open during daylight hours only.

So instead we drove down the forested Interlaken Avenue to the University's Arboretum, parked the truck by the closed entry gate and walked through the grounds in the moonlight. The sky was completely clear and practically blue, the Moon was so bright. We could almost make out the colors of the azaleas, rioting their exuberance; many of the early rhododendrons were also bursting with flower; the soft vibrancy of the silver moonlight gently showered onto us, transforming the Arboretum into a garden of magic.

I felt transported back to a more innocent past -- many times I'd walked through this glorious place, sharing its wonders with my love of the hour, but at no time was it more glorious or wonderful than during this moonlit stroll, due entirely to the delightful ease of Sharon's presence. Gone were the fears and shakes from the ferry; banished were the dark doubts and terrors of the day; I felt younger and more alive than I had in years. As I shyly took her hand, she clasped mine eagerly -- her flesh was soft, fresh, warm; I felt myself falling and did not ever want to stop.

But after I dropped her off at her home (fervently promising to return by 8 AM) and was alone again, my doubts plagued me once more. What if I was being a fool? What if this enterprise really was life-threatening? I had no desire to die for this unknown thing. I wonder if my growing love for Sharon would have been strong enough for me to master this final challenge, promises or no.

Fortunately, Nature was generous with Her messages tonight. When I returned to Lake Forest Park, my mother was frantic, almost in terror. I had never seen her so distraught, not even the day the coroner's call beat the minister to our house by five minutes with the news my father had discovered the hard way it is not always wise to believe advertising. He had quit smoking after his first heart attack, but when the tobacco barons came out with filter kings, he thought he could still enjoy the taste without any side effects. It was a terminal learning experience, that second myocardial infarction.

He should have known better: he owned an advertising agency. He told many laughing stories about the stunts they pulled to popularize unpopular items -- once, when TV was new and yogurt unknown to most, he created a live spot with a local celebrity, had him eat yogurt in front of the camera. This guy was supposed to say how good yogurt was; dad *knew* he would think it was anything but, so he substituted ice cream for it. The commercial was a rousing success as the celebrity declared with sincere amazement, "Hey! This stuff is good! Yogurt tastes like ice cream!" But I digress.

I held my mother to calm her: she was shaking, deeply frightened. As I pieced her story together, she told me two fierce-looking long-bearded Indians in white robes and turbans had come hammering on her door, looking for me.

"Sikhs?" I asked, amazed. I knew there were many of these kind of Indians in Seattle, but I didn't know any.

"Seeking *you*. I already told you that. They were the most fearful men I ever saw! Long beards, never shaved; turbans! Robes! *Fierce* eyes! Why were they looking for you?"

"I'm sure I don't know. Did they say anything else?"

"Something really obscene! They started talking about asses' ends! That's when I said I was going to call the police --"

"Ascension?" I asked, my heart once more pounding at my chest, my stomach once more tying into a hard knot of cold fear. "They asked about Ascending?"

"Is *that* what they meant? Oh dear, I've been a little silly, haven't I? They had such thick accents; you know I don't hear so well... But when I mentioned the police, they started talking fast in some heathen tongue and left at once. What's going on? You selling drugs?"

"No, mom, I'm not. Listen -- I've decided I'm going away for awhile. I don't want you to worry. If those guys or any others like them come around, tell them I've gone back to Missouri, OK?"

"Oh, you're not really going back there, are you? To *that* girl?"

"I'm going, but not to her. I think it's time to face my own personal demons. You tell them that, OK?"

I called Sharon and was relieved to hear neither she nor her aunt had any unusual visitors. I packed in an hour and left to seek a few hours fitful sleep in a motel on Aurora Avenue...

As our 747 gracefully lifted off the ground, I said, "So, now we've ascended."

Sharon grinned and replied, "Off to learn the secrets of the Ancients."

Dave leaned toward us across the aisle and said, "Bon voyage, bold adventurers... Although I'm not exactly sure why I'm attending this mad tea party."

"Time will tell," I grinned at him; I was starting to like this guy a lot. It hadn't hurt that I'd noticed he was forty-something and never married: he probably wasn't much of a threat, in spite of his appearance. The most handsome people, I've discovered, sometimes stay single. It must be hard to find someone willing to look past the surface, someone willing to see beyond the exterior to the person hiding within. I have wondered if that is why some otherwise lovely people choose obesity -- they want to be loved for who they really are, rather than for their bodies.

"Tell me about the Ascendant," he said to Sharon. "I don't think I've quite got it."

"As I understand it," she answered slowly, "the Ascendant is the Universal, non-changing Absolute that underlies all forms and phenomena in Nature."

"Like 'the Force' in Star Wars?" I asked curiously. "I've often wondered whether that existed."

"Sort of, yes, but not exactly, for the Force could be used for good *or* evil. But the Ascendant lies beyond all duality, beyond all opposites like good and evil, right and wrong, hot and cold."

"The *noumenon* of the philosopher Kant, perhaps," said Doctor Dave thoughtfully. "Or Plato's Ultimate Idea, forever beyond the Universe and yet the One Source of everything. Plato said the information from our senses is not only limited but always misleading; it tells us nothing of the real nature of things. Behind the chaos revealed by the senses lies a realm of Eternal Order that alone is truly real. I think he called it, 'The Good.' He said we have all been as if chained in a cave since birth, seeing only the shadows of reality, never the Good, the Ultimate Reality which is casting the shadows. But a fortunate few can escape their chains and see the One Unchanging Light. I don't recall him explaining *how* they were supposed to do that! But he said their job after leaving the cave and experiencing true Light and Living was to come back and help those still imprisoned by the false life of the shadows.

"St. Paul echoed this when he said, 'The things which are seen are temporal; but the things which are not seen are eternal.' I've always wondered if the Absolute were real. The underlying God-stuff out of which everything is made. Philosophers have talked about it for thousands of years, but aside from a few mystics, Christian saints, rare Buddhists and enlightened yogis, I don't know any who could say they have drunk deeply of it. With good reason! If it lies beyond everything, how could it be experienced? Quite a logical quandary, the whole issue."

"Sounds like," I agreed. "Yet that is what the Twenty-seven Ascension Attitudes are supposed to be all about, Sharon said. Experiencing the Ascendant. Right?" I looked at her for confirmation.

"Exactly. Each of the Twenty-seven is like a mine shaft into the Ascendant. Each connects the waking state mind to the Silence and Order within, each in a different way. When one has mastered all the Seven Spheres, Ollie told me, every moment is lived in Awareness of the Ascendant."

"'Praying without ceasing!' That has to be what Paul meant, it has to be!" exclaimed the doctor. "This *really* excites me! I'm glad to be here -- if this is possible, it will rank among the great discoveries in history. It might even be the greatest discovery! It would be the answer to everything. Unlimited knowledge and power must be the handmaidens of the infinite inside, which means--"

"Wait a minute," I interrupted him, "I'm confused. You say, 'the infinite is inside.' How can infinity be within us? Isn't anything inside necessarily limited? We're not that big!"

"Not according to the mystics and Christian founders," answered the doctor. "They've all claimed the inside is larger than the Universe, that God truly is 'a circle with center everywhere and circumference nowhere' as the monks put it in the Middle Ages. Or as Blake said, 'To see a world in a grain of sand, and a Heaven in a wild flower, hold Infinity in the palm of your hand and Eternity in an hour.' In the Upanishads they say, 'That which is smaller than the smallest is larger than the largest.' A wonderful concept, really. Even if it's impossible to understand with the waking state mind."

"'Our senses lie to us.' That is what Ollie said," added Sharon. "He said that our three-dimensional Universe is a cunning deception, an ingenious lie. The senses keep us from recognizing we are all One -- that God is within every one of us, that we are all Universal Beings of Light, miraculous, wondrous Eternal Beings, Co-creators with God, not limited animals who live a short while, suffer and die...

"I don't know. I feel Ollie more with me now than when I was with him. I don't know. I think the belief that our bodies are our most important part is false. So many go to any length to protect their physical structure, but never give a moment's thought to their inner Being. I wonder if Ascension might not be opening us to a whole new way of living, a way that puts us back on track with the original intention of the Creator."

"I guess we'll find out soon enough," I commented, then turned to stare out at the Cascades passing below. We were already through the thick clouds that covered the Puget Sound basin today. The tips of the high mountains were poking through; it was a glorious, sunny afternoon.

Up here, I thought, *the Sun always shines. Could healing all of life's problems be as simple as this ascension in altitude? Was this the coming wave of the future? The entire human race, bored at last with its pointless wars and ego-based conflicts, shrugs it all off and Ascends to a new perspective, bringing peace and progress and prosperity on a global scale? What a sweet thought! Then Ascension would be the ultimate gift to the world. No wonder they attribute it to Christ. I suppose a devout Hindu would say it came from Krishna or Shiva and a Buddhist, from Buddha. Only the greatest one of our belief system would be capable of creating such a Teaching.*

I turned back to Sharon and said, "Thank you for permitting me to accompany you. I don't know how I could deserve this."

She looked startled, then smiled sweetly at me and squeezed my hand. "You're welcome. And don't worry -- you deserve this because you're you. I would have no other sitting at my right hand

on this incredible journey." She leaned into me and kissed me --
neither long nor passionately, but with a sincerity I had never
known before. I was surprised I felt no carnal desire with her, not
now nor at any other time. Was this pure love being born? I didn't
know, but I knew I had never felt so uplifted by anyone's soft
caress before.

"I can't wait to learn to Ascend," I said, then put my chair back
and stretched out my legs. I had never felt clearer, calmer or
happier.

I wonder just how calm and happy I would have felt had I
realized that riding this same plane, quite far back, were two
fanatical and intense Punjabi Sikhs and, further back still, one not
so fanatical but perhaps even more intense Mark Edg?

Part 11
Greece

*"Life, like a dome of many-coloured glass,
stains the white radiance of Eternity."*

-- Shelley

5

Three Planes and a Taxi

Plane travel blurs together for me. Only a few experiences of this journey stand out in memory. We landed in Cincinnati at eight, boarded passengers and took off again before nine. Dave was less lucky this time: an enormous German lady settled in beside him. Looking desperately at us, he moved to the single seat in row four. 747's are a rather strange construction, there are five seats in row four -- two on each side and one like an island in the middle. I wondered how he would like sitting out there, exposed to everyone else on the plane, but he didn't seem to mind -- compared to the alternative.

Sharon was ecstatic to discover this flight included an enormous fruit buffet spread all over the front of the plane like a gift from an ancient God of Plenty -- Dionysus, perhaps. She filled her tray greedily again and again as I watched her in amazement. "You always eat like that?" I asked her after her third return trip.

"Whenever it's this good!" she purred. "Someone must have told them I was coming."

"You never eat any meat or dairy?"

"Sometimes fish or rarely some chicken or cheese -- if I really want it. I'm not rigid, just eating what *feels* right. My body is so much lighter when I eat this way. I suppose eating low on the food chain is good for the planet, but that's not my primary concern. I've not been sick a day since I changed my diet -- in more than seven years."

"It obviously works for you. You radiate health and energy. You, in fact, are gorgeous."

"Well, thank you," she said, coloring. "That's nice to hear from anyone, but particularly from a hunk like you. It's funny, I've never adjusted to hearing I'm beautiful -- I was plain when I was growing up. Or at least I thought I was: my father was abusive; I had a weak self-image."

"Abusive? He hurt you?" I was surprised how much this angered me.

"Not physically -- well, not often. He was an alcoholic; my mother, a classic case of codependency. When he was wild with moonshine, he was pretty crazy. I think he loved me, but only when he was sober; that happened less and less as I was growing up. The bank took the farm when I was six. That was almost a good thing: losing our family homestead shook him up pretty badly, almost turned him around. He admitted himself to a recovery clinic; when he came out, he got a steady job as a security guard. My mother's parents bought us a cute little home in Tulsa. I thought his love for my sister Linda and me would save him. But I guess he loved his whiskey more. Mom landed in the hospital, he beat her so badly. A week later, he killed himself in a car accident. It was... it was my sixteenth birthday."

She stared down at her sliced pears, tears glistening in her eyes, half-sobbing. She shrugged at last, looked at me desperately and continued, "Fool! He had it all. My mother was beautiful; we all loved him; he could have had a wonderful life. Instead he threw it all away."

"Alcohol is highly addictive --" I began, but her feelings were churning around too strongly to accept any trite answers.

"Hah! No one is a victim unless they desire it. First the mind is addicted, then the body. Our love wasn't enough for him, or he would have stayed off the liquor. I should have loved him more."

"Maybe you're being too hard on yourself, Sharon? A little? It's not your fault he was weak."

"Oh, maybe, I don't know. I need to forgive him, I do know that. I just wish I could have helped him! If I could only go back in time, teach him to Ascend before he got so fouled up... I don't know, the world can be so harsh." She looked at me pleadingly.

What was I to say? I had not exactly mastered Earth. In fact, as far as I could tell, the only real difference between me and her father was that I had run away from Missouri after the divorce. He at least had stayed with his family and tried to make it work. Could I have done any better? Thinking of nothing useful to contribute, I asked instead, "What about your mother? Still living?"

I hoped that might bring some joy, but I missed the mark. She shook her head sadly and said mournfully, "Suicide. The second year after dad died. Couldn't live with him, couldn't live without him. Linda and I lived with my grandparents until we went away to college... They were good people, but old. They had my mother when they were both nearly fifty. They never quite made the transition to the second half of the twentieth century. They always seemed totally amazed at the world. Yet it was an amazement born from innocence, not ignorance. They were good to us, even if they could never understand us. I dearly loved them."

Dave suddenly walked up to us -- he'd been wandering around the plane, stretching his legs. It was fairly early in the evening; they hadn't turned down the cabin lights yet or started the movie. He knelt in the aisle beside us and said excitedly, "Did you say two *Sikhs* came to your mother's house last night?"

"Well, yes I did. Why do you ask?"

"Because there are two Sikhs on this plane! Way in the back. Probably just a strange coincidence, but when they saw me, they pretended to be furiously busy! It was bizarre. Why would those Sikhs be interested in us, or in Ascension?"

"Did you ask them?" said Sharon in a tone that made it difficult for him to say no.

"Well, ah, no, I didn't. Too surprised. I'll go do it now."

"I'm coming with you," I said, and followed him back down the plane.

The Sikhs were gone. We waited fifteen minutes, then a flight attendant said the movie was about to begin and asked us to sit down. We returned to our seats and announced our failure.

"Curious," mused Sharon. "I wonder what it all means."

"Motion sickness, perhaps," said Doctor Dave. "Hiding out in the bathroom, too sick to leave. Probably just a random event... Guess I'll turn in. Not interested in the movie." He returned to his island seat and wrapped himself in a thin airline blanket. "Lots of leg room," he murmured, closing his eyes.

I followed his example, hoping to reset my body clock through sleep, but Sharon said, "I think I'll Ascend instead. Maybe the deep rest will help balance time. Worth a try."

"Lucky you," I said, closing my eyes.

The remainder of that flight passed in a dream-haze of surging engines, half-sleep, inadequate rest. When dawn's unnaturally early light made further sleep difficult, I got up to stretch my legs and see if the missing Sikhs had yet returned to their seats or had instead jumped from the plane out of terror of the good doctor.

They were there, but were asleep -- their turbans leaned into each other, their open mouths were drooling on their long beards. The thought of waking them flitted through my mind; instead I concluded it was all nothing and decided to forget them. They looked young and innocent.

When I returned to my seat, Sharon was awake and seemed completely refreshed. "I don't think I've ever felt better," she confided to me.

"Well, I personally have felt less rested," I answered, noting my mouth felt like old sandpaper, "but I don't recall offhand exactly *when*."

She laughed gaily, "Poor boy. Here, try some of this orange. See if it doesn't make you feel alive again."

I did and it didn't.

We landed in Frankfurt on time and changed planes for Athens. Another 747; this time we were in row two. I walked throughout the plane after takeoff, seeking Sikhs. There were quantities of tourists and plentiful Greeks, but not a Sikh in sight. Gratefully, I returned to my friends.

The doctor was waxing profound to Sharon about Greece. "-- A poor country. Not much arable land. What there is left has been eroding for more than three thousand years. Large areas are useless to all but lizards and snakes and the hardy ubiquitous goat. The Renaissance paintings of satyrs and fawns in verdant Greece are largely myth. It's semi-arid or desert, three hundred days of sun a year, mostly dry, largely barren. Fairly inhospitable everywhere -- but its saving grace is that almost all of it is within thirty miles of the sea. Not that it helps the economy much -- even the fishing is lousy. Sponges and octopuses, mostly. Not enough in the clear Aegean for the fish to eat, I guess."

"Seems like countless islands and peninsulas," I volunteered, looking at the airline map.

"Countless is about right. Practically all of Greece is mountains and rocky coastlines. And islands. Patmos is over there, see it? In this group called the Dodecanese because once there were only twelve occupied. Now there are about twenty, I believe, including the largest, Rhodes. Patmos is at the northern end of these. Not much to it. Small, sparsely populated. In fact, the fellow who founded the Monastery of St. John there a thousand years ago chose it because it was so austere and ugly, not because the Apocalypse was written there."

"Why did John go there?" I asked. "Why go to a small Greek island, at the time all but deserted, when the entire Roman world was there for him to convert? I don't understand."

"Desiring solitude?" suggested Sharon.

"No, he was banished there by Domitian, one of the more despotic of the Roman Emperors. His wife murdered him -- in AD 96 -- but the year before, he banished John to Patmos. The Empire didn't know what to do with the Apostle -- they boiled him in oil at the Latin Gate, but it didn't hurt him. One fairly Ascended fellow, that Disciple John, I guess."

"I guess," I said without much enthusiasm, deciding the view of Europe out the window was more interesting than such fairy tales. Hearing it made me question again my presence on this journey. Here I was, flying over the shattered remains of Yugoslavia, and I didn't believe a word about Ascension or John or Revelation. Well, at least Sharon was sitting next to me. Of all the experiences of my last few years, none could compare to the sweetness of that single kiss from her last night. Thinking of that, I closed my eyes and tried to catch a little sleep.

Athens looked different from my expectation. I'd thought it would be a lovely, classical town; instead, I saw a sprawling wasteland of poorly designed, riotous urban growth. "Looks like a cancer," I muttered as we descended.

"But look at the Acropolis, floating like a dream above the city," said Sharon softly. My perspective shifted with her words; I saw the ancient beauty below rising to meet us rather than the mindless modern ugliness.

We landed at Ellinikó Airport, cleared customs, changed dollars to drachmas ($1,000 each, as we all assumed the rates would be better here than on Patmos), secured a hotel near the harbor, then caught a taxi into the city, choosing our driver by his fluency in English. He was a largish Greek named Georgios, elegantly dressed in a black suit that had a red carnation in its buttonhole. He wore a luxuriant handle-bar mustache and black slicked hair and had an obvious affection for the ladies from the way he ogled Sharon. But he seemed nice otherwise and sincere as he loaded our bags. Sharon and I got into his back seat, Doctor Dave sat beside him in the front.

"Oh Athens, Athens!" exclaimed the doctor as we pulled out of the airport. "Here democracy was born, here the first great plays were performed, here the philosophers of antiquity walked and endlessly talked, here Pericles ruled and created a Golden Age unequaled in the world before or since, here St. Paul stood to preach his new religion. Oh, Athens! I don't know guys, pinch me, see if I'm dreaming. Have I died and gone to Heaven?"

Our driver commented, "It's so sad you've come during Holy Week. Athens will be still. The *tavernas* will be closing early, most by one. Little *kefi,* the -- how do you say it -- dance of the joy of the heart. All this fasting and seriousness for Lent. *Vradi,* night, is so boring now, no one drinking *ouzo,* no one enjoying the *retsina* -- it is a dark week you have come to Athens, my American friends."

As he spoke, he jerkily accelerated his taxi. Everyone else on the road was doing the same -- it began to feel as if we were in some sort of mad race. His right hand was often on his horn, his left hand clacked his amber worry beads at a frightening pace. Were these drivers all lunatics? How did anyone survive a trip across town? I had driven in Rome and New York City; this was far worse.

"It *is* Easter week, isn't it?" said Sharon dreamily, apparently oblivious to the mad chaos outside. "I'd forgotten. What an auspicious time to come to Greece!"

"I would *love* to tour this city!" exclaimed the doctor, also unaware of our impending death at the hands of a mad Greek taxi driver. "The Acropolis! The Parthenon! I don't suppose we could spend a couple of days here?"

"I think sightseeing is a little low on our priority list," I reminded him as I stared with terror out the window. "I think we need to report to Patmos ASAP."

"Patmos!" exclaimed Georgios, swerving around a car and narrowly averting disaster from a large fruit truck coming at us in the opposite lane. "Holy Patmos! Where John the Blessed drove the wicked magician Kynops into the sea -- Patmos of the Seven Stars! Patmos of the Seven Candlesticks! Patmos of the Seven Seals! I love Patmos!"

"You've been there?" asked the doctor excitedly.

"Myself? Well, actually, myself -- no; but my wife's brother's father-in-law lives on Patmos."

"Really! You know how to get there?"

"Of course. The boat leaves Mondays, Wednesdays and Fridays at noon from the Grand Harbor in Piraeus. It's about a twelve hour trip. Leave tomorrow, Wednesday, and you'll be in Patmos by midnight!"

"Assuming we survive this trip!" exclaimed Sharon, suddenly realizing how recklessly he was driving. She dug her fingernails into my arm as Georgios narrowly missed two elderly pedestrians, a child and a bicycle. His worry beads flipped riotously up and down as he cursed in Greek.

"These people must have invented tailgating," I said, digging my own hand into my leg. The one object of this insane race was apparently to see how close you could come to being wrecked or killed without succeeding.

The doctor, however, was having the time of his life -- he laughed joyously at every near disaster, chuckled with glee whenever we accelerated. "What does that sign 'ΑΛΤ' mean?" he asked Georgios curiously. "We speed up whenever we see it."

"Oh that?" our driver replied gaily. "That says, 'ALT.' It means 'Stop,' my friend."

6

Athenian Interlude

Miraculously, we reached our destination alive. I'd never felt more like kissing the ground in my entire life.

During our riotous run, I hadn't had much time to look at the rapidly passing city, but my primary impression was identical to my thought in the plane -- Athens was built of chaos, unadulterated chaos, surpassing any city of my experience with its unplanned squalor. It seemed a congealed concrete sea, covering all of the land from the mountains to the ocean. Two to seven story ugly buildings sprawled everywhere, stone tumors of poor foresight and unattended growth. Had the modern Athenians any plans at all when they erected their capital? Perhaps they were trying to counterbalance the glory of the old by the vulgarity of the new. Characterless cubes of concrete seemed the dominant building motif. The air was heavy with smog; garbage and sewage were but marginally controlled. Too much immigration from the surrounding countryside and impoverished islands, too many refugees from the wars, too much rapid and unplanned growth -- as with so many twentieth century cities, these were the unfortunate roots of modern Athens.

And yet, in spite of it all, the wonder of being here in Greece, in Athens, percolated through the disarray. The occasional glimpses of the graceful marble works of the ancients poking through the modern transported us instantly between wildly divergent worlds. I couldn't help but feel that in spite of its flaws, Athens was still one of the most romantic cities in the world.

Our hotel, the Cavo d'Oro, was part way up Vas. Pavlou on Kastella hill, near the Turkish Harbor in Piraeus, the ancient port of Athens. It was a thoroughly charming place with a magnificent view of the harbor below. Every room was well-appointed, even elegant, but the little touch of fresh flowers everywhere meant more to Sharon -- she was enraptured on first sight.

There were only two baths per floor; Sharon took one; Dr. Dave and I played "rock-scissors-paper" for the other. I won (my scissors slicing up his paper) and settled into the hot water with a long sigh. The good doctor upon losing decided to postpone his bath, instead gave into the intense feeling that the Acropolis and the Parthenon desired his immediate attention. "The most beautiful structure in the world!" I heard him exclaim rapturously as he asked the landlady to order him a taxi.

Sharon and I shared a delightful evening. It began at one of the many excellent restaurants overlooking the Turkish Harbor. This was a small bay, mostly for anchoring the sleek racing yachts. Pericles, greatest Athenian statesman of antiquity, used to visit there to watch boat races, or so our matronly landlady informed us when we asked her where to eat. "The young in love *always* eat on the quay at *Tourkolimano*, the Turkish Harbor," she said; I blushed but did not release Sharon's hand. There was no question I was falling in love.

The restaurant we chose looked out over a riotous color of pennants, sails, awnings, umbrellas, flowers -- the entire harbor melted together in a kaleidoscope of wonder. I did not feel even a little tired. This was Greece! We had traveled almost halfway around the world to be here tonight. Gardenia vendors strolled by our table, displaying their wares; fortune tellers walked by to prophesy; sponge sellers, pistachio salesmen, a hundred overfed cats -- it seemed all of Athens was lining up just for us. An old violinist accompanied by a heavyset man playing a *bouzoki,* a kind of long-necked mandolin, serenaded us, and then -- wonder of wonders! over Mount Hymettus rose the Moon, three days past full, but glorious as it streamed its silvery light over the Aegean harbor, creating a radiant, sparkling pathway to Heaven.

"I don't know if any of the Ascension Attitudes deal with the Moon," I said, full of emotion and scallops, "But I'm sure at least one *should.*"

"Oh, I'm sure one *must,*" she answered gaily, filling her mouth with the succulent seafood. I was amazed at the pleasure she displayed with the prawn soup and then the scallops, but she laughed gaily and said, "I *told* you I always eat exactly what I want! All this travel -- my body asked for something heavier." I had never met anyone like this Oklahoma beauty before; I was grateful to be with her, grateful to be alive.

It was a long, lazy dinner. We sampled the *retsina,* the wine flavored with wood pitch so many Athenians like, and found it definitely an acquired taste. When the Athenians abandoned their city to Xerxes and his Persian hordes, they poured turpentine into their wine casks to make it unpalatable, hoping the invaders would grow so thirsty they would go back home. They did leave soon enough, but only after they were defeated by the Athenian fleet in the narrow bay of Salamis. Like the Spanish Armada against the English many centuries later, they could not maneuver their bulky ships as well as the smaller Athenian galleys. The iron-tipped Greeks rammed the Persians and sent them to the bottom of the bay. Xerxes set his golden throne on a hill to watch his invincible navy discipine the upstart Athenians only to find he was the owner of the losing team.

He leveled Athens and went home. The Parthenon and most of the city's other temples date from the subsequent rebuilding phase, the Age of Pericles, Athens' short-lived Golden Age. The Athenians, wild with joy at their impossible victory against insurmountable odds, came back from exile and, being thirsty, sampled their turpentine-spoiled wine. They found it not so bad. Or so the story goes. The rather more boring and probable reality is they used pitch to line their wine casks, it helped preserve the wine and caulked the seams. They got used to the flavor.

I thought this an extremely odd custom, but then Sharon informed me that Italian Chianti takes its unique flavor from the giaggiolo lily that once twined its roots around the grapevines. The Italians liked that taste too; now the Chianti makers add lily root just as deliberately as their neighbors across the Ionian Sea add resin to their retsina.

As she smiled hauntingly at me over the yellow gardenia I bought her, I felt transported to a new world of wonder, of joy, of Love. I could hardly think of words, but stared at her like an infatuated schoolchild.

"I hope you will be able to join me soon in Ascending," she said sweetly. "Then we can really start growing together."

"Tell me more about the Ascendant, Sharon," I said in an effort to think about something other than my wildly growing feelings. "I didn't understand what Dave said to us on the plane."

"See my pretty flower?" she asked, holding it out toward me. "Its beautiful color, its perfect form, its delightful scent? This is the surface form of the gardenia, the part we see, the part we appreciate with our senses. It is lovely, but there is more to the flower than our senses perceive.

"There are many levels of reality we can't see or touch or taste or smell. My flower contains molecules; the molecules are made of atoms; the atoms are made of protons, neutrons and electrons; these are composed of sub-atomic particles. We used to think atoms were solid building blocks of matter, little tight individual balls. But we have learned they are not -- almost the entire inside of every atom is empty -- about 99.9999% in fact. If we took any atom and expanded it to the size of the Roman Colosseum, the nucleus with its protons and neutrons would be the size of a beebee in the center, the electrons would be infinitesimal ghosts of energy flitting at enormous speed in and out around the outer walls -- and the rest of the atom would be nothing, nothing at all."

"Most of matter is just empty space? Yes, I recall hearing that. That is one of the stranger facts of modern science. So the Ascendant is the space inside the atoms?"

"Yes -- and no. It is the space, but it is also the essential reality of the electrons and the nucleus. I'm just trying to help you understand by observing there are different levels of reality we don't normally see. At the deepest or subtlest level, everything everywhere is composed of nothing other than the Ascendant.

"And energy increases at deeper levels. If I were to throw this flower at you, I might manage with enough force to scratch you or even raise a bruise. But if I could excite my gardenia on the molecular level, we could probably destroy this lovely restaurant -- there is more energy contained on subtler levels. Einstein theorized and modern physicists proved the power locked in the atom is exponentially larger -- if I could release the power of the atoms in this flower, we could annihilate most of Athens. And quantum physics tells us that the power contained at the Planck scale -- 10^{-43} centimeters -- a decimal point followed by 42 zeroes and a one -- which is very, very, *very* small -- the power at that tiniest possible scale is so great it could create a Universe. In fact, our entire Universe is supposed to have come out of a region just that large in a fraction of a second in the Big Bang."

"You sure know a lot about physics," I said, impressed.

"I should know a little," she smiled; "I received my doctorate from Princeton in sub-particle studies."

"You're kidding! Hey, I always wanted to go into physics. Why didn't you tell me?"

"Well, for one thing, you never asked... The point is: as one approaches the Ascendant, the power increases. The Ascendant is the Source of all energy, therefore infinite energy lies within the grasp of anyone who can tap it.

"Ollie told me the human nervous system is the most wonderful machine in the Universe, because it can stretch from the perception of the boundaries -- the surface experience of the senses -- to the unbounded, the infinite Ascendant lying within. That is the goal of Ascending, to experience the Absolute."

"Anyone who could do that would gain unlimited power?"

"Yes, but that is only one quality of the Ascendant. It is the root or basis of *everything*, remember, so for one who can master that, all knowledge must also be the result. And all love," she added dulcetly, smiling again at me over the flower.

"This is incredible! The average human lives such a limited life of pain and despair. Can our nervous systems really be that flexible? To experience infinity?"

"That's what Ollie told me. And he also said he'd seen some pretty amazing demonstrations of that -- right here in Greece."

"Patmos... Sharon, do you think Ascension came from St. John?"

"I have no idea. But as I said, all knowledge. So let's be patient, learn how to Ascend, master it well enough to contact the Ascendant at will ourselves, then ask. I'm sure we'll find out then!"

"But, wait a moment -- if the Ascendant is so powerful as you say, why was Ollie killed? Why die so young, at such an untimely moment?"

"Oh, can we truly know it was untimely? Just because we didn't like it doesn't mean it wasn't the right time for him. I don't know, though, that sounds like rationalization. I don't understand it either, I don't understand much of life. Who knows? Maybe he hadn't Ascended long enough to master it. He obviously knew he was going to die, or at least had a strong intuition about it, but he didn't know how to prevent it. Maybe awareness of the Ascendant grows in stages. There are Seven Spheres, after all; maybe one doesn't have all the answers, all the mastery of the Ascendant, until one has learned all the Twenty-seven Attitudes and worked with them for awhile. I don't know!

"Oh, this is too depressing. Let's walk for awhile." She finished her second glass of ouzo with a flourish. The anise-flavored wine had proven much more to our liking than the retsina. She tossed her curls, laughed and added, "I want to keep feeling this light inside. I feel so warm and cozy tonight, so like I'm in Heaven. Let's walk; this place is just too magical."

And so we walked along the waterfront of Piraeus, ancient port of Athens. We passed shop after shop, selling (it seemed) every possible kind of food in the world. Many of them were closed for the night, but a surprising number were not. Sharon bought a bag of African blood oranges, three pineapples and some bread and cheese for our breakfast tomorrow.

We wandered around the next harbor, Zea, lined by ancient walls; several old fisherman were still on their boats, mending their nets. *Do these people never sleep?* I wondered. At the far end of the harbor, there was a submarine's conning tower and a sign which I laboriously spelled out only to discover an English translation a few feet away -- "The Maritime Museum of Greece." Doctor Dave explained the next day that Zea began Piraeus' importance in 500 BC by turning out one hundred galleys a year for the new Athenian fleet -- the fleet which stopped Xerxes and Persia and changed the entire course of Western civilization.

Such historical thoughts were not large in my mind tonight; I was walking with the beautiful Sharon through an ancient land of wonder. We discussed the idea of visiting a taverna; instead decided to climb farther up the Kastella hill past our hotel.

The houses terraced into the hillside were graceful and charming; the view of Piraeus' three harbors and the bay beyond made our climb radiantly worthwhile. But then, as we reached the top, we saw five miles away the floodlit Acropolis and the Parthenon, golden wonder of Athens' stellar past. I felt a rush of ecstasy for the extraordinary way my life had changed; not knowing what to do with so much feeling, I hugged Sharon and kissed her passionately.

She responded warmly but without passion; I blushed and released her from my embrace. "Just hold me," she said; together we stared over Athens, ancient city living still in this modern world. The beauty of the view quickly banished all destructive moods before they could really begin; I think I understood then the glory that was Greece. Standing on Kastella, overlooking a city at once ancient and modern, site of much of the best and the worst in our world, I wondered if it truly would one day be possible to weed out the terminally corrupted from our garden Earth and raise instead a new crop of Truth and Beauty and health and joy.

Piraeus below did not answer my question; we returned to the Cavo d'Oro and our beds, anticipating the morrow's journey to the Island of St. John.

7

The Island of the Seven

Our steamer, strangely also named *Georgios,* was blue, white, huge, beautiful. She pointed her sharp nose toward the East; we departed Piraeus within an hour or two of "on schedule." Which is considered exactly on time for Greece. A hundred terns flew with us as we churned the water; their forked tails made a fitting symbol for the divided past I so longed to leave behind. I took this to be a grand omen.

Soon we passed the ruined Temple of Poseidon, standing proudly atop Cape Sounion, furthest tip of the Attic peninsula. It was of white marble, mostly fallen, still majestic. As we rounded Sounion, the waves grew at once larger -- the waters lifted by the wind coming down the Strait of Chalcis to the Northwest here meet the waves raised by the winds funneling down between the long island of Euboea and the smaller Andros. Now the large ocean swells began. The water looked darker here: the azure and clear Aegean suddenly became three shades more mysterious.

"This marks the spot," said the good doctor as I remarked on the change in the water. "Yes, the very spot. There on the promontory above, where Poseidon's ruined temple now stands, stood Aegeus, king of Athens, the father of Theseus. Theseus, you may recall, with the help of the princess Ariadne, threaded his way through the labyrinth in Crete and killed the Minotaur. A desperate struggle, that; Theseus in his exuberance for his victory neglected to change his sails. His father had instructed the crew to fly white if Theseus was successful, but if he was dead, they should unfurl black. There had been a storm, I suppose; the white sails were ruined. Or perhaps in their joy, they simply forgot.

"At any rate, Aegeus saw the black sails on his son's ship and, assuming Theseus slain, leapt to his death from above, changing the water's color here forever after. Thus is this called the Aegean Sea."

"Your stories are so marvelous!" exclaimed Sharon, clapping. "You went into the wrong field. Why'd you do that?"

"My father mostly. He wanted me to be rich and successful, not just a poor professor as he was. 'No money in the classics,' he told me often enough to become a mantra. 'No money in love. Don't waste your life as I have, son, make something of yourself.' Thus did my heart split, for I loved ancient Greece as much as did he; I followed his commands, but always longed for a life like his. Curious, how we model our parents' repressed lives."

"How was your evening in Athens?" I asked him, thinking the stunning beauty of this Aegean day simply too pleasant to spend on childhood regression therapy.

"Oh! It was glorious! Glorious! I started at the Temple of Olympian Zeus, finished by the Roman Emperor Hadrian on a foundation laid centuries earlier, then walked up Dionysus Avenue to the Acropolis..."

The ferry was filled mostly with Greeks, including a dozen or so Orthodox priests with their black robes, long beards and black hats, heading to the monastery of St. John on Patmos for Easter weekend. Some of them spoke English tolerably well; after the good doctor told us at great length about his night in Athens, he sequestered himself with two of them and became enthralled in a discussion of classical history. This was fine with me, for it left me more time alone with Sharon.

The trip across the Aegean was delightful -- the blue blue sea was deep, rich, clear; the air was alive with a light like magic, with a peculiar lucidity I had seen before only in paintings and thought existed nowhere on Earth. "I didn't know light like this was *real*," I commented to Sharon with awe. "It's so full, so *alive*. My words can't describe it. It feels as if we've entered a painting by an old master."

"You too?" she asked, surprised and pleased. "I thought I was appreciating it more because I've been Ascending. But since you haven't and are seeing it the same way, maybe it really is different somehow. It's so clear! It's as if I can really *see* for the first time."

"Yes! All the world is fresh and new, as if just born. The springtime of the world. It feels like that."

"It may be the springtime of our lives at least," she smiled at me.

"How I hope that's true!" I answered, far from sure. Was I really going to be able to make a new start? "What's our next step? Find some rooms in Patmos, then inquire if anyone knows Alan Lance and company? Sounds a little complicated."

"Oh, I doubt it will be too hard, or Ollie would have given us more directions. Patmos isn't large, remember, fifteen or twenty square miles."

"That's pretty big when we're looking for someone!"

"It's not like a city! There are only a few thousand there; surely a group of a dozen foreigners will be known by the local merchants. I think it'll be easy."

"I hope so," I said without much conviction.

When we landed at the old harbor town of Skala on Patmos about 1:30 AM, we learned Sharon's optimism was not only warranted, it was, if anything, too conservative. As soon as we stepped onto the dock, a tall, pretty Englishwoman with long red hair and wearing a white Grecian outfit walked up to us and said, "Welcome to Patmos! You are, I presume, Ollie's friends?"

Sharon recovered the most quickly and replied, "Why, yes we are! How did you know we were coming?"

"Well, I didn't. Not exactly. Alan said to expect you, but he didn't say when. Where are the rest of you?" She glanced curiously at the other passengers, as if she expected to see more than us three.

"We're all there are," answered Doctor Dave, staring at her with a look I'd never seen on him before. It was like hunger, a deep, primal longing that surprised me -- was she reminding him of someone he'd once known? "You were expecting more? That's odd. But then, how did your Alan Lance know we were coming? That's beyond odd. We didn't tell anyone."

"Oh, he often knows things. He said to expect six from Seattle... What's happened to the others? Regardless! Welcome, each of you, to Patmos." She hugged us warmly, not in the slightest stiffly as I had learned to expect from the British, then continued, "I am Lila, a Novitiate of the Ishaya Order. Alan asked me to meet you here and take you to the villa. We can take one of Patmos' three taxis, if you wish, or we can walk up the donkey trail, if you don't mind carrying your bags... They don't look too heavy."

"Is it far?" I asked.

"That depends on your definition!" she laughed gaily. "Nothing is far on the Island of the Seven. It's about two thousand meters, one hundred and fifty meters up. It's there, up the hill in Khora, the new town. 'New' meaning it was built by refugees from the fall of Constantinople, five centuries ago, not before the birth of Christ. Whichever you prefer, really."

"Oh, let's walk," said Sharon. "Feel the land better." The harbor was all yellow lights and closely packed buildings, arcaded in the Italian colonial style -- Venice had conquered Patmos once. There was some singing from a taverna or two, but other than that the place seemed dead.

"'Feel' is about right," I muttered. "Won't be able to see much at night." I was wrong -- the waning Moon had risen and well lit our way up the hill.

"You should see the stars here when there's no Moon!" exclaimed Lila after we'd climbed about half way up the steep path. "They're more brilliant than I've seen anywhere else; the Milky Way is so bright it really looks like it's made of milk."

The waning Moon eclipsed but could not entirely hide the majesty above. How glorious it must be here on a moonless night! "What's that bright group called?" I asked Sharon about a constellation low in the East. "There, past the Moon, near the horizon. Looks like a lopsided rectangle with two triangles attached."

"Which? Oh, that? That's Sagittarius. Also called the Teapot. That triangle to the left is the handle; the spout is the triangle on the right. Away from the city when there's no Moon, it looks like the Milky Way is pouring out of it. The center of our galaxy is over there, in Sagittarius A, so the radio-astronomers say: it's a huge black hole, with mass millions of times greater than our sun's."

"You probably can't see it well in the dark," said Lila, which Dave and I both found an extremely funny remark. We laughed uproariously and almost missed the rest of her sentence, "*But* the Chapel of St. Anne is just here, to the left of the path. Inside is the Grotto where St. John received and wrote his Apocalypse."

"Do you suppose Alan Lance might still be up?" asked Sharon suddenly. Her tone sounded urgent; I peered at her through the darkness. What caused this sudden transition? Our laughter? It wasn't meant meanly; we were just having fun. Or was it the mention of the Apostle?

"Oh, I'm sorry! I forgot to tell you. Alan's not here. He and Ed Silver and Mira have gone ahead to Amritsar to prepare rooms for us. We're all leaving Patmos in the next few days. He said you're all welcome to accompany us -- if you would like."

"Amritsar?" I asked. "Where's that?"

"It's in India, in the Punjab --" she began, but we all interrupted her in surprise.

"The Punjab! Why there? India?"

I continued, "Why go to the Punjab? Isn't the Monastery of St. John that imposing looking fortress up there?" The moonlight made the thick walls and battlements look ominous. Whatever the original intent of its founder, that place had the look of being built for defense from pirates.

"Why, yes, of course it is, but what difference does... Oh, I see. You think Ascension has something to do with the monastery, is that it?"

"Well, doesn't it?" asked Dave, echoing all our confusion. "Ascension came from the Apostle John, didn't it?"

"Most assuredly, my dear doctor. But *this* monastery knows nothing of that. It was founded in the year 1088 by Christodoulos, a Bithynian abbot."

"Why are you all here then?" he asked, still confused.

"Why? Because of the Chapel of St. Anne, of course. That's a *very* special place... Here we are."

The villa had white-washed walls (as did most of the houses on Patmos, I learned the next day) but was atypically quite large. We entered it through a pleasant courtyard lined with dozens of potted hydrangeas. Lila opened a door on the left; we entered their sitting room and promptly sat. It felt as if the ground were still rolling, moving up and down as though we had not yet left the boat.

No one else was still up. Lila offered us some chamomile tea but Sharon said, still sounding urgent, "Who's in charge while Alan is away?"

"Well, I suppose I am," answered Lila. "Why? Is something the matter? Can't it wait until tomorrow? You must be tired."

"We are, but I feel we have to explain why we're here and give you Ollie's message at once." She told our history of the past few days simply and with little emotion.

Lila listened carefully, also without showing much feeling. Even hearing of Ollie's violent death caused no physical reaction other than a slight frown as she commented quietly, "So *that's* what Alan meant."

"What do you mean?" Sharon asked. She was bleary-eyed, but in control of herself. "Alan Lance knew something would happen?"

"When Ollie left, Alan told him if he went out from us, he would never return. Ollie replied of course he would return -- he wanted the other four Spheres; at the most he would teach Ascension for a few months, then be back. He said he wasn't going to Seattle because of his mother's passing but because he felt some people there needed him. Alan agreed that might be true, but repeated that if he left us, he would never return. He must have foreseen this."

"Why didn't he insist Ollie not leave?" snuffled Sharon.

"Alan never tells anyone to do anything. He holds the individual's free will sacred. If Ollie was adamant about going, it was because he had to. Even if he was just going to Seattle to die. But then, it wasn't just to die, was it? For here you are -- he found the three of you, didn't he?"

"You don't seem much affected by this," I said curiously. "Didn't you like him?"

"Oh! You don't know. I love -- loved Ollie dearly. We came to Patmos on the same day -- we were among the first Alan invited here. We were -- we became intimate before I took my Novitiate vows. Please understand! I shall miss him for the rest of my life. But I made my peace with never seeing him again when he left. Alan's words were plain. And I also believe all things work together for good in this world. So even though I don't understand and will mourn him, I know there must be a higher reason for all of this; I choose to rest content with that...

"Later, while I'm Ascending tonight, I'll let the grief wash through me and carry me where it will. I'll learn from it and master it. Through that, I'll reintegrate on a higher level of understanding. I owe him no less than to see the beauty of his passing. And rejoice in it for him. My dear love Ollie Swenson has graduated: he is free.

"Enough of this. You mentioned a message? What did Ollie say?"

Sharon and I exchanged a glance; she answered, "He said we were to tell Alan, *The Opposition is real.* We don't know what he meant."

"Opposition?" Lila asked curiously. "Nor do I. What was he talking about? What Opposition? Didn't you say Ollie was killed in an accident?"

"I said I *thought* he was. We don't know who was driving that limousine."

"You didn't tell me that!" exclaimed the doctor, paling. "I didn't sign up for that kind of adventure!"

"I was afraid if I told you my fears you might not come," Sharon replied, wringing her hands and looking as if she were having a hard time not crying. "And I didn't know and I don't know if I had any reason for them. I was wrong. I'm sorry! Please forgive me. I should have been completely honest. I felt three might have an easier journey here. If you want to return home, I'll understand."

"I never said I wanted to leave," he said, looking at Lila with the hunger still plainly visible in his eyes. "I just wish I'd known the danger from the beginning."

"I apologize for not trusting you better. I was quite distraught Sunday -- was that only three days ago? I should have followed my intuition, not my intellect."

"Forget it," he said, still looking only at Lila. "I'm sure I would have come anyway. I only wish you'd told me."

"I wonder if this is related to those guys who showed up at my mother's house," I said, thinking this series had run its course. "They asked about me. And about Ascension. From her description, they sounded like Sikhs --"

"Sikhs!" cried Lila, deeply concerned. "*Now* I understand. Oh my."

"Can you explain this?" asked the doctor, strain in his voice. "Who are these Sikhs? Why would anyone oppose this Teaching? Isn't Ascension from St. John?"

"Yes, it's from the Apostle John. After he dictated *Revelation* here on Patmos to his disciple Prochorus, he traveled to Epheseus in Asia Minor to have it published -- Epheseus where he had laid Mary to rest some fifty years earlier. Gathering his closest students, he then traveled to the East -- following, some say, the route both John the Baptist and Christ took before they taught in Galilee. The Apostle desired to set up a monastery high in 'the Backbone of the World,' the mountains we today call the Himalayas. He found a secluded valley there, isolated from the rest of the world, and established his Order, the Ishaya Order. Isha is a name for Christ, you see: it is often translated Jesu or Jesus. Ishaya means, 'of Isha.'

"The Ishaya Monastery has preserved this Teaching for nineteen centuries. The monks kept Ascension alive, but for hundreds of years, they have all believed it is too good for the people of the world. All, that is, until now.

"The chief monk, the Custodian, was in every age chosen by his predecessor by a 'laying on' of hands. This occurred just before the previous Custodian died, making an unbroken succession of authority from the days of St. John himself.

"The unrest of the modern world invaded even that peaceful valley. During the India-Pakistan war, the Custodian and all but two of the monks were killed, leaving no clear direction who the new Custodian of the Twenty-seven was to be.

"One of the final two monks, Durga Ishaya, holds firmly to the old ways and says Ascension must remain the exclusive property of the recluses, that no householder is worthy of this knowledge, that only those willing to renounce everything of the world are entitled to it. He was of Sikh background before he joined the monastery; therefore he went out to find his Novitiates from among that people.

"The other, Nanda Ishaya, is convinced the age long ago prophesied by John is at hand -- the time is here to bring Ascension into the world. In fact, he believes Ascension is *the* tool that will heal the world; he thinks it is the secret Teaching Isha passed to John for this precise moment in history. So he journeyed to the West, to the Greek Isles, and found Alan Lance. Thinking his task well accomplished, he returned with him to the Himalayas; he has trained him in six of the Seven Spheres.

"Unfortunately, some of Durga's followers have grown extremely angry that Alan has been teaching Ascension to anyone, regardless of vow."

"Would they murder?" Sharon asked quietly.

"I wouldn't have thought so. Definitely not Durga, he is much too evolved for that. He could never even think of it. And that should be true for his Novitiates as well. But the Sikhs have a long tradition of violence, you know; many of them have misunderstood their founder's intent. Might some of his followers turn to violence? To save Ascension from what they consider profanation, might they go so far? I don't know, but it is not quite inconceivable, regrettably. Most of the Durga Novitiates are good people, some are close friends of mine, but a few are true fanatics. Oh, I do hope none of them is that misguided! To make a religion out of these techniques is to miss their point. Ascension opens one to new experience; outmoded beliefs should fall away, die a graceful death. They should not be allowed to pervert the simplicity and power of this Teaching."

"So, what do we do?" asked the doctor, looking stunned.

"Well, we're leaving here Friday by private yacht for Athens. Saturday, we're touring Delphi, then Saturday night is the Easter celebration on Mt. Lykabettos, an experience like no other. You can join us for all of it. Then Sunday, we're flying to Amritsar... And tomorrow, if you'd like, I will teach you two gentlemen how to Ascend, say at eleven? And Sharon, for you the Second Technique."

"Oh yes! I'd like that!" she exclaimed. The doctor and I both agreed, but with rather less enthusiasm. He sounded more interested than I did. A war with a fanatical group of Punjabi Sikhs was a great deal more than I had bargained for.

As I lay to sleep in my room (formerly Ed Silver's), I wondered if I should just quietly leave on the next boat... But then, there was Sharon. And Ascension. I had come so far, I might as well try it. If it didn't work for me, I could split off in Athens and head back to the States. I once had desired to visit Greece, but never in my wildest dreams had I thought of visiting the strife-torn Punjab state of India.

With that thought whirling around in my head, I drifted off to a rather uncomfortable sleep.

8
A New Attitude

The next morning, the three of us met Lila in the "Teaching Hall" -- a pleasant apricot-colored room lined with soft white and comfortable looking couches and chairs. Many of the villa's rooms had stunning views of the harbor and of Skala below; this one, however, was on the back side: the light was subdued, outer sounds were muted. It looked like a good place to learn to Ascend.

Breakfast that morning was plain, fruit and dried cereal, taken outside, on the dining verandah. It was a beautiful, sunny day; the fragrant wisterias and clematises climbing around the iron trellis on all sides and overhead covered but did not eclipse a magnificent view of the harbor below.

My prime entertainment came from meeting the other residents. There were a few other Novitiates, monks in training, but most were normal worldly householder types. All of them appeared deeply happy; the news of Ollie's death passed like a momentary cloud over their faces. Had they all been prepared for this? Who was Alan Lance that his words held such power? Nothing in my memory of him could explain this -- for that matter, nothing in my experience could explain it. These were like no people I had ever known. They reacted differently to tragedy; they remained in peace when anyone else would be in agony. Were they unshakable?

There were three Americans. Two were Novitiates, Satya and Devindra, twins from New York. They had black beards and long black hair tied in pony tails. Both had blue eyes that twinkled when they talked, as if they found life truly fascinating. The third American was aptly named Steve Young -- he was a handsome young guy in his early twenties with short brown hair and no beard. For some reason, he took the news about Ollie harder than the others. He was the only unhappy-looking one of the lot.

There was also a couple from Holland, Charles and Linda Vanderwall. They were quite friendly; he was tall, skinny, blond and Dutch and she was short, plump, dark and Indonesian. I also met another English woman, Mary Brown, who had curly dark hair and sparkly eyes -- she looked to be in her early sixties -- and two Germans, Hartmut Sorflaten (beardless with long blond hair and steel-blue eyes) and another Novitiate, Balindra, who had thick black beard and hair, the longest of any of them.

Best of all was a pretty young Greek named Aphrodite Kambos who spoke flawless English. She happened to be eating her breakfast just as I emerged from the kitchen into the bright sunlight on the verandah; through her I met everyone else. "Why those strange names?" I asked her curiously after meeting the others.

"Oh, the Novitiates are given new names when they take their vows," she explained. "They are apprentice monks and nuns. Five here have taken the preliminary vows to join the Ishaya Order. Those of us who haven't know we will one day marry and have families." She looked at me with barely disguised longing when she said that. I felt like a potential meal.

"So those with their birth names still intact like 'Alan Lance' or 'Aphrodite Kambos' are not planning on becoming monks or nuns? Is that it?" I asked hurriedly, wishing to derail her intent.

"That's right. And those who have changed their names like Lila or her sister Mira have taken vows as a year-long experiment to see if they wish to become life members of St. John's Ishaya Order. In fact, that is why we're leaving now for the Punjab. Balindra and Lila and Mira are committed to taking their life vows. Alan wants them to do that in the presence of his Teacher."

I wasn't sure how I felt about anyone becoming a monk or a nun -- my family had long sundered from the Catholic Church. But then I shrugged mentally: it didn't matter to me; let them do what they wished, if they thought it would make them happy. I at least was sure the life of a monk was not for me.

Sharon entered the dining room just then, looking for all the world like the Spirit of Spring. She had plaited some daisies in her hair and was wearing a white outfit similar to Lila's. She looked like my vision of a Greek Goddess.

"Up at last, sleepy head?" she practically sang to me. "You should see the poppy field on the hill out back! I thought you'd never get up! I've *missed* you." She kissed me lightly on the lips, glancing out the side of her eye at Aphrodite.

"Jet lag," I explained, glad she wasn't jealous about my conversation with the gorgeous Greek. Or at least -- not *too* jealous.

Lila was speaking earnestly to the doctor when we arrived in the Teaching Hall. He looked up at us, flushed and excited. *What's going on with them?* I wondered. *Last minute doubts about her vows?* That didn't seem very likely.

"You don't need to hear this again if you don't wish," Lila said warmly to Sharon. "I can meet you alone after; the Second Technique is much more quickly taught than the First, for you already know how to Ascend."

"No, I want to hear it all again, if that's OK. I want to learn it completely."

"Of course, that's fine," she smiled. "So, gentlemen, what do you know about Ascending?"

Dave and I looked at each other; he said, "Not much. There are Twenty-seven Techniques to experience the Ascendant, divided into Seven Spheres; each Sphere is said to be more powerful than the one before. When does one graduate to the next? When one masters the previous?"

"Yes, but not exactly. Full mastery of any of the Seven is probably impossible until *all* are mastered, but there are general guidelines of progress. We'll talk more about that later... And why are *you* interested in Ascension?" This was to me.

"My life wasn't working. I couldn't stop shooting myself in the foot. I'm tired of that! If by settling down my mind, I can rewrite the old destructive programs in there, that'd be great -- and if not that, even having the deep rest I've seen when Sharon Ascends would be wonderful. If it works for me."

"Oh, it will. Ascension produces rest about twice as deep as sleep even for a beginner; this allows stress to be thrown off gracefully by the body. Properly practiced, it will work for anyone, because it is based on the natural functioning of the mind and body, not on belief."

"So you're saying," commented the doctor, "Ascension taps us into a natural but unusual operation of the nervous system?"

"Yes! Everyone is already Ascending all the time, to some extent. Today you'll learn how to make it systematic."

"So we can Ascend at will," I said.

"Exactly. Whenever life becomes hectic or crazy or you feel stressed out, you can Ascend -- with the eyes opened or closed. And from Ascending, return to silence, to peace, to innocence."

"Like a child," breathed Sharon. "Life in the present moment. No worries about the future; no regret for the past."

"Lots of potential in such a mind," observed Doctor Dave.

"Yes!" Lila beamed at them. "Because the baby hasn't been caught by the past or the future, the power of its mind is awesome. This is what Ascension gives back to us: the innocence and power of life in the present."

"I see," said the doctor. "The adult, abstracted away from the present, is often caught by self-defeating beliefs and habits. And I suppose we learn those from our family, our friends, our schools, our society -- from all life experience."

"Precisely; and these habits freeze life into patterns which are beyond conscious control."

"Yes," he agreed thoughtfully. "The problem is: some of the beliefs we've adopted are useful, some habits serve us, but many do not. It's useful to remember how to read. It's useful to remember who our friends are. It's useful to know our names. But so many of these internal programs serve no one in any way. So many of them are damaging. So what do we do?"

"We learn how to use the mind differently! Instead of incessantly thinking, chattering away, never ever stopping for rest, thinking the same thing we thought yesterday and the day before and the day before that, over and over and over again, pointlessly noisy, going nowhere -- instead of all that, we rediscover silence inside. We learn to experience the present. We stop regretting the past, we stop worrying about the future. We begin to be Here and Now. Then the full power of the mind is available every moment."

"I think I'm with you," I commented. "You're saying the mind is like a pond. Thoughts are like waves in the pond. We've all dropped a single stone into a quiet pool -- it creates gentle, beautiful ripples across the surface of the water. This is like having only one thought moving through the mind, isn't it? The mind is coherent, it is orderly, it is powerful. But if several stones, a whole handful, fall into the water? Chaos. The waves become choppy. Some troughs are on top of crests; many get canceled out. This is like the mind when it is caught by those continually running internal programs. It keeps going and going and going and nothing comes of it except fatigue."

"Exactly! And further: a clear mind creates a healthy body. Your body is already creating trillions of chemical reactions every second, did you know? For example, when your mind is tense, anxious, nervous, your body produces tense, anxious, nervous molecules."

"Like adrenaline and noradrenaline," agreed the doctor. "That's so. And when the mind is calm and peaceful, the body produces calm and peaceful molecules -- like Valium. The body is already producing chemicals similar to any I can prescribe, but it is doing it without the side effects. When my body creates Valium, it means I feel tranquil but don't also feel spaced-out. When our bodies produce immune-stimulating agents or anti-cancer drugs or anti-aging hormones, these have no damaging side effects. Our bodies do this all the time, when we're not stressed... So that is the effect of Ascending. *This* I can understand! So, how do we learn?"

"Simply," said Lila, smiling affectionately at him. "And soon. But first, I have three requests to make of you, three requests Alan says are necessary to ask anyone desiring to learn Ascension.

"One. It is necessary to make a commitment of time. Ascension is powerful but subtle; it may take a few days or even weeks of regular practice to notice the benefits overtaking your life. So, will each of you do this?"

"Of course," both the doctor and I declared willingly.

"Very good. Two. Ascension works best if we are innocent with it. Believing in it is not necessary, nor is it necessary to expect any kind of experience when we are Ascending. In fact, even the slightest expectation slows down the innocent inward movement of the mind. Belief is not required, it is positively not required. So, to the best of your ability, no expectations, OK?

"And three. I have to ask you to keep this confidential until you are trained to teach it. Ascension is delicate; the First Attitude is so simple, it seems anyone could do it. And anyone can, yet without proper instruction, it could be misunderstood. If you give it to people before they are ready for it, not only will they not appreciate it, they will criticize it and condemn you for practicing it. They will judge you and reject Ascension without ever giving it a chance. So: *do you agree to keep this technique confidential until you are trained as Teachers of Ascension?*"

"Absolutely," I agreed with complete sincerity.

The doctor said again, "Of course."

"Great... I want you to know, I'm so pleased you're doing this, I'm so happy you've come all the way to Patmos to learn this age-old Science. You're going to love Ascension.

"Please understand: this is quite ancient. It's not an invention from some recent person's mind. I believe it came from Isha, the Christ, through his Apostle John. But you don't have to believe that; you don't have to believe anything. I'm just putting it in an historical context for you.

"These Twenty-seven Techniques were preserved throughout the centuries by the Ishaya monks, but the understanding that this Teaching is for *everyone* became confused. Somewhere down the long centuries, the monks began to consider the average person unworthy of Ascension. In order to learn, it was required to become a recluse and devote one's entire life to the practice.

"But Ascension is and always has been completely natural. Ever since humans have existed, we have had the ability to rise in our thoughts, to Ascend. It is easy to imagine this Teaching coming up at different times in different parts of the world, when anyone realized it *must* be simple and natural to return life to the innocence of the child, to life in the present moment."

"Sure," the doctor agreed. "Examples of Ascending can be found in all cultures by people of all ages and all religions. Since this is so, Ascension *can't* require belief of any kind."

"That's right! People have experienced it jogging, staring at the stars, at the beach, while praying, during childbirth, over a full desk on a crowded day -- everywhere throughout the full range of human experience. Ascension comes to people at any unpredictable time. So it *must* be something built into the fabric of the human nervous system. Anyone anywhere at any time can and does Ascend. As I said, we're just making it repeatable and systematic.

"OK." She paused a moment as if gathering her mind. "So, let's begin. Most of the Twenty-seven Attitudes have three parts: one for the heart, one for the mind, and a focus for our awareness.

"According to modern science, our emotions are centered in the right hemisphere of the brain. In most of us, the right brain is spatial, holistic, intuitive, creative, artistic, emotional. Of these, it is the emotions that most cause us to Ascend -- or descend. Negative emotions, for example, cause a lowering of our life, a descension."

"That's undoubtedly true," agreed the doctor. "Anger shuts down the brain and internal organs so more blood can go to the muscles. It speeds up the heart and increases blood clotting factors. This is the classic 'fight-or-flight' response. Once it was needed -- when you were about to be eaten by a saber-toothed tiger, for example. You don't need to be digesting lunch if you are about to be someone else's! Fight for your survival or run away. Useful response. Still is, when faced by a crack addict with a switchblade in a dark alley. But the problem is: fight-or-flight is turned on all the time in our modern world -- when someone cuts us off on the freeway, when our boss yells at us, when we miss a traffic light. Our blood pressure goes up and stays up; the internal organs remain shut down until they fail."

"Precisely!" Lila beamed at him again. "But there are also built into everyone positive emotions; these cause Ascension."

"Such as love," said Sharon, gazing at me. I blushed.

"Yes, and it *is* love that is the most powerful of the Ascending emotions. This is why almost every culture in the world has said, 'God is Love.' Love is the most powerful way to Ascend."

"I've often believed that," said Dave. "Whenever we feel love, our minds function more effectively, our bodies respond by producing the molecules of health."

"Yes," agreed Sharon warmly. "And you don't notice surface imperfections when you're in love. Your vision is broader.

Happiness is greater. If you stub your toe when you've fallen in love, you hardly notice it. But break up with your boyfriend and then stub your toe! 'Why is God so cruel to me! Life is hell!'"

"The difference is obvious," said Lila. "How you feel when you're in love -- this is the sweet influence of Ascension."

"There's a problem with love," I protested, thinking I saw a flaw in her logic. "It's hard to manipulate. You can't turn it on at will. If I were to tell you and Dave to go out on the verandah and fall in love -- maybe you would, but maybe you wouldn't... Well, *you* two would! But there are no guarantees. Christ said, 'Love your enemies,' and 'Love thy neighbor as thyself;' look what happened to his Teaching. No one does it, no one *can* do it. It doesn't work."

"Actually," said Lila slowly, "you're right -- for most people. Love is hard to *make* happen. That is why we don't start with the Love Attitude. The Love Technique is third. Of the three primary Ascending emotions, Love is the hardest to create at will. But there are two others.

"Similar in strength to Love is Gratitude. Thankfulness produces similar changes in the body and the mind. And Gratitude is easier to culture than Love -- if I were to give you one thousand pounds sterling, for example, you would most likely feel some thankfulness to me."

"But again!" I exclaimed, continuing my skeptic's role. She had said belief was *not* required; I wanted to put this to the test. "Gratitude has earned a bad name in the world. We've been told to be thankful so many times when we don't feel it. I so much wanted an electric train for Christmas when I was seven, and what I got was a fuzzy ugly olive green sweater -- and then I was told I had to be grateful anyway! I guess I don't feel thankful very often."

"Well, you're right again! Many of us have been told to be grateful so much, we would rather eat nails. So even though it's easier to develop than Love, it's still not altogether easy, which is why Gratitude is part of the Second Attitude, not the First."

"OK," I said, chuckling. "I'll be good. What's the emotion in the First Attitude?" My curiosity was larger than my skepticism.

"Appreciation. Or in one syllable, Praise. Appreciation is almost as powerful as Love and Gratitude, and it's a *lot* easier to turn on at will. You can simply shift your mind toward appreciation instead of criticism; your body responds by making you healthier as your mind becomes happier. We can choose to be sad that a glass is half empty or choose to be happy a glass is half full. It's completely within our power; it's all a matter of choice. And the simple truth is that condemnation never helps anyone improve, whereas appreciation always does."

"I've seen this in action," said Sharon. "With my niece Liza. One time when I was staying with them, Liza came home from school with a drawing she'd made. But my sister Linda was tired, she'd had a hard day at work; instead of thanking her for it and praising her for her creativity, she was short with her and criticized her for it. And you know what? The next day, Liza dragged home from school with a worse drawing.

"But that day Linda had changed her thinking, decided to appreciate, and was lavish in her words. And the *next* day, Liza bounced joyfully home with a third drawing, by far the best of the three. It was amazing. Every part her mother had praised was drawn better than the first day."

"Exactly! Praise works like magic for anybody, for anything, always. And it's just a choice: a choice for joy and life. It is the easiest of the Ascension emotions, because it grows from *simply making the decision* to appreciate rather than condemn. Our society may have programmed criticism deeply into us, but whenever we find ourselves moving down that descending path, it's easy to turn upward, simply by finding something to appreciate. Anywhere, about anything, to anyone, always."

"So, for the right brain, we choose to appreciate rather than judge?" I asked. That didn't sound too difficult. "This seems pretty simple."

"It is. It's simple and basic. The Cathedral of Ascension is built on the rock-hard foundation of perfect simplicity, the sign of unalloyed Truth...

"So, for the right brain, for our emotional side, Appreciation is the force, the driving emotion, that causes Ascension. OK? Good. Now, the left hemisphere of the brain also has certain thoughts that cause Ascension. The left brain is logical, verbal, analytical, mathematical, rational. Thoughts that cause Ascension here are those of awe-inspiring wonder."

"Like staring at the sky in January on a moonless night?" asked Sharon dreamily. "When you think there are as many as four hundred billion stars in our Milky Way? When you remember some of those points of light are really distant galaxies and there are as many as one thousand billion galaxies in this Universe, each one containing an average of two hundred billion stars -- the whole thing is so huge? Who wouldn't feel the awe of this?

"And it all proceeds with such perfect order! Who keeps the natural laws functioning so the atoms don't implode? Why does the ratio of a circle's circumference to its diameter equal 3.14159-265? Such magnificent order, everywhere! It stuns my mind."

"Right," agreed Lila, looking pleased. "*Your* left brain is awed by such thoughts, which causes a slight degree of Ascension for you. But it's different for everybody."

"I see this," said the doctor. "For me, I feel awe when I think of the order in the human body. Fifty trillion cells, all operating in harmony. And inside each of the fifty trillion is the wonder of the DNA molecule -- a molecule so complex that it contains life itself -- a molecule so compressed that were one from any cell stretched out, it would be six feet long!

"The exalted mystery throughout the body! You inhale a bacteria, one of a kind you've never met, but your great-great-great-great grandmother did, 200 years ago or 2,000 years ago or 20,000 years ago and your DNA remembers how to educate your defensive machinery, your macrophages and killer T-Cells and lymphocytes, to destroy it! Such intelligence there is in Nature! Such brilliance!"

"Yes," agreed Lila again, "these are all examples of left brain Ascension thoughts. Do you see how they work? They involve some sort of analysis of life to create expansion, awe, wonder. It is an incredible, magical universe; everyone sees this in a different way, through the filter of his or her own left brain."

"So what I want for Ascension," I said, a little bored by their examples, "is not any old awe-inspiring thought, but the *Ultimate Thought* of my rational side, personally chosen by me for me, like..." I offered my conception.

"Exactly, yes!" agreed Lila, chuckling at my choice. "Very good. And for you, dear doctor..." She helped him discover his private vehicle for Ascension.

"What if you don't believe this will work?" I asked, playing skeptic again.

"No problem! It doesn't matter. We don't have to believe in Ascension for it to happen. Part of the mind would like to believe in it, part of the mind would like to reject it; this makes no difference. Belief is from the surface of the mind, which we Ascend immediately anyway. We're creating your most effective path to the Ascendant. Ascension is built of a series of individualized techniques; it's not a belief system."

"Can we change our Ultimate Thought as we're Ascending?" asked Dave.

"Of course! The idea we choose need not remain the same; it will change as life-experience changes. You've just picked one now to begin with: it's necessary to have a starting point.

"Now we take these two, appreciation for the right brain and our Ultimate Thought for the left brain and add one final concept and we will have our first Ascension Attitude. Remember I said most of these techniques are built of three parts? The first two parts together cause a slight Ascending... Do you feel this, by the way? Some upliftment from these two? I don't mean the *words*, I mean the feeling behind the words?"

"Yes, I do," I agreed, surprised that I actually did feel lighter. The doctor and Sharon murmured their assent.

"Great. So now, we want to take this Ascending motion and focus it onto the root stress of modern life. When this happens, the whole structure of our old internal programming falls apart."

"How does that work?" I asked curiously.

"Did you see any of those wonderful old arches still standing in Athens? In Greece and Rome, the great arches were created by building up a huge pile of sand under the stones for the legs. No arch could stand until the final piece, the keystone, was installed. When the keystone was in place, the sand was removed; since the opposing tensions were equal, the arch would not fall; many of these still stand, 3,000 years later. That is why your Pennsylvania calls itself, 'the Keystone State,' by the way. They felt they were the indispensable link in the Colonies' Rebellion.

"Similarly, some of the stresses in our lives are supporting others. If we can remove the root stress, all the others will leave, for their support will be gone. It's hard to destroy a building by shoving it over. But it's easy to collapse it by removing the foundation. It's hard to break addictive and self-destructive habits in their own space. But it's easy to undermine them by erasing the fundamental stress that gives them life. To kill a tree, kill the root; the leaves wither and die...

"So, what do you think is the root stress of modern life?"

"Separation," answered the doctor.

"The ego," I answered.

"Yes, to both of you! So the antidote to our deepest stress is to apply the movement of Ascension back onto it..."

She explained exactly how to do that and continued, "These, then, are the three parts of the First Ascension Attitude: Appreciation for the heart; our Ultimate Thought for the mind, then a focus back onto our subjective self. Just this much, no more, no less. We move upward, we Ascend, then we apply the Ascendant onto the fundamental root stress, back onto our belief that our lives are separate, ruled by the ego. We expand to Universality then contract back to individuality; this dissolves anything standing in the way of our connection with the Ascendant in the process."

"So," I said slowly, "This First Attitude simply adds one new triple thought to the ocean of thoughts we already have."

"Like a needle in our hand to remove all the old painful thorns," commented Sharon.

"Like a catalyst to precipitate out our stress," added the doctor. "One new thought with three parts to replace the 50,000 thoughts we normally think throughout the day. And, since the mind can only do one thing at a time, if we continually introduce this new thought, we replace all the old thoughts."

"You've got it!" exclaimed Lila. "By choosing over and over again for the Ascension Attitude, all the other thoughts race away. This becomes the new root thought in the mind; all the small and mean and false thoughts are erased. The Ascension Attitude is like the big fish in the pond. When the big fish comes, all the little fish run away. You feel lighter, clearer, calmer, more peaceful."

"I've been finding," said Sharon, "every day, at each and every moment, I always have a choice, which kind of thought I wish to have. I introduce my Ascension Attitude all the time; I'm discovering silence, coherence and peace where I never thought I would. I may never understand *why* life happens as it does; but

I've realized that's not my job. It *is* my job to make the most out of every moment; Ascension is the key for me to do that."

"That's the way it works," agreed Lila. "That's why you're ready for the Second Technique; the First has become a deep groove in your mind. Since you've been Ascending any time you remember to, it has been rewriting your outmoded judgments, beliefs and habits. Well done!

"Now, the greatest value of Ascension comes from taking it inward, to use it as a tool for inner exploration. This makes the new paradigm stronger in the brain and rewrites the old programs more and more quickly."

"Isn't that hard to do?" asked the doctor. "Many people have written it's difficult to Ascend. They've stood in ice water up to their necks in the middle of winter. They've bent their bodies into pretzels. They've sat between four fires with the summer sun burning golden overhead as their fifth. They've forced their minds eighteen hours a day to experience the slightest degree of Ascension! It is hard to do, isn't it?"

"No, its the simplest thing you'll ever do! It takes *less* effort to Ascend, not more. Those who think it's difficult believe the mind is like a monkey, jumping from branch to branch. They believe the only way to stop its erratic jumping is to beat it and whip it and force it to be still. But this tires the mind and raises the metabolic rate. It is not and never will be effective for Ascension."

"That makes sense to me," I said. "If I have a dog I want at my back door, I could chain it there, but it wouldn't like me much. It would howl and moan and complain *all the time* and bite me if it got the chance. Forcing the mind seems like that to me. I don't want to do that."

"But suppose you open the door from time to time and put out dog food, the dog will never leave your porch!" exclaimed Sharon. "And he'll be your best friend for life."

"So, what's the favorite food of the mind?" I asked. "No, I already know. It's the Ascendant, isn't it?"

"That's right," agreed Lila, smiling at us. "You see, the mind *is* like a monkey, jumping from branch to branch, but it jumps *because* it's seeking an Ideal Banana. The mind jumps because it's seeking an Ideal Experience. Only the Ascendant is capable of satisfying this wanderlust of the mind, for only the Ascendant is the home of all intelligence, happiness, energy, and wisdom."

"The mind follows its bliss, as Joseph Campbell put it," said the doctor. "You're saying that the bliss is already there, deep inside; Ascension points the way to it."

"Yes, this brings us full circle back to the Ascension Attitudes," agreed Lila. "Each of the techniques of Ascension has a meaning on the surface of the mind. But because of their Source, each also has the unique quality of being *more true and more enjoyable* at deeper levels of thinking. Because this is so, the mind is drawn inward effortlessly.

"Therefore, *no effort is required to Ascend!* In fact, even the slightest effort, even the slightest desiring for the experience to be like something, or to be specific somehow, will slow down this process. From our side, we must *always* be innocent about Ascension. This is the first and most important rule. In fact, it's the only rule. We never, ever *try* to Ascend.

"So, you're prepared. Now we'll do it.."

I felt a little silly and self-conscious at first, but only for a moment. Gradually, I sank deeper and deeper into Silence. A few thoughts came up, but the comfortable repetition of the Ascension Attitude soon banished them. I slipped effortlessly inward on a soft, warm cloud of golden light.

I had come home for the first time in my life; I was alive and well in my soul, more so than any time since I was a tiny, tiny child.

I was a stranger no longer.

I was no more lost and alone.

I had come home.

9

The Grotto of the Apocalypse

Sharon stayed in the Teaching Hall with Lila to learn the Second Technique. Doctor Dave said he wanted to Ascend in his room; I was feeling restless and decided to walk around the island, go exploring. I had more energy than I'd had in years. If this came from even that much Ascending, I knew I was going to like this new thing a lot. I felt like a young tiger. Plans for new homes were bursting through me; I couldn't recall the last time I'd felt as creative. If I stayed in the villa, I knew I'd scrounge up paper and start scribbling home designs. This seemed inappropriate; instead I decided to investigate Patmos.

The sun was brightly shining, but a sea mist had rolled in and was hanging low over the water, making this appear the only island in the world. My impression last night about the monastery looming overhead had been, if anything, too reserved -- the place looked as if it had been built to withstand a siege of thousands. Who had they been, those Middle Age monks? Soldiers of God? Were they so fearful of the end of the world they built their walls to keep out the devil's legions? Or had the pirates as the Byzantine Empire slowly decayed been so dangerous?

Patmos was a stony, all but barren island, composed mostly of three hills of congealed lava. The field of poppies behind the villa was nice, but smaller than I'd imagined from Sharon's ecstatic description. The primary plant life on the hill was a low heather with fragrant pink blossoms -- the shrub arbutus. As I climbed through the low heath, legions of small lizards ran everywhere frantically to avoid my feet.

From the top of the hill, just beyond the monastery walls, I could see down both sides of the narrow isthmus that divided the island. The port of Skala was on one side and a lovely harbor was on the other. There was a large private yacht there; a feeling of foreboding flowed through me when I looked at it. My gut tightened up, my heart accelerated. *Classic fight-or-flight,* I thought. Discovering no reason for my feelings, I denied them and continued my leisurely stroll.

The low fog gradually burned off; in the far distance, floating above the water-hugging mist, there was a large mountain on the next island, Samos. I also gradually made out seven little islets surrounding Patmos.

From up here, the "new" town of Khora was a blinding surgical white. Most of the houses were square and flat-roofed. There were some green vineyards scattered here and there, a few olive trees, some cypress, a small herd of goats and sheep on the northernmost hill. I could just make out a small village there, built around a white church.

Two people were walking up the hill from Khora toward me. At first I thought I preferred to be alone, so I turned away and strolled toward the northern slope. But at the last minute, I decided not to go down -- if they wished to speak with me, so be it.

Ascending had heightened my senses -- everything seemed worthy of my attention -- my appreciation of the island, the Sun, the sky, the plants mingled with an intense wonder at my being there at all. How could my life have changed so quickly? From my dark bedroom to the bright sunlight on Patmos! Maybe there really was a Divine Order in the Universe -- maybe our one purpose was simply to enjoy the gift of life, to appreciate it.

Was this not what the First Ascension Attitude was teaching? To reconnect us with that rising current of Creation, the upward flowing river of appreciation? Surely the Ultimate needed no praising for itself -- but perhaps our human minds needed to appreciate it -- to align with it, for the sake of our mental, emotional and physical health. I decided to ask Lila about this in the evening, then turned to see if the couple was still climbing up toward me.

They were; it was Aphrodite and the American, Steve Young, walking hand-in-hand, deep in conversation. I thought they hadn't noticed me and decided to make a graceful exit by hiking down the north side toward the other harbor, but just then she looked up at me, waved and smiled. So instead I waved back and waited exactly where I was.

Steve still looked unhappy. In fact, he looked as if he had been crying. I don't often inquire of other men's feelings, especially those of near strangers, but this time I found myself asking, "Hey! You all right?"

"Sure, fine," he answered gruffly.

But the young Greek scowled at him and said, "Now, Steve. Pretense is not the answer. You know that isn't the doorway to peace." She looked at me and added, "He feels bad about Ollie. I brought him up here because you knew him well. I thought it might help."

"We were best friends in high school," I began, but Steve interrupted me with a flood.

"It's so unfair! He was the best friend I've ever had! Saved me from myself. I was going down, hooked on wine and drugs, lost, wandering alone through Europe. No light in my tunnel -- except the train of Death coming at me full speed. I tell you, I was one messed-up kid. I was lying there, passed out in a back alley in Athens; next thing I know, I'm being carried aboard a ferry by a complete stranger. It was Ollie; he brought me here, to Patmos.

"That was six months ago; I've been Ascending since then, gotten the first six techniques. But I tell you -- none of this makes sense! Ollie was the nicest, most generous guy I've ever known. My own parents were never there for me -- my dad's a lawyer, my mom's a broker -- they were never home. I couldn't wait to move out. Soon as I was eighteen, I left for Europe. Hitchhiking was good for awhile, but I started hanging around a bunch of guys with their heads stuck in the powder. And then I got into alcohol and crack.

"My folks sent me money every month, hoping I'd come home, but I'd just spend it within forty-eight hours and be busted for the next four weeks. I was diving down fast, dying young.

"Ollie saved me from that! Then I hear he's dead... I almost went with him, you know, back to Seattle. I like Alan and the others, particularly Ed Silver and Mira -- and of course you, Dite -- but Ollie was my Teacher! It's so meaningless, so unfair!"

"See how it is?" asked Aphrodite. "He won't listen to Lila or any of the others. Says he's going to go back to Chicago. Can you talk to him?" Her eyes pleaded with me. She obviously had long plans for him -- of which he was completely unaware.

I smiled to myself about the ways of the heart, but answered, "I'm no expert on Ascension -- I only just learned the First Technique today. I like it and think I'll like it even more as it imprints deeper on my nervous system, but I don't know much about any of this."

"I know that," she answered with a touch of impatience. She didn't seem the kind of woman that could easily be refused anything. "Experts on Ascension are all around us. I'm hoping you can give Steve something so he'll remain with us."

He had sat down in the heather after his long speech; his head was drooping. Was he listening to her at all? It didn't look like it. What was she asking of me? To take Ollie's place as his personal mentor? How could I? Ollie had had twelve techniques, I a single one -- Steve had six times as many as I did! What could I do? My heart went out to him in his pain, but was that enough? Well, I *was* older than he; that might count for something. But what could I say?

It occurred to me this kid might just need attention. He'd been all but abandoned by his parents -- probably it was not so much Ascension that inspired him to turn his life around, rather the compassionate attention of my friend.

"Look," I said, sitting beside him, "I don't have any answers. I don't have any idea why anyone ever dies. If I were God and were designing the Universe, I think I'd change many things. There's an awful lot I don't quite see. I have noticed people often get stuck in their thinking; they don't know how to bend with the storm and shatter and die when the world changes around them. They get rigid and inflexible and brittle. Their deaths I can kind of understand, can kind of feel why such people need recycling, but a guy like Ollie? Young, vibrantly alive, moving ahead at an incredible pace? That I can't grasp, at least not yet. Maybe after I've Ascended more and my understanding has deepened. Maybe I'll react more like Lila did when we told her last night. But not now. Now it makes no sense at all.

"Since I don't understand, the best thing I can do about those who die is remember the joy of their lives, the love we felt flowing between us. We keep them alive in us; we honor their memory by living as they would have wanted us to.

"Ollie, *particularly* Ollie, would he have been depressed if anyone died?"

"Ollie? No way! He was always up, always cheerful -- even when he heard his mom was gone. But I always figured that was because he'd Ascended so long -- for three years."

"Well, maybe. But there must have been a moment or two in those three years when he chose to be happy -- when he chose to look for the good in life and appreciate it rather than dwell on the bad. I think we could all find bad everywhere if we looked for it. But what would that do to us?"

"I think I see your point," said Steve, looking at me earnestly. "Some fanatics for example -- they spend all their time looking for Satan in everything. Sure they find the devil working the world -- that's what they're seeking everywhere."

"But if they would start looking for the Good instead -- that's what they'd start to find. And I'm beginning to see that a choice as simple as that has incredible consequences for us -- our mental stability, our emotional well-being, even our state of health responds to this simple decision -- to appreciate or condemn."

"You know," said Steve slowly, "I've had the First Attitude for six months, but I don't think I've ever understood how I can apply it *all* the time, regardless of what happens. I was pretty foggy when I got it; I never really understood it until now. Thank you! I'm starting to feel much better. I really am."

"Don't mention it," I said, resolving to talk to him again whenever he asked me. "What else is there to see on Patmos? The view up here is lovely, but I'm ready to move on."

"We'll take you to the Grotto!" exclaimed Steve, standing up and sounding almost cheerful. "Right Dite? He'll love it."

"Sure," she said, and winked at me.

We walked back down through the white, white Khora. I was charmed by the pots of hydrangeas, begonias and sweet basil everywhere. The stone arches spanning the street stood out for me, since I'd so recently heard Lila talk about keystones.

Everything was so charming, our walk to the Chapel of St. Anne was extremely slow. Was Khora truly so lovely, or was the First Attitude working its magic on me? My Ascension had been restful, but was the technique really so profound? *Anyone could have come up with it,* I thought. *And many may have. Perhaps it is the power in this simple technique the charismatic Christians plugged into, for example. If so, their entire movement is based on the First Ascension Attitude! How would their understanding deepen with the increasing subtlety and power of the next six*

Spheres? Were the other three techniques of the First Sphere so simple and obvious as this one? Could finding the solutions to all my problems truly be so simple as regularly using the First Attitude? To appreciate rather than condemn? I had no answers to my questions, but my curiosity had grown larger, not less from my experience so far with Ascension.

We reached the Chapel of St. Anne at last. The doorway opened to the east; from the threshold, there was a stunning view over the harbor. The inside of the church was filled with flowers -- it looked like a hothouse conservatory. We were greeted by a Greek Orthodox priest, attired typically in black robes with a black hat and long beard. He evidently spoke no English, but Aphrodite chatted with him for few moments; after that he left us alone.

The Grotto was a great, gray sea cave. It must have been quite wild once, but now it was leveled and formed the inside of the south part of the building. The northern aisle was dedicated to St. Anne, the mother of Mary. Aphrodite showed me a lovely twelfth century icon of her there and told me the monastery possessed several such magnificent works of art, the like of which would be hard to find elsewhere outside of Russia. In spite of the past thousand years of warfare in the Aegean, the monastery had never been looted. She also said it had a large fragment of the Gospel of St. Mark, dating from the fifth century. "It is written in silver uncials on purple vellum, with the sacred names of God in gold. It is a work of the greatest beauty and delicacy. I doubt you'll have time to see it this time, but it's wonderful."

"I'm sure it is," I said, impressed equally by her English and her sincerity.

The southern aisle was called the Church of the Apocalypse: here John received his Revelation. The building there consisted of the Grotto itself; the roof was the stone of the rock. There was a large, triple crack in the ceiling; Aphrodite said that was created during John's vision. "Represents the Trinity, you see," she said earnestly.

She explained that a slope in the rock wall had served the disciple Prochorus as a desk as he recorded John's words. Nearby there was a silver halo on the wall over a hollow in the rock where John was supposed to have slept. "Many villagers have seen the Blessed John's face in that sea-hollowed hole where he used to sleep," she said. There were several channels in the floor; she commented sharp-scented water had flowed through them until fifty years ago.

"Sharp-scented? Like what?" I asked, amused by her credulity.

"They say it smelled like roses or lemons. I know what you're thinking, Mr. Skeptical, but you know what? I was up in the monastery, reading some of the books in their library, and I saw a record from the seventeenth century that said the same thing. This is a place of wonder! Every old person on the island saw these streams running; most of the islanders have also seen the face of the Apostle just there, where I told you.

"Patmos is a wonderful place. I have heard there was once a fig tree outside that had the word 'Revelation' written in Greek inside every fig. John fought with a wicked magician, Kynops, when he came here and turned him into that large rock called *Yelopas* in the harbor down in Skala. The monastery was built on top of an altar to the Moon Goddess Artemis, the Huntress, who still roams the hills of this island, forever seeking her twin, the Sun God Apollo. I don't know where to draw the line, but some of these stories are probably based in truth."

I had to agree the place had a soft peace and a grand wonder about it; I could see how the Apocalypse would have been written there. I suggested we Ascend for a while; they agreed readily.

Here I am, about to Ascend in St. John's Grotto, I thought as I closed my eyes. *Just last week, only seven days ago, I believed my life was over. Now I'm in Greece, in love, practicing a technique that may be two thousand years old. Who says life isn't strange and mysterious?*

I felt a thrill of excitement. But this time, Ascension started slowly. I had lots of thoughts; the more I tried to push them out, the stronger they became. I decided to quit and try again later, but then I remembered Lila saying the only rule was *not* to try; therefore I continued a little longer, but without using any effort. I stopped forcing the Ascension Attitude and just drifted with the thoughts.

As soon as I stopped fighting them, they became less strong. There was a sudden and clear memory of the expensive yacht in the harbor on the other side of the island, accompanied by my stomach tightening and my heart speeding up again. I almost felt ill, but suddenly the image drifted away; my body at once relaxed, my heart slowed. *The mind and the body are one*, I thought, then found I could easily think my Ascension Attitude now. Other thoughts kept drifting through, but they no longer bothered me. As long as I was completely easy with it, I became more and more relaxed. I felt as if I were floating inward, riding a fleecy golden cloud, feeling as comfortable as I ever have. The world was OK, I was OK, everything was going to work out: I was learning to experience Silence.

I felt as if I were expanding through space, becoming larger and larger, becoming huge. I was bigger than the Chapel, bigger than Patmos, bigger than the Earth. Still outward and onward Ascension led me -- suddenly a bright golden sphere appeared before me. It expanded around me; inside were seven rings of fire, each a color of the rainbow, each more brilliant than our sun. These also expanded around me; inside were galaxies, stars, planets -- I was seeing the entire Universe. It was before me but also in me; it was part of me, yet I was also observing it. I stared in wonder, forgetting the Ascension Attitude, forgetting who I was, forgetting everything I had ever known, so glorious was this Universe, expanding around me...

10

The Last Supper

I have no idea how long I Ascended, but when I at last opened my eyes, Steve and Aphrodite were gone; it seemed late. From behind me, someone started softly chanting, *"I was in the Spirit on the Lord's day and heard behind me a great voice, as of a trumpet, Saying, I am Alpha and Omega, the first and the last: and, What thou seest, write in a book, and send it unto the seven churches which are in Asia..."*

It was the doctor. "I wondered if you'd ever finish," he chuckled. "I've waited over an hour for you. Sharon sent me to find you, thought maybe you'd fallen into a cave or something. I felt you might be here: I always get my man."

"What time is it?" I asked. My mouth was dry; my voice felt as if it hadn't been used in days.

"Early evening. Time for dinner, in fact," he answered, looking at his watch.

A little unsteadily, I stood up and followed him outside. It *was* late, the Sun was behind the monastery; it would set soon.

"Nice day?" he asked.

"Unbelievable! Ascension *is* magic. How about you?"

"Some of the times it was kind of flat. I didn't seem to go anywhere. But now with you in the Grotto it was *very* still. Didn't feel like I had a thought other than the Ascension Attitude."

"Really? It changes every time, doesn't it?"

"Makes sense. The body is always going to be in a different state -- different foods being digested, different fatigue toxin levels in the blood, changes in circadian rhythms, different hormones -- all these will make for a different experience."

"I guess that's why we're told to be easy with it. No trying, no looking for some kind of experience. Right?"

"I suppose. A different state of body means a different state of mind. The mind and body function as one. It's all perfectly logical... Wow! Smell that? They must be making a feast in there!"

They were -- since it was the final meal, there was much to eat before the morrow. It was a smorgasbord of pure delight.

Sharon looked, if possible, even more radiant. Before I could comment on this, she cried, "I'm so proud of you!" and threw her arms around me and kissed me without the slightest reserve.

Yes! I thought, but said, "Why? What'd I do?"

"Don't be so shy! Aphrodite told me how you helped Steve. That was brilliant!"

"Hah? I didn't do much. Just reminded him to Ascend with his eyes open, that's all. Nothing to make a fuss over."

"Hah yourself! Everyone else *tried* to tell him that; you're the one who got through. I think you're a natural born Teacher."

She looked like she was about to kiss me again, but there were a few too many others around for me to be altogether comfortable with that. The New York Novitiate twins were grinning at us; I said hurriedly, "Well, I doubt that. I've never had any interest at all in teaching. Seems like a pretty thankless task to me."

"Oh, we're teaching all the time," commented Lila, coming into the dining room behind us. "Can't help it. Our only choice is, do we teach from the ego, from the belief in separation, in suffering, in death? Or do we teach from the Ascendant, from the experience of Unity, of joy, of life? In every moment, everyone chooses one or the other."

"Teaching is not memorizing facts and figures and then spewing them out. Teaching is the example we're living," agreed Devindra.

"Well, let's eat," I said, feeling unsettled about this. Whatever they called it, teaching was far from my desire. Just a week ago I had been on the verge of catatonic withdrawal from the world. I did not feel worthy to teach anyone anything, nor could I imagine ever being worthy. For someone who had fouled up his life as much as I had, what could I possibly offer others?

Lila, looking as beautiful as a China doll, sat at the head of the table, blessed the meal and said, "I want to tell you all! I've been having dreams for over a week about our journey. I think we're all going to move to a higher plateau of understanding. I don't know exactly why, but I feel tomorrow is going to be one of the most important days of our lives."

As if in comment on her words, a sudden gust of air blew open the door behind her. Five napkins flew into the air and landed on the floor. Lila laughed with joy and started serving the meal as Aphrodite and Sharon bent over to pick up the truant napkins.

After dinner, we met again in the Teaching Hall.

"So, how was the Second Technique for you?" Lila asked Sharon.

"Wonderful! Just wonderful! I spent all afternoon Ascending with it, as you suggested. I've never felt more balanced in my relationship with my body and my world."

"That's its purpose," Lila grinned at her. "That technique is designed to heal all physical problems. And how did you two find your Ascensions?"

"Different each time," said the doctor. "Sometimes still and relaxing, sometimes noisy and jumpy. I thought it must have to do with the body. Right after lunch when my stomach was full, it was hard to settle down. Is that it?"

"Yes. Food in the stomach raises the metabolic rate, the opposite effect of Ascending -- which, as you have seen, produces deep rest."

"Do other physical factors also effect it?" he asked.

"Sure. That's why it's important to learn right away that the experiences during Ascension constantly change: they are determined by the state of the body, which is never constant. Sometimes Ascension feels deep, sometimes it feels less deep. From our side, it doesn't matter, we just do it -- but always easily."

"I had some interesting things happen at the Grotto," I said. "When I started, my thoughts were intense; I tried to push them out. Then I remembered you said it had to be effortless; I relaxed and stopped pushing it; it became *much* easier."

"That's right: since we're not forcing the mind, thoughts can *never* stop or even slow Ascension. Sometimes there are many thoughts; sometimes there are few. It depends on what's happening in the body when we Ascend."

"For me, it's always different, every time," said Sharon.

"Yes," agreed Lila, "and that's why we evaluate the success of Ascension by the changes in our lives, rather than by our experiences during it. I can't emphasize this enough. The one all-important rule is: *never force it.* Don't quit, thinking it's not working, if it doesn't feel as deep as the last time. It just means some stress is leaving."

"I think that happened at the Grotto too," I said. "After I stopped pushing it, one thought became particularly strong; my heart speeded up, my stomach tied itself in a knot -- fight-or-flight, I guess, Dave, but I was just sitting there, not doing anything!"

"No, you were *Ascending,*" smiled Lila. "The deep rest caused stress to dissolve; this caused the discomfort and the thought. What happened next?"

"I let it wash through me. It peaked; my body stopped feeling uncomfortable; the thought faded away. Then the most amazing thing happened -- I expanded through space, became larger and larger; I saw the whole Universe in front of me and inside me at the same time. I don't have words to describe it properly -- it was the most incredible experience I've ever had. What was happening? Was that the Ascendant?"

"Not exactly -- the Ascendant lies beyond *all* boundaries. You were seeing the subtle state of your nervous system. Contained within you is the entire Universe."

"That's what it felt like, but I don't understand how I could be that big!"

"The Ascendant underlies *everything*. You touched one of the most basic expressions of the Ascendant. I suppose you could call it a Cosmic experience, for you saw the cosmos inside you."

"Whatever it's called, it was *highly* enjoyable."

"Sure. When we're effortless with Ascension, it's pleasant and relaxing. It may seem deep or not, but that isn't our concern. What *is* our concern is just to do it, easily. Then the silence and the rest will come, as much as the body can experience at the time, and the stress will go...

"I'm curious. Did any of you notice a time when the Ascension Attitude had faded out *completely,* it was no longer there in any way, and there were also no other thoughts of any kind, and yet you were still awake, you hadn't fallen asleep?"

"I think I did, after that expansion I described," I said.

"I'm positive I have several times," said Sharon.

"I may have, I'm not sure," said the doctor. "Why?"

"Because that state of silent awareness is the first stage of experiencing the Ascendant clearly," answered Lila. "That's good."

"I don't understand how it's possible to experience the Ascendant at all," said Dave. "If it's infinite and beyond all boundaries, how can it be experienced?"

"Good question! The reason it's possible is the same reason you *will* experience the Ascendant clearly sooner or later: you *are* the Ascendant. Consciousness is what you are; that is what the Ascendant is. The beliefs in limitations of body, mind or ego are beliefs merely; you are, as are all humans, Unbounded Beings, living the Ascendant in human bodies. It's just that we've forgotten; from birth we've been identifying with the boundaries.

"This is necessary at first, to survive in the world; but the truth is, we're not different from the Ascendant. It may be completely covered up, so much so that even hearing this simple Truth sounds impossible; nevertheless, this is true."

"Are there ladders back to the Ascendant?" I asked.

"What do you mean?" she asked curiously.

"I mean, is the way to remember who we are built into Creation? When I was talking to Steve today, it occurred to me that maybe we're tapping into a fundamental principle of Nature when we use the First Attitude. I don't know if I'm putting this well, but is appreciation like a huge vortex of energy that is part of the structure of Creation; we connect with that when we Ascend?"

"I see what you're saying!" exclaimed Sharon. "You're saying we're hooking onto the primary Ascending emotions that already exist -- we're flowing with the River of Life; that is why Ascension so rapidly transforms us. Right?"

"That's what I was wondering," I said, smiling at her. She was so brilliant.

"You're exactly right," commented Lila. "Well said."

"How long until Ascension's clear?" asked the doctor.

"It will be clear when the stress is gone from the central nervous system. What helps most is regular practice. We normally Ascend with the eyes closed two or three times a day -- before breakfast, before dinner, before bed.

"And we Ascend with the eyes open whenever we happen to think of it during the day. Both these ways are invaluable. The eyes-closed way gives us deep rest and starts strengthening the new groove in the brain; the eyes-open way enables us to meet challenges directly as they come up. This means we don't have to waste time in old reactive behavior patterns; new stress doesn't lodge so deeply."

"When we Ascend with closed eyes, is it better to sit up straight?" asked the doctor.

"Only if it's comfortable! The key thing is comfort. If the body is rigidly upright and this is a strain, it will distract the mind, keep it from innocence. The secret, physically, is to be comfortable. Naturalness is everything. It's even OK to lie down to Ascend."

"Wouldn't that encourage sleep?" he asked.

"Not as much as you might think! Meditations that are hard and involve concentration or those that are boring recommend sitting up, because the mind prefers the blacking out of sleep to continuing. Because Ascension is effortless and fascinating, you'll only fall asleep when the body really needs it, even if you are lying down."

"So many people in the world are running on empty," mused the doctor, "chronically fatigued. Wouldn't they fall asleep a lot as their bodies take advantage of this rest?"

"They might. At first, until their bodies normalize. For such people, the simple decision to take time for themselves could be a real challenge. There are so many 'workaholics' in the world. Rearranging their priorities enough to Ascend is their great challenge: they need to do it for awhile, until they discover for themselves how enjoyable and relaxing it is."

"I feel so rested all the time now, I'm starting to sleep less," said Sharon.

"That's normal -- because of the deep rest, the body begins to be more efficient; less sleep is required. So by going *away* from activity, the ability to be *more* active results. Once active people realize that, they'll start taking the time to Ascend so they can work better. And then, with new experience, their priorities will change. Their 'type A' personalities will settle down, they'll live longer, healthier, happier lives...

"Well, folks, I need to go down to the harbor. Our chartered yacht, the *Marylena*, is due in tonight. I need to talk to the skipper."

"I saw a yacht on the other side of the island," I said.

"Odd." She scowled; a dark look clouded her eyes. "Not much tourist traffic at this time of year -- rarely in that harbor. Never, in fact, except when there's a gale blowing from the East. Someone visiting the monastery?" She shrugged and looked as if she were forgetting it.

"May I come with you?" asked the doctor. "I want to hear more about becoming a Novitiate."

"You're not thinking of doing that, are you?" I asked, incredulous. "Becoming a monk?"

"Well, I don't know, probably not for life, but *something* about it fascinates me; I'm thinking about trying it for a year."

"Why did you do this?" I asked Lila.

"Why become a Novitiate? Because I wanted to devote my entire life to God. There is nothing else that interests me. Having realized that, it was an easy decision. For me."

"I can't even begin to relate to that," I said, looking at Sharon curiously.

She smiled back at me and said, "As a matter of fact, neither can I. I want to be in a relationship -- but an Ideal One, this time, with someone who shares my priorities, someone who's as dedicated to Life and Truth as I am. I believe it's possible for two to grow together into God -- even if it's rare in the world."

"That's what Nanda Ishaya says," agreed Lila. "'The life of the recluse is not for most.' He also said, 'Many people have an easier time carrying the Ascendant on four feet'... Well, I've got to go. Dave, coming?" She stood, smiled warmly and held out her hand to him.

"You bet," he said, grinning back at her.

11
The Passion

Our Good Friday began strangely. White as a ghost, trembling all over, Sharon ran into my room, crying. I held her for five minutes before she could speak. Finally she calmed enough to tell me: "I dreamed of Ollie. No -- it wasn't a dream. It was a nightmare: he was as smashed and broken as I last saw him.

"He told me not to take the Marylena, instead wait for the regular ferry this afternoon. When I asked him why, he pointed his arm at me and -- oh God! -- it was decomposing! It was so real, so frighteningly real! Then he said again, 'For no reason take the Marylena!' I've never had a dream like this. Why did it happen?"

It was 6 AM, we were supposed to be carrying our bags down to the yacht by 6:30 for our departure, and here was Sharon, deeply shaken, talking about a bad dream. It didn't make the slightest sense and I told her so.

"I'm *not* going on that boat," she said firmly. "I'll find you in Athens later tonight."

"Hey, wait!" I exclaimed, startled by her words. "I didn't say I wouldn't stay with you; I only said it doesn't make sense to follow dreams. They're unpredictable, can't be trusted. Come on, let's take our bags down to the harbor and talk to Lila; maybe she can give us some advice." I was hoping the Novitiate would dissuade her.

"All right. But forget about my suitcase. I'm *not* going on that boat. Half a minute while I get dressed."

"No problem," I said, wondering if my girlfriend was having a bad day or if the Moon was in the wrong place for her at this time of month or if she knew a whole lot more than I did and I was too dumb to recognize it. Shrugging, I finished dressing and joined her in the hallway.

Lila was sympathetic but did not understand either. Sharon remained adamant; as we stood on the dock and watched our new friends boarding, I realized with a sigh I would be taking the ferry again today. Yesterday's mist was gone; the waning Moon was hanging in the West; the early sun streamed over the harbor. It was fairly hot already -- a beautiful Aegean day in the making. What would be so bad about waiting on Patmos with Sharon for a few more hours? Nothing at all, I decided, feeling settled with our plans for the day.

"We'll go back and Ascend in the villa after they leave," I said softly. "Or in the Grotto. It'll be a fun morning."

She squeezed my hand and beamed at me. "Thank you for being you," she sang sweetly to me.

Aphrodite and Steve were the last to come down the hill. As soon as the young Greek saw the Marylena, the day turned strange again -- Aphrodite screeched in fear and started babbling in Greek.

"What's the matter?" Steve asked her incredulously.

"Stormy petrels!" she cried. "*Five* of them! There, on the bow! Don't you see them?"

"Stormy what?" he asked, looking curiously at the boat. "Those little black and white birds? So?"

"I'm *not* going on that boat," said Aphrodite firmly. "Not for any amount of drachmas. No way. I'll take the ferry and meet you later in Athens."

"Hey, if you're staying, I'm staying. But this sounds awfully dumb because of a couple of birds."

"I'm not going," she said fiercely and started carrying her two suitcases back up the hill.

"OK, OK, just wait up, will you?" he said, grabbing his backpack and hurrying after her.

"Shall we go back too?" I asked Sharon, astounded by this unlikely coincidence. "Guess we'll have some company on the ferry after all. Strange day, this."

"I wonder... Here, half a minute. Let's ask Dave if he wants to wait with us." She walked over to the edge of the dock and called to him, asking him to stay.

"I don't think so," he called back cheerfully. "I'm too much enjoying Lila. Thanks anyway. See you in Athens!"

He walked to the stern to talk to the Novitiate while the others disappeared into the hold of the ship. *They're going to Ascend,* I thought. *It's early.*

"See you in Athens tonight!" I shouted to him as the crew began casting off. He waved, apparently not hearing. Sharon and I waved back, then walked back up the hill. I was looking forward to Ascending; it felt like I hadn't had nearly enough rest yet.

Just as we reached the Chapel of St. Anne, the day went completely insane: there was a terrific explosion out in the harbor. Several windows near us shattered from the concussion. We spun around to see what could possibly have happened; there was a huge fireball on the water where the Marylena should have been but definitely wasn't!

"Sharon, isn't that -- !" I exclaimed in rising fear, but she was already racing back down toward Skala.

Was someone in the water, stroking back toward the shore? I wasn't sure, but if there was, it was only one.

There *was* someone: the doctor. He reached the pier just as we did, pulled himself out and started cursing. He was bleeding from his head, one ear and both arms.

"What happened!" we cried as we ran up to him.

He kept cursing, stamping his feet up and down on the dock, screaming in rage, completely wild.

"David!" exclaimed Sharon, managing to put an arm around him. "Dave, it's Sharon. You're OK. Here, sit down, let me look at you. You're here. We're here. You're OK, David. Dave! You're OK. *David Tucker! Sit down!"*

He heard her finally and looked at her blankly. She told him a third time to sit down; he did, clumsily; she examined his wounds as I said, "What's happened?"

"I -- ouch! Careful! I have no idea. One moment, Lila and I are talking about the Novitiate vows, the next she screamed and pushed me into the water, then Boom! A second's difference and I'd be spread all over the harbor like they are. Damn! Why the hell didn't she jump too?"

"Maybe she didn't have time," I said. "But how did she know there was going to be an accident?"

"How did I know in my dream?" asked Sharon. "You and I weren't meant to be on that boat, that's why. And neither was Dave... Oh God, poor Lila. And the others. What a nightmare." She started sobbing.

Aphrodite and Steve ran down the hill, shouting in fear. The local residents were lining up along the harbor, looking blankly at the remnants of the yacht. There wasn't much left to see. A couple of half-dressed scraggly policeman were in an old launch, struggling to get their motor started and cursing it in Greek.

Some sixth sense caused me to look over my shoulder -- there was someone in the shadows, staring at us from an alley. He was dressed like an Orthodox priest, with long beard, black hat and robe. When he noticed I saw him, he disappeared into the shadows.

My stomach was churning; it felt like I was about to throw up. Steve Young beat me to it. Leaning over the edge of the pier, he wretched his breakfast into the harbor.

"Damn," said Dave. "I'm bleeding. Had some bandages in my bag, too. Anybody got anything?"

"Back at the villa," said Sharon dully.

In a daze, the five of us walked back up the hill.

"Well, now what?" asked the doctor. "Back to the States?" It was mid-morning; after bandaging his arms and head, we had all Ascended together. It was pretty choppy for all of us, with lots and lots of hammering thoughts. But afterward, we felt calmer -- or at least, I did.

"Not for me," said Sharon emphatically. "We haven't delivered Ollie's message to Alan Lance yet. I'm going ahead with the schedule as Lila laid it out for us: Easter Sunday, off to India."

"I kind of expected you'd say that," I sighed. "And there's no use pretending I won't go with you. I know that tone. So, I'm coming too. How about the rest of you guys? Steve?"

"I'll go if you go and Dite goes," he answered, looking at me with trusting innocence. *Do I deserve that?* I asked myself, and decided I probably didn't. But I didn't see what to do about it, so decided to ignore it. For now.

"I'm terrified of India," said Aphrodite in a small voice. "I hated it the last time I went. But I want to see Nanda again, and I want to learn more about Ascension. I want to finish the training to teach the nine techniques I've received and I want the other eighteen. I guess I have to go and find Alan Lance and Mira and Ed Silver."

"Don't *any* of you feel this wasn't an accident?" the doctor asked plaintively. "Don't you think so many bad things happening to Teachers of Ascension is a little improbable?"

"Well, look here," I answered slowly. "I've been thinking about Ollie's death almost constantly since Sunday. And that last Ascension! There was nothing else *but* thoughts about this morning. I don't remember if I introduced the Ascension Attitude even once. No, I don't believe either one was an accident. We're all in danger. We should get lost in Athens as soon as we can. We're like sitting ducks here on Patmos. I think these Opposition guys are totally ruthless. They're determined to destroy Alan's interpretation of Ascension. I don't believe we're safe anywhere.

Ollie was walking down a street in Seattle. Lila was on a boat in the Aegean. Where could we possibly hide?"

"I have no idea," said Dave, "but heading straight to the Punjab? Isn't that exactly what they'd expect?"

"I have no idea what they'd expect! They may think we all died on the boat, although I doubt that. I think one of them was watching us from an alley down there in Skala."

"No! This is too terrifying. We can't trust anybody! How do I know some of you might not be working for the other side?"

"Well, how can you? How can you trust anyone? You only met Dite and Steve here yesterday and Sharon and I in Seattle Sunday night. How can you trust us? For that matter, how can we trust you? How do we know you're really David Tucker? Whoever killed Ollie might have intercepted my call and replaced the real Dr. Tucker. You're as likely a candidate for treachery as anyone. You survived the Marylena, after all. How could you do that?"

"That's preposterous!" he shouted indignantly. "I'm Dr. David Tucker!"

"Of course it is and of course you are. I was just showing you how, once you start down the road of suspicion, it leads to any kind of madness. Let's not get completely unplugged here. There are obviously some people trying to end St. John's Ascension, but I'm learning to trust my feelings. And I feel strongly about each of you. I am, in fact, willing to stake my life on my intuition. For I agree with Sharon -- we've got to find Alan Lance before they do. And then, who knows? Maybe this Nanda fellow can do something, can stop that other guy, Durga. They used to be Novitiates together, didn't they? So maybe Nanda can convince him to call off his dogs. Then we can go back to the States without having to watch our backs for the rest of our lives. And also learn more about Ascension. There's something to this stuff, something that maybe *is* worth dying for. I don't know; but if I don't go ahead now, I'd always wonder what might have happened if I'd been a little more persistent, you know?"

"Oh, all right," agreed the doctor glumly. "I'll come too. I hope I'm not being a fool."

"Fine, it's settled then," said Sharon, looking relieved. "This feels right to me -- I think we five need to stand together. Let's scrounge some lunch, then catch the ferry."

It was difficult to leave Skala. The military officials that appeared in the harbor were extremely curious how Dr. Tucker managed to escape the Marylena. Aphrodite had to translate at great length; finally they agreed he could take the ferry on his promise to report to their superiors in Athens first thing Monday morning. We didn't bother to tell them that with luck we'd be in India by then.

12
Aftershocks

The trip across the Aegean was as beautiful as the crossing on Wednesday, but today I could hardly appreciate it. In spite of my strong words to the doctor, I was full of fear at the prospect of continuing any further on this quest. It was obviously lethal. I knew I didn't value Ascension enough to face death. At least, I didn't think I did; yet whenever I was presented with the choice of dropping out or continuing, I found myself pursuing the path that led more deeply into this Teaching. It felt that my rational mind hardly had anything to say about it -- I was hearing a quiet voice inside, directing me in every situation. I could choose not to listen to this, my voice of intuition, but I was finding the more I listened, the more automatic my life became. And the more spontaneously right were my decisions.

Steve needed my attention early on this crossing. The New York twins had been his good friends; he had felt close to each of the others and was struggling to understand why they had died. Like it or not, I found myself again in the role of counselor.

"Can you explain to me," he said as we found a place to sit on the crowded boat, "why life has to end in death? It's senseless to me." Sharon had gone off with Aphrodite to talk; the doctor said he wanted to be alone, to think. That left me to try to help the young American.

I sighed and answered, "What can I tell you? I'm as mystified as you. I haven't any idea why those moving ahead should die. I don't know! Maybe we're in the middle of a great Cosmic War we only dimly perceive. Maybe Earth is pivotal; perhaps there is more at stake here than our own happiness.

"If Ascension truly is as important as Alan thinks, it makes a kind of twisted sense some of the Powers in Creation might be trying to keep it from the world."

"What do you think?" Steve asked, sincerity flooding his brown eyes.

"I don't know. I guess I don't see any need to invoke other Powers as an explanation; we humans seem perfectly capable of fouling up our world all by ourselves. If there is a God who is all good? I don't know. I would like to think there is. And I'd like to ask Him -- or Her! -- why He/She permitted that tragedy today. Or any tragedy anytime. But until I meet God face-to-face, about the only thing I can do is the best I can to help make the world a better place. As far as I can tell, Ascending makes perfect sense; it seems to be able to help anyone live a better life."

"I think," said Steve with great emotion, "if someone is trying to end this Teaching, they should be stopped. I don't know how, but they should be stopped! Someone should pay for what happened today!"

"Well, I feel exactly the same way, but you know what? We're looking at this from a fairly narrow perspective. Losing my home and family in Missouri was a nightmare, a living hell -- but if I hadn't, I wouldn't have met Ollie or Sharon and learned to Ascend. And Ollie's death still seems pointless to me -- but if he hadn't died, I wouldn't be here with you now. It wouldn't be today anymore, it would be some hypothetical Universe that doesn't exist. I'm not pretending to understand, for I don't. But I *can* see, there *may* be meaning hiding behind all of this; if I could be innocent, if I could stop *all* my beliefs and judgments, I might see it. I don't know!

"I don't know -- but I *do* know Ascending is making me feel better about myself and my world than I ever have; I want to learn more about it and I want to Ascend a lot more. It's the brightest hope in my Universe; if I have to continue a little longer without understanding everything, I guess I'm no worse off than before I learned the First Attitude; and really, I think I'm far ahead of where I was before yesterday. What about you? Would you trade in what you've learned and go back?"

"Go back? No, I don't think so. No, of course not! I'd be dead. I guess you're right, I *do* know a lot more about life than I did six months ago; it's unreasonable to expect to learn it all at once. But I've sure got some questions for Nanda when we get to India."

"Me too. Have you met him?"

"Not me. But Dite did once, spent a week with him, a year ago. She said he was unlike anyone she'd ever met -- filled with peace, love, wisdom."

"I'd like to hear more about him! Maybe it would inspire us. Want to find the girls?"

"You bet," he said, grinning at me. "And again, thanks. I always feel much better when I talk with you."

"Well, you're welcome," I said, uncertainly. Why should he? I hadn't said anything much.

We joined Sharon and Aphrodite in the crowd at the bow. There were Greeks everywhere, traveling to Athens to spend Easter with their families. As in our own country, the population of Greece has dramatically shifted in the twentieth century. Just as we have abandoned our family farms and small towns so that some of our rural states' populations are actually shrinking while our metropolises explode, just so, the Greek islands have suffered greatly as Athens has swollen from a steady influx of immigrants. "All the best young people leave the islands," moaned one aged islander to me in the restroom on the ferry. "I don't know what will become of us." The population on board the boat was certainly old: most of them were traveling to visit their children and grandchildren in the capital for Easter.

Sharon and Aphrodite looked up at us and smiled. They both seemed OK. "How are you doing?" I asked Sharon.

"Actually -- well. I feel the pain, the shock, the horror, but another part of me remains calm. I feel as if I'm watching it all happening. And the part watching *knows* everything is all right. I wonder if I'm turning schizo or something."

"Well, if you are, I must be too, for I feel the same way. My emotions are different now. It's not that I'm feeling them less -- in fact, I'm experiencing them more than I ever have. But there is a bigger part to me now, a silent part, huge, forever at peace. I don't understand it, but I'm sure it's real."

"That's called 'Perpetual Consciousness,' I think," said Steve, uncertainly.

"No, you're right," Aphrodite agreed enthusiastically. "Alan explained it to me -- he said that as the mind becomes saturated with the Ascendant, it becomes completely peaceful, deep inside. He said that's called Perpetual Consciousness. It's like having an anchor at the bottom of the sea -- the waves on the surface don't bother you so much any more, because you're grounded in infinite Stability. He says this naturally grows in anyone. As the stress decreases in the body, the nervous system starts functioning differently, as it was designed to do. Part of the mind looks inward to its ground, its Source in the Ascendant; part of the mind continues to look outward, into the world revealed by the senses."

"So Perpetual Consciousness is a dual style of functioning of the mind?" I asked curiously. "How odd. Yet, it does describe my experience. I feel split between this new inner peace and my old normal feelings."

"Alan says the old way of reacting is the *abnormal* way. He says that in time, the Peace and Love grow so strong, outer experiences can't shake you at all. You become like a rock. And that's called Perpetual Consciousness. Or so he told me."

"I can't believe how fast Ascension works! I'm changing so quickly!"

"I suppose that's because the Ascension Attitudes are built into the fabric of Creation," said Sharon. "We're not *adding* them, we're *aligning* with them. Praise and Gratitude and Love exist everywhere, always; we're learning to flow with them all the time. As we discussed last evening, this explains why the growth with Ascension is so fast. We align with the root tendencies in Creation; then our lives become significant. Our limited individual selves melt into our Unlimited, Universal Self."

"That scares me," said Steve. "I don't want to lose me."

"Oh, I don't think you will," laughed Sharon. "You'll truly *become* you. Once the self-destructive beliefs melt away, what will be left is the Real Steve."

"I think that's right," I agreed. "The Ascension Attitudes are stairways back to the Real Us."

"More like escalators," said Dr. Dave, joining us. He looked a whole lot better -- clear, relaxed, peaceful. His eyes looked red, as if he'd been crying, but other than that he seemed fine -- or, more than fine. Ascension was obviously working for him too. "I say escalators because they're moving upward already. We only have to get on board for the ride. I just hope it's not a roller-coaster."

"My life *was* a roller-coaster," said Sharon. "I couldn't stop a bad mood when I was caught by it. Somebody would say something nasty to me or something awful would happen and I'd spiral down for days or even weeks at a time. *Then* I was out of control; *now* I feel as if I have an ocean of patience and love inside. And I've only been Ascending a week! What will I feel like in a month? Or a year?"

"I'm sure I don't know," I said, "but I'm finding this adventure *very* exciting. I'm looking forward to my next chance to learn more. Neither of you can teach me the next Attitude, can you?"

"I haven't completed the training," answered Aphrodite quietly.

Steve said with intense feeling, "I haven't ever desired to be trained as a teacher, but I'm thinking I would like to now. I feel calm inside too, but I'm angry on the outside. I guess anyone telling me I can't do something makes me want to do it. And somebody sure seems to be saying that about Ascension. So I'm beginning to want to help spread this... There may be no better way to change people like my parents. It might make them more loving, more compassionate... Oh, they may be loving enough, they just don't know how to express it. I'd really like them to learn. Yes, I've made up my mind: I'm going to ask Alan to train me."

"What's it take to become a teacher?" asked the doctor.

"About six months of in-residence study," answered Aphrodite. "That's the minimum. And clear experiences with the first three Spheres. I've got about a month of study left and three more techniques to learn. I hope that by summer, I'll be qualified to teach in Greece... Although I doubt *my* parents will ever be open enough to learn. My dad runs a shipping company, my mother is the only daughter of a wealthy vintner in Thrace. They're both extremely traditional. They sent me to the States to school, but that's the limit of their involvement in the last part of this century, I think. I was engaged to the son of an oil billionaire on my twelfth birthday. They laid out my whole life for me... Maybe that's why I was so attracted to Alan when I met him in Athens. He showed me a whole new way of living. He's the only man I've ever known who thinks of me as a person, not just a body. Present company excepted," she added, blushing.

"Tell me about Nanda Ishaya," I asked, partly to change the subject. "What's he like?"

"Oh, he's wonderful! Short; in his sixties now, I guess; wears saffron robes. He's always laughing, always happy. I don't think it's possible to move him from his peace. It's unshakable."

"How's his English?" asked the doctor.

"Excellent! The last Custodian insisted he finish college before he join the Order. Majored in Philosophy and English. The British ruled India for a long time, you know. English is the official language. Most of the peasants can't speak it much or at all: they hold to their native dialects, but they can't understand other regional groups without using English. The wealthy and the college educated prefer it; it sets them above the herd, I suppose."

"Tell us about the Ishaya Order," the doctor asked. "Why does everyone think it came from the Apostle John?"

"I asked Nanda that myself," she said. "He said they have preserved the records in the monastery for nineteen hundred years. He has studied them. In fact, he told me St. John never died; he simply retired to a cave farther up in the mountains. He was such a perfect master of Ascension he could stop his heart and breath and translate his body at will. He mastered the aging process and gained immortality."

"Oh, now, come on --" I began, feeling this absurd.

But the doctor interrupted me, "No, I believe that's possible. In fact, the leading edge of modern science is close to verifying this. Please continue." He was completely earnest; I looked at him with amazement.

"Well, the point is," she continued, looking uncertainly at us both, "Nanda-ji says John comes out of his cave every century or so to check up on his monastery and the Ishaya Teaching. So says the historical record. And if that's true, as Nanda believes it is, he may come out again soon, for it has been more than a century since the last time. Nanda and Durga both feel John will appear and install one of them as the new Custodian, the new Maharishi of the Ishayas."

"Couldn't someone go to the cave?" I asked, not believing for a minute this highly unlikely story, but willing for the moment to play it out. "Go there, find the Apostle John and ask him? Surely

Durga would stop his opposition to Ascension entering the world if John told him he must."

"Sure he would," agreed Steve, "but what if John decides for him instead of our guy? Then where'd we be? If St. John wanted Ascension available to people like us, why'd he go to so much trouble to hide it? The middle of the Himalayas is not a friendly environment, from all I've heard, not a logical place to put a Teaching designed to revolutionize the world."

"Well," I said thoughtfully, since no one else was answering him, "let's assume for the sake of argument it's *all* true. John would, I presume, have been able to foresee the fall of Rome and the Dark Ages about to descend over Europe like a cloak of despair. He would also have known what was going to happen to Christ's Teaching, how it would become so distorted -- maybe the only way he could see to ensure Ascension's survival was to hide it away from the world until now. Today with mass communication, the whole Earth is united in a global electronic network; it would be difficult to stop Ascension once it was made available. Once a book about it is published, for example, who could ever hope to contain it again?"

"*That* explains why Durga's followers are so violent!" exclaimed Sharon. "They know once the Secret of the Seven Spheres is out, there will be no stopping it. From their perspective, that must seem the ultimate blasphemy. They're trying to stop an avalanche before it begins."

"But it's an avalanche of good!" protested the doctor.

"To us it is, sure. But to them it might look like the end of the world. Infidels with infinite power? Think about their background! Their entire tradition is built on fear. The thought of us crude, barbaric Westerners with the world's most precious and secret Teaching must be giving them nightmares."

"But how can they be Ascending correctly?" asked the doctor. "Even the First Attitude shows all life works together for good. How could they not see that?"

"I wonder if they're Ascending at all," mused Sharon. "There's no guarantee their master taught them anything True. In fact, seeing the way they operate, I would have to say he couldn't have. Maybe he's waiting for approval from John before he teaches anything authentic."

"Second guessing these guys strikes me as being difficult," I said. "I'm not sure it's worthwhile."

"I guess you're right," agreed Dave. "All we really have to go on is our own experience with as many techniques as we have. Ascension seems logical and consistent so far; I've begun to notice profound benefits in terms of inner calmness and deep rest. That's all I can verify, for now. It's even possible we've all developed intense group paranoia -- we could have seen two accidents, disastrous, coincidental, but accidents none the less."

"Maybe," I said, not convinced. "Well, let's continue to be cautious, OK? Dite, where did you tell those police Dave was staying in Athens?"

"Why, the Grand Bretagne, where Lila made us reservations. Aren't we going there?"

"I think that would be a very bad idea. I think we need to get lost in Athens -- take a hotel up in the center of the city some-where, disappear. I'd prefer it if you got a different ID, Dave; they may try to keep you from leaving Sunday."

"I can help with that," said Aphrodite. "I know some people we can see tomorrow. It's pretty easy. I can get visas too: my aunt used to date the Indian Ambassador."

"Good!" I exclaimed, relieved. Two problems solved.

Dave was the only one who had given his name to the military -- I don't think they realized we were traveling together. If we could secure our Indian visas *and* leave Greece with him using a different name, that would make it harder for anyone to follow us. There had been too many surprises on this journey already; I wanted to avoid more.

In that, I was sure to be disappointed.

13
An Oracle

We landed in Piraeus in the middle of the night. There were so many passengers we couldn't catch a taxi, but the railway station was nearby, just to the north; as luck had it, the train to Athens departed fifteen minutes after we arrived.

Our journey of five miles ended at the north side of the Acropolis, where Athena Avenue ends in Hermes Street. We walked through this lovely part of Athens, known as the Plaka, seeking a hotel and craning our heads at the stunning view of the Parthenon up the hill. Most of the boarding houses and hotels were full, but finally we discovered a nice-looking place on Apollonos called the Omiros. Three hundred yards to the Southwest was the Parthenon; about five hundred yards to the Northeast was Mt. Lykabettos, site of the world famous Easter celebration that evening.

The landlord, a large and phlegmatic Greek, was *not* overjoyed to be awakened at 3 AM by five weary travelers. The beauty of Sharon and Aphrodite mollified him somewhat, as did the news we wanted five rooms *me bánio* -- with private baths.

He imagined we were here for the grand celebration of *Páscha,* Easter; we replied we were grateful to find rooms on such a weekend.

"Very fortunate you are indeed! I had five rooms *me bánio* reserved until midnight -- but they never arrived. I was afraid I was going to lose money this Holy Week. I'm so glad you've come."

"Many thanks for opening to us," said Sharon as we climbed the stairs to our rooms.

I put her bag by her door and started to look for mine. But she said, "Let's go to Delphi tomorrow, please? It's important we do that, I think."

"Sharon! It's so late! Doctor Dave has to get a new ID; we need visas; we're flying to India Sunday. Don't you think it would be better to spend the day here, relaxing and Ascending? It's going to be a hard journey."

"Dite and Steve will help the doctor get his papers; they'll get visas for us too. I'm going. You don't have to come if you don't want," she said, downcast.

"Hey, I never said I didn't want to go with you," I said, frustrated, "just that there might be wiser uses of tomorrow. Rest here during the day; watch the Easter celebration at night; be better prepared for traveling Sunday. It's been a grueling day."

"Oh, we Ascended through most of it. You can't be *that* tired."

It was true -- most of the voyage had been devoted to Ascension; I actually felt quite rested. But I wasn't ready to give in yet and said, "I didn't get deep *at all*. Just thought after thought after thought, mostly about the accident. I hardly had a chance to introduce the Attitude all day."

"But how do you feel *now*?" she asked with wide-eyed innocence.

I could not continue pretending, seeing those amazing blue eyes. "In all honesty, quite well. Rested, in fact. Astonishingly so. But why go to Delphi? It must be at least three or four hours by car. Is it *so* important to go sightseeing?'

"I'm not sightseeing! It's *important* for us to go there. It's just intuition -- but if I ignore it, we won't learn something we're meant to learn. That's what I think."

So 8 AM found us renting a car and driving northwest toward the suburbs. Even at such an early hour on a superhighway on a holiday Saturday, the Athenian motorists were savage. They all seemed to believe they owned the road and were deeply offended if anyone dared to be in front of them, even on the freeway. It was a terrifying experience, driving in Greece.

I was happy when the city ended and happier still when we were out of the suburbs; we entered a countryside of sparse olive and almond trees as we gradually started climbing and winding around several ridges. Sharon Ascended for an hour or so, equally disinterested in the amazing views and the potential carnage from the other motorists doing their best to kill us and each other.

She opened her eyes about the time we came to modern Thiva, site of once famous Thebes. There was little of interest to the town now, not much left of its historical grandeur when it challenged Athens and Sparta for control of the Greek world.

"Thebes was the city of King Oedipus," said Sharon as we drove by the disappointing place.

"Who killed his father and married his mother," I said gloomily.

"Why does that depress you?"

"My father died when I was fourteen. I had fairly recently before discovered my sexuality. At the time, I was perversely hoping he'd go away so I could have my mother all to myself. When he died, part of me was afraid I'd caused it."

"What a time for him to die! That must have been awful for a young adolescent."

"It was horrible. He was a great fool, my father. Like yours. If he'd only loved me more, he would have changed his habits and not died. Not that I was much to love in those days! Pudgy, glasses, an anti-social little nerd-in-the-making of the highest degree. I didn't have many friends before high school. I'd learned contempt from my family, but little of successful interpersonal relationships. I was a lonely kid.

"That's one reason I wanted my children to grow up in a small town. More personal, a real chance for life-long friends. Not like huge Seattle... Sharon, how do you feel about step-mothering?"

"Why -- why, I think it's a hard job: the children need not only to get past their jealousy, they have to accept the authority of the new parent. But if I loved a guy enough to marry him, I'd make it work, through unconditional love... Why? Have you thought of asking me to marry you?"

Her forthright sincerity shocked me to silence. I locked my hands on the wheel and stared at the road, trying to control the sudden waves of fear rolling through me.

The olive trees of the Attic peninsula had given away to fields of wheat. The snow-capped peak of Mt. Parnassus, site of Delphi, appeared more and more awesome as we drove Northwestward. We were passing many little chapels along the side of the road; they ranged from tiny mailbox-sized on stone posts to small temples with icons inside. I realized they were marking the sites of fatalities. Their vast difference in construction style and quality implied each had been built by the relatives of the deceased. Considering how all the Greeks drove, it was likely that someday every road in Greece would be solidly lined with these little buildings.

As the road started winding up the north side of the narrowing valley, multitudes of bright blue beehives appeared -- thousands upon thousands of them. I'd never seen so many beehives in my entire life. The gentle slopes of the mountains were covered with arbutus and heather and other low shrubs that looked like they might be huckleberries or blueberries. I wondered what the honey from such a mix might taste like; later Aphrodite told me this region's honey was famous throughout Europe.

In many places, the road passed alongside steep cliffs, typically without guard rails. As we climbed higher, we passed large herds of white and black curly-horned goats, tended by shepherds that looked like they belonged in an Old Testament painting, complete with crooked staffs, Greek peasant dress and dogs. There were rough stone houses here and there -- shelters, perhaps, for the shepherds during winter storms.

I pretended everything I saw was utterly fascinating so I could avoid thinking or answering Sharon. The whole time I was thus repressing my feelings, she sat silently, patiently waiting.

After almost an hour of this, the mountains started closing in more and more; we came to an intersection of three roads near a gorge between two high hills. There was a jumble of signs; on impulse, I pulled off the road to read them. "'Schiste,'" I spelled out laboriously. "'Triodus.' 'Distomo.'" Then I saw one in English, "'Here Oedipus killed his father.'"

"Blast it!" I shouted, hitting the steering wheel so hard it cracked. "I'm not worthy of marrying you; I'm not worthy of marrying anyone! I can't even afford child support. Of course I've thought of it. Yes, I love you. I adore you! I can't imagine living a day without seeing you -- but my life is *ruined!* I've *nothing* to offer you."

"Well, *I* think you do, you know," she said warmly, not in the least affected by my outburst. "You've accompanied me boldly on this quest, an adventure which is at the least frightening and probably extremely dangerous. So, you are brave.

"You've taken to Ascension. Though you fuss about it, I can tell you love it. You want to pursue it to the end. So, your priorities are straight and clear.

"You've also taken to *me*. I see that, even though you hide it. I can see your love in you. Your self-image tries to block it, but your heart knows what it knows. It is deep and it is strong. So, you love me.

"I don't care about your past. It doesn't exist. Your current financial woes don't concern me either, for we are moving ahead, you and I, into a glorious new future of magic and wonder. Everything *is* going to work out for us, you'll see.

"Here, let me drive. You enjoy this wonderful mountain scenery for awhile. Or, better -- Ascend and see what happens, OK?"

I followed her suggestion and Ascended; within a few minutes, I did feel much better, but was no closer to resolution of my core issues.

Within another half an hour or so, we came to a picturesque little town called Arakhova, perched high on a rocky spur of Mt. Parnassus, above a large gorge. The white houses rose in several terraces to a church at the top; the town was pretty and unique -- several large streams of water ran down the mountain along the sides of the streets. We decided to stop and buy a picnic -- bread and cheese and lots of fruit -- to eat at Delphi.

As we drove down the other side from Arakhova, we saw that the valley was covered with silver-green olive trees, some of them huge, ancient. "I've heard the olive can live thousands of years," said Sharon, admiring them. "Some of these may have been alive when Christ taught in Galilee. Some of them may have been here when Xerxes was defeated. That is amazing to me."

Parnassus was starting to show lots of color in its rocks. As we "S" curved down the mountain, I saw a shining ribbon of a river below, winding its way to the azure Gulf of Corinth. Our road kept high above the gorge on our left; the view of that was often obscured by vineyards and olive and almond groves. Suddenly two eagles swooped overhead; Sharon said, "I've read that Delphi was called 'the navel of the world' by the ancient Greeks. Zeus released two eagles to find the center of the Universe; they flew in opposite directions and finally met at Delphi."

She drove us slowly down the mountain until, without warning, we rounded a sharp corner past a cemetery and arrived at the ruins. A modern and ugly museum of white concrete with a large parking lot beckoned to our car; we exited into the noonday sun of the ancient shrine.

Two of Parnassus' immense gray cliffs, streaked with rust, towered over us to the North, their fissured faces brilliantly reflecting back the dazzling sunlight. To the South was another mountain; the gorge we had followed from Arakhova expanded out at its foot, covered with olive trees, until it reached the bay below. Such were the physical surroundings of the heart of Ancient Greece; but the grandeur and living silence went far beyond words.

"We have to begin at the Kastella fountain," said Sharon with great seriousness as she studied the guidebook and map we purchased in the museum. "There are several springs here, but Kastella was *the* sacred water. Those coming here seeking the oracle's advice were told to purify themselves in it first. Most washed their hair, but murderers had to bathe."

"I wonder how long I should soak in it," I murmured, but the glory of this colossal ruin made it impossible for me to dwell in dark moods for long.

The spring was near the gap between Parnassus' two cliffs. A large stream was running between them; I thought at first it might be coming from the sacred fountain, but soon realized it was flowing from plateaus farther up the mountain; Kastella was a little to the east of the cleft. Its ancient façade, carved out of the rock of the mountain, was still visible, but the original tanks and basins were long since damaged and broken. There were some steps carved in the rock leading down to it; we put our hands in its clear pool and dripped the water over our heads. Nearby was a shady grove; we decided to sit there, close to the sacred fountain, and have our picnic. For some reason, few other tourists were walking there today.

"Where to next?" I asked as I held a chunk of cheese and bread in one hand and the open guidebook in my other. "There is a Temple to Athena and a famous round temple called the Thoros over that way to the Southeast, see it? And down this way in the other direction is the Sacred Way and the Temple of Apollo, which once had the phrase, 'Know thyself,' inscribed on its walls. The whole of Delphi was dedicated to Apollo, the Sun God of creativity, art, music and prophecy. He came here from Crete, so the story goes, riding on a dolphin. Hence the name Delphi -- Delphinos means dolphin in Greek.

"There are dozens, maybe a hundred ruined temples here. Each city-state of ancient Greece had its own treasure house at Delphi, it says. It really was the navel of the world to them, the center of their Universe." So much to see, so little time.

"You know," she answered slowly, "I don't think we came here to see Delphi. I think we're here to learn something."

"What's that?" I asked curiously.

"I haven't the foggiest idea! Where was the oracle? I'd like to go there next; maybe we'll have some sort of inspiration."

"It was in the Temple of Apollo, I think," I said, reading rapidly. "Yes. Let's see, the *Pythia*, the priestess-oracle, was a peasant woman of at least forty years. The Pythia ate bay laurel leaves, then breathed the vapors rising through a fissure in the rock -- it's volcanic here, you know. There've been many earthquakes. It says one came just in time to stop Xerxes from sacking the temples... The Pythia smelled the vapors, then fell into a trance and uttered mystic phrases which the priests translated into verse to answer questions. Sounds like a BC version of speaking in tongues, doesn't it?

"More often than not the cryptic answers didn't help much. One emperor, Croesus of Lydia, asked if he should attack Persia -- this was before Xerxes, I guess -- and the oracle answered, 'If you march into Persia, you will destroy an empire,' which sounded like a pretty clear, 'Yes.' So Croesus did and was soundly defeated -- it was his empire Lydia that was destroyed.

"The Athenians asked if Xerxes would defeat them; the oracle said everything would fall to the Persians except a wall of wood --

they interpreted that to mean their wooden fleet would stop him. Which of course it did.

"I begin to see why Dr. Dave is so moved by the history of this country. It just keeps creeping up on you, doesn't it?"

"Why was the priestess called the Pythia?"

"Let's see -- here we are. Pythia means pythoness. Apollo killed the python that owned this place when he came here."

"Hey, this all means something, I'm sure of it!" Sharon exclaimed animatedly. "Apollo was the God of the Sun, of consciousness, of creative inspiration, of music, of poetry. And where does inspiration come from? From deep in the unconscious, that's where -- which is why the symbol of the unconscious is often a dolphin, diving beneath the waves, or a serpent, living in the ground. In India for example, the power of life, the Kundalini, is often represented as a coiled snake, lying at the base of the spine, waiting to rise through the nervous system and bring enlightenment. So the dolphin Apollo's Pythia, the daughter of the python, inhaled vapors rising from the Earth, from Gaia, and that gave her the power of prophecy, of pure divine inspiration. That *is* wonderful! Do those vapors still rise?"

"Apparently not. One of the earthquakes probably shut them off. Unless it was all metaphorical. It says here that Julian the Apostate, one of the last Roman Emperors (he lasted only two years, from AD 361 to 363) sent to Delphi in 362 AD to ask how he could best serve Apollo. The oracle answered,

Tell him: Emperor, the laurels are cut down,
the fair-wrought house is fallen to the ground,
Apollo no longer wanders here;
Even the water sings in silent fear.

"I guess they all packed up and left, a long time ago."

"I'm frustrated," she sighed. "That collection of ruined temples over there is no doubt fascinating, but hardly worth the drive. It may be the best ruin in Greece after the Acropolis and the

Parthenon, but it's still just a bunch of old ruined buildings. What we're discovering is a living tradition. Ascension is today what Delphi was to those Greeks -- a means of communicating with Divinity. Only instead of looking outside, seeking advice or counsel from others -- from oracles, priests, ministers, doctors -- Ascension teaches how to contact God directly, by looking within."

"Why did we come here then? You would not have insisted so strongly last night unless you thought it could tell us *something*."

"I don't know! Oh, let's walk down to Apollo's Temple. Maybe an idea will jump out at us."

We followed the Sacred Way along the base of the mountain. It was obvious why Delphi had been built there -- the huge cliffs above made a magnificent backdrop to the greatest church in ancient Europe. The sun striking full on the cliffs glowed the colors in the crevices, purpled the shadows and drew every crag on the mountain sharp against the bright azure sky. I could see why these twin cliffs were called *Phaedriades,* the Shining Ones. I had read that those guilty of sacrilege were thrown to their deaths from the eastern cliff. *How could anyone commit sacrilege against an oracle?* I wondered, then remembered with a shudder yesterday's explosion.

Before we reached the old wall around the cluster of ruined and partially restored buildings, Sharon stopped suddenly, cocked her head to one side and looked over the gorge below. A huge golden eagle was circling there. Had the other two been golden? I didn't think so, but was more concerned by the changes in her. "Sharon," I said alarmed, "are you all right?" All the color had drained out of her face; she was staring over the valley as if in shock.

"The Second Ascension Attitude! I know what it *means!* That eagle... the beauty here... my heart swells with Gratitude... I see! *I see!* This is all a projection of me! It was all created for me! I built Delphi! I built Athens! I built Rome!"

"What do you mean? Reincarnation? You remember being here?"

"No, that's not it, but yes, yes! I've been here! I'm every one of the those millions who came here to the City of the Dolphin, seeking answers in a confusing world. I'm everyone of the Pythias who breathed the vapors of Gaia and prophesied. I'm the Christians who defaced the ancient temples, misunderstanding Christ's Teaching from day one; I'm the tourists; I'm the timeless Greek peasants; I'm Gaia, the Mother! I'm Delphi! I'm Parnassus! I'm the Earth! This is all coming out of me! That eagle is me! The ground is me! These trees are me! You are me! All this world is a part of me, of my body. It's all me, it has all been me, it will never be anything other than me! It all makes perfect sense. Oh, my words can't describe it as I see it. Oedipus blinded himself when he learned he'd killed his father and married his mother and his wife/mother hung herself, but what was blinded? And who died? It's all fitting together in a perfect tapestry of wonder! It's all in me! It was all created for me! I created life! I created Love! I created death!"

"Sharon!" I exclaimed, not knowing what to do or say. "Sharon. Are you all right?" I took her hands and stared into her eyes. Was she having some kind of a breakdown? From the strain of traveling added to the two accidents? She didn't seem unhappy, rather wild with a frenzied emotion that might be ecstasy. Her pupils were completely dilated, amazing in this bright sunlight. Had one of the oranges she'd eaten been bad? Or the grapes? She hadn't had any bread or cheese. "Should we start back to Athens? Or stay here, explore more?"

"It doesn't matter where we go! I am Athens! I am Delphi! I tell you: I'm creating the whole Universe, this instant! The whole of it, the whole of its history. I've made it all! I am you! Nothing other than you, nothing other than a thought in you. You don't see me, you see your projection onto me, which more or less resembles who I am, but is not *me*. You're creating your own Universe! You're projecting the whole thing! And I'm creating mine. Sometimes our creations overlap; we call that communication. Do you see?"

"I don't have any idea what you're talking about," I answered, discouraged and frightened by the changes in her. "I think we should go. If we leave now, we'll travel mostly in the light. Driving in Athens after dark doesn't appeal to me. We might even get back in time for dinner with the others, then be with them for the Easter celebration at midnight. Does that sound all right, Sharon?"

"Fine. Whatever. Don't worry about me, OK? I'm having a wonderful day. I've just discovered one of the greatest secrets of the Universe. The Second Attitude is a lot more powerful than I realized. Believe me, I'm fine. I'm *immensely* pleased, in fact."

This was the Sharon I knew, returning from wherever she'd gone. I breathed a sigh of relief; we walked down the Sacred Way past the ancient temples and treasuries and returned to our car by the poorly designed museum.

"Would it be all right if you drove again?" she asked cheerfully. "I want to continue exploring this as long as I can. I'm learning so much."

"No problem," I said, opening the door for her.

14

The Resurrection

By superb driving skill married to *extremely* good luck in surviving the Greek motorist mentality, we made it back to the Omiros in time for dinner with our friends -- barely. They were leaving through the front door as we hurried up the steps.

"Glad you're here!" they exclaimed, embracing us.

"We were just going to Mt. Lykabettos for supper," said the doctor. "Dite has a special place where she likes to eat whenever she's in Athens."

"Wait while I change?" asked Sharon, hurrying to her room.

I was content with what I had on, but it seemed wiser to follow her example. I somehow managed to return to the others in the lobby more quickly than she; I asked them about their day.

"Very successful," answered Dave. "The passport was easy: only took a couple of hours. And the visas were even quicker. We bought me some clothes, then spent the rest of the afternoon on the Acropolis, Ascended up there. I had a wonderful day."

"So did we," said Aphrodite, holding Steve's hand and looking at him with love. "I'm so pleased to tell you: we're *engaged.*"

"Hey! No kidding! That's *great!*" I said and meant it, but at the same time felt guilty for poorly answering Sharon that morning. The trip home from Delphi had been quiet; she Ascended through most of it, changing with me after we passed Thiva so I could also Ascend before dinner. We hadn't talked more about her experiences at Delphi or about marriage; I felt on one hand relieved and on the other disappointed. Had I lost my only opportunity with her already? What such a brilliant beauty could see in me was beyond my comprehension.

Sharon walked down the stairs from her room, ravishing in an evening gown of sky-blue with a shawl of cashmere gold. *How does she keep so much in her small bag?* I wondered, mystified by the ways of women. *She likes me? Impossible!*

We took a taxi to the northern corner of Mt. Lykabettos -- it was about thirty blocks from our hotel. Aphrodite's special taverna there, curiously enough called the *Pythari*, was supposed to have great food *and* music.

After we found a table (mostly through forceful persistence) and followed the Greek custom of visiting the kitchen to select our dinners, we settled down to a leisurely evening of food and music: it was three hours before the celebration on the mountain. No one felt like alcohol tonight; we all sipped lemon juice or Turkish coffee and sampled Aphrodite's recommended snacks: *dolmádes,* grape leaves stuffed with rice and chicken and seasoned with grated onion and herbs, *dzadzíki,* a tangy yogurt dip with garlic and grated cucumbers, and *taramosaláta,* a pink spread made of gray mullet roe mixed with mashed potatoes, olive oil and lemon juice. We ate these with dark Greek bread and wondered how we'd possibly have room left for everything else we'd ordered: *saláta choriátiki* -- Greek salads with sliced cucumbers, tomatoes, green peppers, onions, radishes and olives topped with féta cheese, *avgolemono* soup made with chicken, rice and eggs and flavored with lemon juice as well as red mullet for Sharon and me, squid for the doctor and octopus for Steve and Aphrodite.

"How was your day?" asked Doctor Dave as he covered his third piece of bread with the pink taramosaláta paste.

"Delphi was amazing!" I exclaimed. "I'm learning your passion for ancient history. But my discoveries were small compared to Sharon's."

"Oh? What were they?"

"We were walking there," she began in a dreamy voice, "at Delphi, just past the sacred fountain Kastella. I was wondering why we'd come; finding no reason, I was feeling more and more frustrated. I stared over the valley and the gulf below, crying out in my heart to God for meaning; from nowhere a golden eagle appeared! It seemed as if it materialized from thin air.

"Something clicked inside; I understood the Second Attitude more deeply than ever before. It washed through me with perfect meaning -- I was connected to everything; the entire world was part of me. This doesn't say it properly -- the entire world was coming out of me, from deep inside me. I was the Creator of it all. It was amazing. I've never experienced anything like it."

"That's called Unity, I think," said Steve slowly. "But I always believed that Unified Consciousness came after Perpetual Consciousness."

"Well, you're right, it does," said Aphrodite, "but it's possible to taste Unity before Perpetual Consciousness becomes permanent."

"How does that work?" I asked, intrigued. "How many states of consciousness are there?"

"I know of seven," she began, but the doctor interrupted her.

"Seven? Really? To be a unique state of consciousness, not just an altered state, there have to be distinct physiological characteristics, not just subjective experiences. Sleep exhibits deep rest and mental dullness; dreaming, much higher physical activity, often rapid eye movement, and illusory experience; waking, still higher activity and mental alertness. That makes *three* distinct states and seems an exhaustive list; I assume anything else must be some kind of alteration of these three."

"Ed Silver, a physiologist by training, explained this all to me," she answered, looking embarrassed. "Would you like to hear what he said?"

"Sure," the doctor agreed and we echoed him.

"Well, Ed said people who don't Ascend *do* regularly experience only three states of consciousness -- waking, dreaming and sleeping, each with different subjective experiences, each distinct physically as you just described.

"But Ascension produces a fourth state of consciousness. It's not an altered state, it's different enough from the other three to be classified separately."

"To be a major state of consciousness, it has to be different physically and subjectively," persisted the doctor.

"Yes. Ed says the rest from Ascending is much deeper than sleep -- about twice as deep as measured by oxygen consumption, carbon dioxide elimination, basal skin resistance, blood pressure, heart rate and breath rate. He also said fatigue toxins like lactic acid and plasma cortisol drop more in twenty minutes of Ascension than they do in eight hours of sleep at night."

"Well, I've certainly experienced the deep rest of Ascending," agreed the doctor, "*and* I'm still awake when I do it, so the Ascendant State can't be either waking or sleeping. It is similar to both and yet different from either. Fascinating."

"Ed also said, during the clear experience of Ascending, the mind is still, but not asleep. It's perfectly coherent, alert but not thinking other thoughts. He said he's measured this with the EEG, the electroencephalograph, and found that during this stillness, the brain waves become completely orderly."

"Just like my stone in the pond analogy," I said smugly. "One stone, nice clear ripples. Lots of stones, chaos."

"So," continued Aphrodite, "this is the fourth state of consciousness, called Ascendant Consciousness. Ed says Ascendant Consciousness has been known about and written about in all parts of the world by all the great traditions. They call it *satori* in Japan, *samadhi* in India, *the peace which passeth understanding* in our own tradition, often simply *the Fourth* in ancient literature. But only recently have medical professionals and physiologists studied it and found it real."

"Well," said the doctor thoughtfully, "now that I've heard some more about it, I do seem to remember somebody at Harvard Medical School was studying this -- a Dr. Benson, I believe. Called it the 'Relaxation Response,' I think. He theorized anyone could experience it. I read about his findings in the *New England Journal of Medicine* -- or was it the *Lancet*? Fascinating work. So, OK. I can understand this fourth state; I'm experiencing it myself. Deeper rest than sleep and more mental clarity than waking. But you said there were *seven* states? What are the other three?"

"Perpetual, Exalted and Unified," answered Steve, as if reading from a textbook. "Sleeping, dreaming, waking, Ascendant, Perpetual, Exalted, Unified," he counted on his fingers. "Each distinct physically and mentally. Seven states, Seven Spheres. Makes perfect sense."

I didn't like that idea. Seven Spheres for seven states? Surely there were no Spheres for dreaming or sleeping. But I said nothing. Steve obviously meant well, and who could say? Maybe one of the Seven Spheres *did* relate to dreaming, and one to sleeping. I couldn't be certain that they didn't.

As this was flitting through my mind, the doctor was saying, "I want to understand this in great detail. This knowledge would revolutionize our understanding of the human body. And mind."

Our dinners started arriving; all conversation ended for a long time. The band -- two bouzokis and a guitar -- started playing while we were eating; after dinner, Sharon and I danced, so did Aphrodite and Steve; the doctor was left alone to contemplate the seven states. I was curious about these, but less than he; I was content with my progress and certain that, since it was all unfolding naturally, whatever developed in me would have to be good and certainly better than the stressful life I was leaving behind, a life impossible to change until I met Ollie again -- was that truly only a week ago today? It seemed like a thousand years.

The musicians abruptly stopped playing at 11:30; everyone stood up and started for the exit. "What's going on?" I asked Aphrodite.

"You'll see," she said excitedly. "Come on!" She led us into the Athenian night.

"Half a second," said Sharon, pulling some flats out of her purse. "Don't like hiking in heels," she explained, grinning at me.

The streets were already thronged. "No Athenian misses this night," Aphrodite said as she threaded us up the slopes of Mt. Lykabettos. There was a small church at the top, the Chapel of St. George, already filled to overflowing. I had never seen so many Greeks in my entire life. With difficulty, we managed to squeeze through the outer gate into the small courtyard surrounding the church. I noticed that everyone was carrying an unlit candle and asked Aphrodite, but she was prepared: she pulled five long tapers out of her bag and gave one to each of us.

The crowd was mostly quiet, silently expecting the stroke of midnight. "All over Athens," Aphrodite whispered to us, "the priests are leading services. Every church is full; all the streets around every church are full. Everyone is outside, waiting, waiting. The heavy air that began with Lent forty-eight days ago is about to lift. The fasting is ending; joy returns to Athens!

"It has been particularly sad here since yesterday. Every year, on Good Friday night, there is another candlelight celebration, this one with a big parade beginning and ending at Athens Cathedral. It is more of a funeral procession than a parade. Everything is somber and sad. Incense smolders, marching bands play the funeral march from Beethoven's *Eroica* and Chopin's solemn *March Funèbre*. Soldiers march, their flags at half mast. Sailors march, boy and girl scouts march, all escorting the body of Christ. Violet robed acolytes and a bare-headed bishop holding aloft an empty wooden cross are last before the great bier. A hush falls as the coffin passes by, borne by white-robed priests.

"At the Cathedral, the archbishop, crowned like a Byzantine emperor and carrying a golden crosier, leads the body of Christ into the Inner Sanctum. He removes his crown and comes back out, now wearing his regular black hat. As he sits on his throne, the people flock forward to touch his robes and kiss his hands. Then he quotes St. Paul's letter to the Corinthians:

'Behold, I shew you a mystery: we shall not all sleep, but we shall all be changed, in a moment, in the twinkling of an eye, at the last trump: for the trumpet shall sound, and the dead shall be raised incorruptible, and we shall be changed. For this corruptible must put on incorruption, and this mortal must put on immortality. So when this incorruptible shall have put on incorruption, and this mortal shall have put on immortality, then shall be brought to pass the saying that is written, Death is swallowed up in victory. O death, were is thy sting? O grave, where is thy victory?'"

As Aphrodite spoke, the dimly lit chapel plunged into total darkness. All the lights of the city suddenly went out; even the floodlights on the Parthenon were turned off. This was all planned, I realized, to symbolize the darkness of the grave.

The chapel doors burst open; a priest wearing resplendent scarlet robes inlaid with rich gold and holding aloft a lighted candle emerged and cried with great emotion, *"Christos Anesti! Christos Anesti!"*

The crowd shouted back, *"Alithos Anesti O Kyrios!"*

Chapel bells pealed to proclaim the Resurrection. An artillery battery fired twenty-one rounds. The ships in Piraeus Harbor sounded their sirens. Fireworks blazed across the sky. Quickly, unbelievably quickly, flames from the priest's candle swept to us and around us, then raced down the serpentine roads leading to the summit. This scene was repeating all over Athens: in every church, the priest had appeared in his chapel doorway at the stroke of midnight, bearing a lighted candle, then spread the light to the crowds. All of Athens was participating joyfully in the largest Easter celebration in the world.

As we wound our way slowly down the mountain, everyone was hugging everyone else and crying, "Christos Anesti! Alithos Anesti O Kyrios!" I had never seen anything like this before and doubt I ever will again, unless fate takes me back to Athens on Easter weekend.

The mood of the crowd was utterly infectious. The tears streaming down my face, I cried over and over, "Christos Anesti! Christos Anesti!" My friends all shared my mood -- we were several blocks down Mt. Lykabettos on exactly the wrong side before any of us realized where we were.

"Oh no!" Aphrodite exclaimed without much concern. "Look -- we're at the stadium! Mt. Lykabettos is there -- we've come down northeast! We're supposed to be all the way to the southwest!"

This seemed quite inconsequential to us; we laughed in good humor and started the trek back to the Omiros. *It can't be much over a mile,* I thought, *Nothing to worry about.*

The Athenians vanished as quickly as they had appeared; the candles burned out; the street lights were not yet back on everywhere. We were walking through a part of Athens that no longer felt safe. I grew fearful of the dark spaces between the buildings. Were there gangs in modern Athens? How could there not be?

My worst fears abruptly materialized in the form of a dozen sullen-looking young Athenian thugs, surrounding us on all sides, heckling us in Greek and poor English. We instinctively drew together, trying to look in all directions, not wanting to expose our backs to these street fighters.

One of them jeered, "Why you in Greece, Americans? Coward Americans! Maybe we'll let you crawl home! Give us your money, we'll see."

Aphrodite answered him in Greek but it didn't help. "Hey! These Americans have one of our girls! We'll take her, Americans. And the other one too."

"Keep away from her!" shouted Steve.

"Hey, shut up, American!" he switched out a knife; five of the others followed his example; they started closing in on us. Resurrection eve had abruptly degenerated into a nightmare that was looking like our last night on Earth.

From nowhere, a darkly dressed man leapt onto the leader. The newcomer's arms and feet flew with lethal precision; before I was quite sure what was happening, half a dozen of our assailants were down, moaning, unconscious or possibly even dead; the others were retreating as quickly as they could limp or run. As the stranger turned toward us, the light of a single distant streetlight caught his face.

"Ed!" cried Steve and Aphrodite together at the same moment Sharon and I exclaimed, "Edg!"

It *was* Mark Edg, appearing like a dark angel sent at the final moment to save us. But how was he here? And why? And how did the others know him?

We had a thousand questions and tried to ask them all at the same time, but he said, panting a little, "Later. I'll explain later. Let's move now, before they find more of their friends -- and return."

Aphrodite told him where we were staying; he led us swiftly back to our hotel.

Safely back in the Omiros, we crowded into Doctor Dave's room to hear this story. How was he here? Why had he come? And who was he? For to Aphrodite and Steve, he was Ed Silver, but to Sharon and me, he was Mark Edg.

He sat on the couch, still panting a little, and chuckled. I was amazed to see that after taking out a dozen, he seemed unharmed --

not a bruise, not a scratch from his demolition of our would-be attackers. Who was this guy, anyway?

"That's simple to explain. My full name is Mark Edward George Silver -- the Third, to be exact. Quite a moniker, eh? I've always shortened it, usually to Ed Silver, but lately I've been feeling if all those Novitiates can change their names, why not me? I've decided I like Mark Ed G. better than Ed Silver -- or just Edg best of all."

"Why didn't you tell us who you were in Seattle?" asked Sharon, a little testily. "You might have talked to us better."

"And told you what? You'd never heard of Mark Edg or Ed Silver. I had no desire to tell you what I know of Ascension, for I didn't want to teach you anything more about it. I told Ollie he was making a mistake, some of the Durga Novitiates might be pretty upset if he tried to expand the Teaching -- until such an unlikely time as John miraculously reappears and approves of Nanda's novel interpretation of this ancient practice. But Ollie was too stubborn; he wouldn't listen. I thought that was the last I'd ever see of you two; how'd I know you'd be crazy enough to come to Greece?"

"Ollie asked us to," I said angrily. I too did not like being left in the dark by him. He had saved us now, for that I was grateful; but if he'd told us more last week in Seattle, we might have avoided a lot of trouble. "He left us a video."

"I *asked* you if he'd left any messages!"

"We didn't trust you," said Sharon simply. "You have a violent energy about you, you know."

"I have a *ruthless* energy. There's a big difference."

Leaving that to be understood later, I said, "OK, we've heard the Who from you. Now let's hear the Why. Everyone on Patmos said you went to India with Alan Lance and Mira. Why were you in Seattle?"

"Alan asked me to go, make a last minute attempt to save Ollie. But I arrived too late, as you know. After that, I headed back to India. I was on the same plane as you to Frankfurt, by the way, as were two Sikhs. They weren't any of Durga's Novitiates I knew; still the coincidence of you three being there *and* those two gave me cause to wonder. I followed them in the airport to see where they were heading, but they left the International area; I had to hurry to catch my flight to Delhi.

"I reached Amritsar only to find Alan had already departed for the mountains. He'd left me a message with Mira, asking me to return to Greece and escort you back, for he felt you were all in danger.

"But when I arrived at the Grand Bretagne this evening, none of you had checked in. It made no sense; finally I remembered the Pythari and knew if Dite would be anywhere on Easter eve, it would be at that taverna.

"I arrived just as you were leaving. The crowd kept us apart. I lost sight of you, but reasoned Dite'd lead you up toward the summit. I would've found you sooner, except you came down a different way from the one you went up. It was fortunate I chanced upon you when I did -- those kids were vicious."

"You have *that* right," Doctor Dave agreed animatedly; we all murmured our assent.

"What confuses *me*," said Edg, "is why you're here? And where are the others? Did you split up for some reason?"

We looked at each other for support; finally Sharon said. "Edg. There's been another accident. Or another murder. All the others, Lila, the twins, the Vanderwalls, Mary Brown, Hartmut, Balindra -- they're all dead."

He kind of crumpled into the couch, as if he'd just been kicked in the stomach. "All? Lila? Charles? Linda? Mary? Devindra? *All of them?"*

"I'm sorry, Edg. All of them. The boat Lila chartered exploded in Skala Harbor. They all died."

"But, but! Why are you alive then?"

"I had a dream," she answered, flushing slightly.

"She kept me from going," I said.

"There were omen birds on the bow," said Aphrodite. "Five stormy petrels! That boat was doomed."

"I wouldn't go without Dite," said Steve.

"I was on the cursed boat," said the doctor, "but Lila pushed me into the water at the last instant. Saved my life by sacrificing her own. Heroic, selfless, and stupid! For here am I, and she has walked away from us, gone alone exploring the unknown land of midnight shadows."

Edg looked at us as if he were about to cry. Finally he shook himself and said uncertainly, "So tomorrow morning you're all leaving for India? These deaths haven't scared you off?"

"We have reservations on Delta airlines at 8 AM," I said. "You coming with us?"

"Of course. We're all fools, aren't we?

"Doctor Tucker, might I use this couch for the rest of the night? I'm beat. Seems as if I've been flying non-stop for a week."

Which, of course, he had been.

But that night, I awoke in a cold sweat, remembering the accident on Patmos. What if Edg *hadn't* been flying all around the world? We only had his word for this. *What if he brought that yacht to the far side of the island? What if he sank the Marylena? How can I trust him? For that matter, how can I trust the doctor? How did he escape the explosion? We only have his story he was pushed to safety. And how did Sharon know not to take the boat? Nobody has dreams like that! Or Aphrodite? Birds on the bow! Who can I trust?*

My heart hammered at my chest; I writhed in agony. *They could all be involved! It might be none of them are honest or true! What can I do?* I jumped out of bed and started furiously pacing.

They may all be part of this! Edg may have killed Ollie, then ransacked the Swenson's house, then flown to Greece and killed the others! He knew where'd we be tonight! The doctor or Aphrodite or Sharon told him! Any of them could be working with the Sikhs to destroy Ascension! Maybe it was the Greek. They bought her or bribed her or blackmailed her. Or maybe Sharon was their agent; she set up Ollie's death. None of us has ever heard anything but her story of his final moments. Maybe Dave wasn't really Doctor Tucker. Even Steve might not be what he seemed! They may all be lying to me! I can't trust any of them!

I stormed around the room for an hour, growing ever more desperate, but finally decided to lie down again, think the Ascension Attitude once and see what might happen.

As soon as I introduced it, the terrors stilled, I slept.

Was it a sleep of innocence or one of exhaustion? I didn't know, but morning found me again at peace with all my companions; I doubted none of them. Was I being a fool?

Part III
India

"Be ye transformed by the renewing of your mind."
-- The Apostle Paul

15

A Modest Proposal

Our flight out of Athens was at an inhospitable 8 AM. I wondered how many short nights I could handle on this journey, but had to admit I didn't feel particularly tired, in spite of my rough night.

We had reservations on Delta to Frankfurt and New Delhi, then on to Amritsar via Indian Air Lines. We all flew coach class: Sharon and I were beginning to feel the limit of our cash; Steve and Aphrodite were on tight, parent-controlled budgets; Doctor Dave and Edg opted to ride with us rather than be separated. These last two were fabulously wealthy by my standards -- Edg probably a great deal more so than the good doctor -- but from the bottom of a well, the difference in height of two tall trees is hard to judge.

We filled our Airbus 310 from one side to the other in row 34; Sharon took one window and Aphrodite the other; Steve was inseparably at her side and I at Sharon's; the doctor was to my left and Edg across the aisle to Steve's right.

We all settled in to Ascend and/or sleep on the flight to Germany; the trip passed like a dream. We had an hour lay-over in Frankfurt, then boarded our plane to Delhi at noon. It was another Airbus; we kept the same seating arrangement and were all more or less awake by now. The doctor leaned across the aisle and asked Edg, "Could you describe the seven states of consciousness? Dite says they're distinct; I find this curious. She said you're a physiologist; can you explain them? Can it be possible there are seven different states?"

"Sure it's possible," he answered. He sounded cheerful enough, but something about his voice made me think he was hurting somewhere inside. Was the fight last night as one-sided as it appeared at the time?

"It's more than possible -- it's natural. Life was never meant to be chained to three states of consciousness, one dark, one bizarre, one confusing. The natural development of consciousness is frozen because the world is so stressed. All Ascension does is enliven the potential built into every human being."

"Lila said and you're saying, Ascension taps us into a natural functioning of the mind and body, one everyone can experience?"

"Yes. But because our bodies have been damaged by the intensity of modern life, few rarely or ever experience even the fourth state, Ascendant Consciousness. And without regular experience of the fourth, there's no potential to remove all the stress from the central nervous system, so the fifth state can't develop. And without the fifth, there is no platform on which to build the sixth and seventh."

"How does that work?" Sharon asked. "How does experiencing the fourth develop the fifth?"

"It's the rest, isn't it?" asked the doctor.

"The rest *and* the coherence," answered Edg. "The rest allows deep stress to dissolve -- stress never touched by sleep, because during sleep the metabolic rate stays too high. And the coherence means the mind likes the experience of Ascending *so much* it holds onto it for longer and longer periods of time. The Ascendant is so enjoyable, the mind prefers floating in it; as the stress decreases in the body, it is able to do so more and more. These are two sides of the same coin."

"So the inner peace stays longer and longer?" I asked, trying to understand the difficult concepts. "The stress of living has less and less of an effect -- and eventually, we're grounded in Silence inside, all the time? And that's why it's called, 'Perpetual Consciousness?'"

"Yes, that's it. Part of the mind is *always* coherent. This is the fifth state. The mind has recognized it is forever still, deep inside -- not as an intellectual concept, but as a twenty-four hours a day reality of peace."

"'Praying without ceasing,'" said Doctor Dave dreamily.

"Yes, or permanent samadhi. Or the first stage of enlightenment. We call it Perpetual Consciousness because it's never lost and because those other names create confusion due to previous associations."

"What if you don't believe it's possible?" I asked, trying on my skeptic's role again.

"Doesn't matter. Once the central nervous system is clear of stress, the inner Silence remains with you all the time, if you believe in it or not."

"So it's not just that Perpetual Consciousness is *a* natural state, it is actually *the* normal functioning of the mind and body!" exclaimed the doctor, excited.

"Sure! The waking state as its lived by the vast majority of humanity is abnormal -- pathetically subnormal."

"All of humanity is underdeveloped," I said thoughtfully. "This world is a prison house for the insane. That makes perfect sense to me. No wonder the Earth is suffering today. A whole bunch of retards at the controls."

"Nanda says life was not meant for suffering. Suffering is the aberration, born of false and limited beliefs about who we are; when Perpetual Consciousness is established, all suffering ends."

"People have always said it takes a long, long time to gain enlightenment," said the doctor wistfully.

"The simplest truths are often obscured in our modern world, aren't they?" answered Edg with a chuckle that ended in a cough. "The reality is: there is no distance to be traversed from the waking state to the infinite. Unbounded Awareness is inside every thought, every feeling, every perception, every belief, every judgment. It is what we truly are.

"Since this is so, it *is* surprising how many consider it difficult to grow into enlightenment. Perpetual Consciousness is closer than the breath, closer than the heartbeat -- it underlies and permeates everything, everywhere, at all times. Therefore, no path is needed to realize it, no long years of study are necessary, no devotion at the feet of the illumined is required. What *is* necessary is the willingness to destroy the beliefs in lack, limitation, suffering, illness, pain and death that fill the mind in the waking state.

"By focusing on the Absolute through Ascension, the beliefs in isolation gradually still. This is not difficult; it is an effortless movement of joy that raises the seeker on eagle wings into the continual perception of the infinite. If every moment is filled with appreciation of the wonder of life, there is no longer any space for suffering! Praying without ceasing is not only not complicated, it is perfectly simple, the purest joy to an evolving soul.

"To illustrate this, Nanda tells a story which I like."

One day many years after founding his monastery, the Apostle John walked in the world and chanced upon an old man who had spent many years in rigorous meditation. The recluse cracked open an eye and said, "Oh, it's you, John! Thank you for stopping by. I've been wondering -- how long will it take me to gain salvation?"

The Apostle looked at him with love and joyfully replied, "You are doing well, my son! With only three more lifetimes of similar effort, you will realize the Supreme Ascendant."

The old man, mortified, cried, "Another three lifetimes of this miery! Never would I believe such as you! You are not from the Lord! Begone from me, you impostor!" He threw his begging bowl at him.

John smiled at him with love and walked on. Nearby, he chanced upon a young fool laughing and playing in the river, sing-

ing at the top of his lungs, "God! How I love God! God!" Seeing the Apostle strolling by, he splashed out of the water and said, "Oh, it's you, John! Thank you for stopping by. I've been wondering -- how long will it take me to gain enlightenment?"

The Apostle looked at him with love and joyfully replied, "You are doing well, my son! With only seventy more lifetimes of similar effort, you will realize the Supreme Ascendant."

The fool, in great joy, cried, "Wonderful! Another seventy lifetimes of this bliss! Thank you for this wonderful blessing! You are truly from the Lord!" Because he was so filled with rapture at this thought, the last doubts in his mind were instantly crushed; the fool gained the highest degree of enlightenment instantly.

"So you're saying," said Sharon, "without living life Here and Now, it takes forever to establish Perpetual Consciousness, no matter how hard you try."

"But with what we're experiencing here," I observed, "it shouldn't take long at all -- Ascending is too enjoyable."

"It doesn't take much time," agreed Edg. "It depends on three factors -- how much stress there is in your body when you start the practice; how much stress you put in every day; and how regularly you Ascend. And that's it. Some people are a lot more stressed when they begin; it may take them a little longer. No matter how efficient a filter, a large pond filled with mud is going to take some time to clean."

"I'm sure I was among the worst when I started," said Steve, joining the conversation. He had been quietly and earnestly talking to Aphrodite since we left Frankfurt; now they seemed to have reached a concluding point and were ready to interact with the rest of us. I suspected they would find less and less interest in anyone else as they explored their love for each other; but then again, *I* was finding lots to do besides focus on Sharon. Was that another way to avoid making a commitment to her? Her question from yesterday morning was still hanging in the air. My outburst at

Oedipus' Distomo had been no answer. Of course I had thought of asking her to marry me -- how could I not? She was everything I'd ever dreamed of -- brilliant, fun, spiritual, beautiful, compatible -- *and* she said she loved me. But what had I to offer her? Nothing.

"Why do you say that?" Doctor Dave was meanwhile asking Steve.

"Because of all the drugs. I don't know how long it'll take to make up for what I did to my body."

"Not long," said Edg cheerfully. "Nothing can stop the power of Ascension. You've worked most of it out already."

"I used to be so jealous when I'd hear everyone else's experiences! They'd be telling how clear it was for them, and all I'd be getting was the same dull fog. But a few weeks ago, it started to lift -- lately my mind is still when I Ascend. And I'm feeling calmer during the day: things aren't bothering me as much as they did before. It's working well for me now."

Stewardesses pushing lunch carts divided us; I couldn't hear any more of Steve's conversation with Edg. In honor of our destination, they were serving saffron rice, lentil dahl, curried vegetables and parathas -- a kind of puffy wheat bread.

I decided this as good a time as any to try to defeat my personal demon; I took a deep breath, leaned close to Sharon and said quietly, "Yes. Of course I love you. I can't imagine another day without you. Would you consider marrying me?"

She put down her paratha, stared at me with surprise, blushed and said, "Consider it? I might. Want to ask me?"

I swallowed hard; my throat was *very* dry. "All right, I'll try. Sharon, if we survive this trip, will you marry me?"

"If? Want to try again without any qualifiers?"

"You're not making this easy on me!"

"I've never been married! I've waited my whole life for the right guy, because I didn't want to be like my friends -- married, divorced, married, divorced. When it happens for me, I want it to be permanent, you know?"

"I didn't wait for you!"

"So, you've had some practice! You know what *not* to do. I didn't set as condition my partner never having been with another, just that he loved me with all his heart and desired to grow with me forever. I don't think I would have been ready for you any sooner; nor do I think you were ready for me."

"Why were you crying on the ferry when Ollie found you?"

The suddenness of that transition startled her. She frowned for a moment; I was afraid I'd offended her. But then she laughed, "You intuited that, didn't you? You *know* why, don't you?"

"I think so. But I want to hear you talk about it."

"OK! I came to Seattle to escape my past and discover my future. I'd asked two things of the Universe -- the first was for a Teacher, someone to show me how to find Truth in this confusing world. And the second was for an Ideal Relationship, a relationship that would serve me, my partner, and everyone else in only life-supporting ways. I'd had a powerful sense I would find both in Seattle, but there I was and there I'd been for weeks and weeks and *nothing was happening!*

"I didn't have any rational reason to take the ferry that day. All evening before, I'd felt if I would just go the waterfront, something wonderful would happen. When I was walking down there, I saw one of the big boats pull in and thought, 'Well, why not? Maybe this is it: maybe I'm supposed to take it.'

"But when I was sitting on the top deck looking at the gorgeous day, I started feeling foolish. I started beating myself up, telling myself I was all alone in the world, no one understood me or ever would or even could; my feelings to come to the waterfront and take the ferry had been false, nothing was going to come of it. I felt so alone and cheated. I couldn't believe my life was working out so poorly, when I'd always had such a clear understanding of exactly what I wanted. I put my head down and bawled. I didn't care who saw me."

A little tear hung from the corner of her left eye as she relived the sad moment. I clasped her hands and kissed them, then said, "You believe in me. You believe I'm worthy. Perhaps your belief will inspire mine. I don't know. But I do know this, Sharon Alice Stone: when I'm with you, I'm in Heaven. I adore the ground you walk on. I love every inch of you, from your painted toenails to the top of your curly head. I thrill at your touch. I dream of you at night. I can't imagine not being with you for the rest of my life, whatever may come. I've never felt so strongly about anyone; I know this comes from the best and clearest part of me, not from anything small or mean or distorted. I envision walking into Eternity with you. I see us as two souls uniting in our quest to find God; as the streams of our lives flow together, I see them becoming a river larger and more vital than either in isolation.

"So, yes. I'm going to say it now. Today, this Easter Sunday, I dedicate myself to a new life, a new beginning of commitment and unconditional love. No longer will I accept half a life. No longer will I compromise my desires for an ideal future. So, wonderful love, deepest dream of my heart, I'm asking you without any ifs, ands or buts. Sharon, will you marry me?"

Her azure eyes flashed wonder and joy. She squeezed my hands and replied, "Yes! Yes, I will marry you, for *you* are the one I have sought throughout my life. I knew it the first moment I met you on Bainbridge! Your face has often appeared to me, ever since childhood, just before sleep, or during an idle afternoon's daydreams. I recognized you at once."

"You're kidding! Why didn't you say something?"

"And see you run for the border? Hah! You had to figure this out by yourself, big guy. If I'd whispered a word, you'd still be running." She had me there. How could anyone know me so well?

16
Another Capital Experience

The rest of the flight was uneventful. Doctor Dave seemed content to contemplate what he'd learned of Perpetual Consciousness; he was furiously scribbling notes on a white legal pad. Aphrodite and Steve were happy contemplating each other, as were Sharon and I. Edg said he just wanted to rest, his nine days of flying had worn him out. He was looking worse and worse as the day wore on; I was pretty sure those street urchins last night had not left him entirely unscathed. I couldn't be sure, it had all happened so fast. But the good doctor was at his right hand; I figured Edg would talk to him if there were a real problem.

My personal terrors from last night had not resurfaced; for this I was extremely grateful. Doubting any of these people today seemed insane; my experiences last night appeared as mad thoughts born from an exhausted mind... Except possibly for my feelings about Edg. There was a certain energy around him I did not know or care to know -- that which Sharon called violent and he, ruthless. Whatever it was, I recognized its ability to kill and destroy and was sure I did not wish to get too close to it. Nor to him.

We landed in New Delhi about 1 AM. I had thought Athens slum-like and overcrowded, but soon learned what congestion and squalor really were. Even the airport had a dirty air about it; it was smelly and noisy and *very* hot and humid. Summer starts early in India; it doesn't cool down until the July monsoons.

Our flight to Amritsar didn't leave until the next morning; we had no choice but to find a hotel. But Edg was with us; he knew

Delhi. He threaded us through the crowds of beggars -- red-coated guards tried to keep them off the airport grounds, without much success. There were dozens clawing at us, begging for rupees. Some looked well fed and dressed, but some appeared genuine -- lepers with deformed faces or rotting hands and feet, cripples, maimed children.

Our taxis were filthy and had no air conditioning. As we pulled out into traffic, I rolled down the window, thinking any air was better than none. At the first stop, a small, twisted hand reached in, patted my shoulder, begged for a handout. I was wearing a white coat; her hand was so filthy, it left a smudge on my sleeve. Partly out of compassion and partly to get rid of her, I gave her a hundred rupee note. Fortunately the traffic moved on again; another dozen rushed toward us when they saw her success.

"You really shouldn't, mister sir," said our driver, whose English was understandable with effort. "They don't keep the money; it goes to their begging ring leader, who broke her hands in the first place. It just encourages this."

Our driver was a Sikh -- when India and Pakistan divided, millions of his people moved eastward; many did not stop in the Punjab but continued down the Grand Trunk Road and settled in Delhi. The doctor and I had both become very curious about the Sikhs; we asked our driver about his religion.

He explained his faith had been founded in the 1500's by Guru Nanak, a Hindu of the Kshatriya or warrior caste by birth. Nanak rejected the polytheism of India in favor of a strict belief in One God. He sought to bridge the gap between Islam and Hinduism, abolished the caste system among his followers, never fought with anyone, and apparently accomplished much good.

I asked him how the Sikhs became such good warriors; instead of answering, he launched into a long monologue about the abuses the Sikhs had suffered at the hands of the Hindus. There had been much rioting in Delhi over the years; the Punjab was often the site of terrorist attacks, from both Hindus and Sikhs. Foreigners were often excluded from that state because it was considered too dangerous for them to go there.

During the last riots, he said, the Hindus had actually used the heads of Sikh children for basketballs. As the tears welled up in his eyes, he vowed vengeance and swore some things could never be forgiven. He complained the government had gone too far in forbidding his people to carry their *kirtan,* short sword, which their tenth and last guru more than two hundred and fifty years ago told them they all must wear.

"How did these people become so violent?" I asked Sharon quietly; she had no answer for me, instead continued staring out the window with amazement and horror at the city passing by.

Delhi was noisy and crowded, even in the middle of the night. I was singularly unimpressed by it. If this was the best the third world had to offer, I had seen enough of it already. The air was heavy and foul-smelling, with a peculiar odor I later learned came from the many small fires using sacred cow dung for fuel.

Our driver had apparently flunked driving in Greece. He saw no point in slowing for bicycles or pedestrians and was apparently of the opinion that if a vehicle was as large as a truck or bus, it had the right-of-way, but if it was not significantly bigger than his taxi, it had better get out of his way. Street signs were there but were universally ignored, as were the policemen with white gloves and whistles who vainly attempted to direct traffic.

Our hotel, the Taj, was huge and once must have been a lovely place. The lobby was almost rococo with enormous wall paintings copied from Renaissance works and faux marble columns supporting the ceiling. Since the British left, it and most of the rest of Delhi has been rapidly decaying. But there were vast quantities of fresh flowers in the lobby; the doorman greeted us with leis made from marigolds. There were piles of oranges and mangoes, free for guests; the shops off the main corridor sold everything one could possibly desire of clothing or jewelry.

The Taj was an enigma of enormous contrast. The rugs in our hallway were filthy with ground-in dirt, even though there was an old Indian sporadically sweeping at them even in the middle of the night. The wallpaper was cracked and peeling; the tap water was rusty and smelled. But the bedrooms were huge; each had a private bath; the sheets were clean and lilies were on our nightstands. I settled into my bed with a sigh, at once immensely pleased and utterly terrified at my engagement. I slept fitfully, dreaming of and longing for Sharon all night.

The next day dawned early with Rama chants echoing through my windows. Apparently not all the Muslims had left Delhi with the partition, for there were also songs from minarets of the mosques addressed to Allah. As I dressed for breakfast, a marriage procession passed beneath my window. Indians marry when the Vedic astrologers tell them the most auspicious time is, even if it chances to be in the middle of the night. The bride-to-be, dressed like a goddess in scarlet and gold, was carried in an ornate gold-inlaid and silver-filigreed red carriage pulled by white horses; behind her came the groom, wearing resplendent gold armor, riding a lavishly decorated white elephant. Musicians played for them; Brahmin priests recited the Vedas; dancers danced around them, strewing the ground with flowers; well-wishers walked beside them, laughing and singing. I took this all to be a splendid omen, even as I wondered how wealthy this bride's father must be to afford such opulence.

Sharon saw them too; as we sipped sweet lassis in the dining room and ate fruit for breakfast, she talked lightly with me about marriage customs in different parts of the world. "How about you?" she asked me. "What do you want ours to be like?"

I thought perhaps she might be testing me to see how deeply my resolve had worked itself. I was determined not to disappoint her and replied, "My last marriage was in a living room. My mother did not invite even one of her friends -- she was too embarrassed we'd been living together. I've always felt I've never been properly married.

"What would I like? A large, old-fashioned wedding in an ancient stone church with all the trimmings: ushers, bridesmaids, crowds of people, the whole nine yards. I know it doesn't make any difference, it's only a symbol, after all -- but that's what I want."

"Me too," she smiled lovingly at me. "I've always wanted it to be a *big* deal. Like a fairy tale. I'm worth it."

"You sure are!"

"Worth what?" asked Doctor Dave, joining us. "What's good here?" he added, looking curiously at the menu.

"Oh, the lassi is *superb*," said Sharon. "And so are these papayas."

"What's lassi?"

"It's a sweet drink made of yogurt. Mine has peaches."

"Maybe I'll try their mango milkshake," he said. "Worthy of what?" He asked again.

"A large church wedding, Dave," I answered, thinking he had probably heard the whole conversation on the plane yesterday and was just being polite. "Sharon and I are getting married."

"Really? You too? Ascension really brings out the desire for Union, doesn't it? Congratulations!" He shook my hand and hugged Sharon. "That's great! I'm very pleased for both of you!

"You might like to know, I've come to a decision too. I'm going to ask Alan to make me a Novitiate. As soon as we find him."

"That's beautiful!" exclaimed Sharon. "Beautiful! I'm *extremely* proud of you." She leaned over the table and kissed him on the forehead.

He blushed as I asked curiously, "Why are you doing that?"

"Why? I've never desired to marry. Oh, when I was young, I thought I was supposed to; but even thinking of it always made me feel depressed. A couple of times, I went so far as to get engaged, but I always broke it off, because I knew, deep inside, it wasn't for me. If I'd married either one, it would have proved too hard for them; they would have divorced me eventually.

"Besides, I've never had any sexual desire at all -- or at least, not much. It's not that my equipment doesn't work either, it works just fine. I've never had the drive to use it."

"Desire to be in relationship is all I've ever had," I commented. "I used to be so lonely in high school, I'd stand in my bedroom and stare in all the four directions, hoping to feel *her* presence somewhere, anywhere. I was seeking so desperately, I compromised and took the first compatible person I could find, rather than wait for perfection, for Sharon. Still, I might not have matured enough without suffering to deserve her. I don't know...

"So, you're going to be a Novitiate? That's great! What are the vows you take? I've heard there are ten."

"There are ten eventually, when I complete my probationary year and join the Ishaya Order as a monk. There are only five I take for the first year."

"What are those?" asked Sharon, more curiously than mere politeness warranted. Would devoting her life exclusively to God be more tempting to her than marrying me? I was amazed how much this scared me. I'd known her for only ten days and been engaged only since yesterday, but the thought of her becoming a nun was beyond horrible.

"They're pretty simple," he answered seriously. "The first is Truthfulness. I will vow for a year to tell the truth always."

"That's not all that simple!" I exclaimed perversely. "Suppose you've got a friend you *know* is innocent of murder, but the only way to save him from hanging is to lie. Would you do it?"

"I've not thought about extreme examples," he answered, looking a little disheartened. "I don't know. I suppose my vow of Non-violence would take precedence -- saving someone else from pointless suffering would be more important, I believe. But I'll have to think about this. That was a good question."

"It seems to me," said Sharon thoughtfully, "there must be some order to the levels of truth. Two plus two equals four is true, but not always. Put two Siamese fighting fish in the same bowl with two guppies and two plus two will equal two. Add two balloons to two children with two pins and two plus two plus two will equal two with laughter or two with tears. And I think truth needs to be addressed to the audience as well."

"What do you mean?" I asked curiously.

"If I'd told you I'd seen you since I was nine in my dreams, would you have allowed yourself to fall head-over-heels in love with me?"

"I see what you mean," I chuckled. "Sometimes exclusions are useful -- but was it strictly true?"

"Of course it was. I never said I *didn't* have visions about you, did I? Since you never asked, I had no need."

"Well, it's complex," said the doctor. "I suppose I mean: I will do the best I can never to lie."

"That seems reasonable," I agreed, deciding not to oppose him any more. I was embarrassed I'd questioned his vows. Wasn't this a kind of engagement? Was his joining the Ishayas different from a wedding? My only response should have been to praise him for his courage, not criticize him or try to talk him out of it.

Old habits die hard, I thought ruefully, and added, "You know, what you're doing is brave. It takes a lot of courage. I don't think I could be that bold. I'm impressed you are... So, truthfulness and non-violence. That's two. What are the other three?"

"Non-stealing is the third. This includes never acting as though I've done something when I haven't, never taking credit for another's work, that sort of thing.

"Celibacy is the fourth, Lila said that means: to the best of my ability, all my thoughts, words and actions will be directed upwards, to the Ascendant. And lastly, non-grasping -- to break attachment to things, to possessions, including mental debris. Mastering non-grasping means to become a clean slate, free from pointless beliefs about life."

"That's a lot," I said, impressed. "And the purpose of them is to speed the growth to Perpetual Consciousness? Is that it?"

"Yes. By using my body and mind in alliance with these five, I hope to progress much more quickly."

I couldn't help but think the good doctor was a trifle naive, but I held my tongue.

Edg joined us now. He didn't look good *at all* and complained he was having a hard time breathing. Dave looked at him, thumped his chest a few times, listened to his heart, then proclaimed, "You're going back to bed. Your right lung has fluid in it, and so may your left. You must have received some hard blows Saturday night. Look at these bruises! Why didn't you tell us?"

"Didn't think it was anything. Had worse before. Look, I'm fine. Sorry I mentioned it. I'll rest at Amritsar, OK? We're not scheduled to go to the mountains for three days -- on Thursday."

"Changing altitude in a plane wouldn't be wise in your condition!" exclaimed the doctor.

"The air here's worse! I can't breathe this stuff; I could cut it with a knife. Look, I'll be fine. Don't worry about me. The Third Sphere Love Technique will heal me right away, as soon as I can do some long Ascending. Really."

Aphrodite and Steve joined us now, halting Dave's disagreement. They both looked flushed, as if they'd gotten little sleep. I was glad, seeing them, I'd spent the night in my own bed -- though at the time, I'd had strong desires for a different experience. Regardless of the doctor's plans, my path ahead was clear.

17

The Immortal City

Indian Airlines was like the rest of India -- crowded, dirty, inefficient. I was amazed how such a handsome people could be so impoverished and so slow. The whole country was stuck in a fog, a stupor that left nothing done at the end of the day. Even those moving fast didn't accomplish anything. No wonder meditating had a bad name in the West! I could see the wisdom of calling St. John's Teaching 'Ascension.' No intelligent Westerner would want anything to do with any practice from India, even if it were founded by an Apostle of Christ. Erroneous practices of concentration had made these people other-worldly in a useless kind of way.

Our plane, an ancient prop-driven thirty-seater of a kind I did not know took off two hours late, for no reason anyone could explain. Even boarding was hard -- our international tickets, purchased in Athens, had to be reconfirmed at the airport; the Airline official seemed to have a head made of molasses. He sat in tight-lipped silence, staring at our tickets as if they were from another world. Which, I was beginning to think, they must be. In a move of pure brilliance, Edg borrowed back a ticket and stuck a $100 bill inside of it; that difficulty cleared up instantly.

But another immediately surfaced -- a pudgy Indian military officer with greasy black hair and a soiled brown uniform hauled us into his office and said, "Why are you going to the Punjab? Foreigners should not go to the Punjab. It is not wise. Often forbidden. Shouldn't have relaxed the rules. Dangerous place. Sikhs are a terrible, violent people. Why go there? Especially with girls?"

Aphrodite started to answer, but Sharon nudged her to silence: she concluded, no doubt correctly, this official would listen to no woman say anything.

Edg explained we were going to Amritsar to study; this did not help. "Those gurus are everywhere," the officer said, sneering. "Why do you Westerners waste your time on those fakers? Look what's happened to our country! All this talk of God; no one works; even those who do, don't work well; all the good young people leave; only the poor and the stupid stay here."

The thought of another bribe flitted through my mind, but I dismissed it as inappropriate, possibly dangerous. This fellow was trying to do his job; probably he believed every word he was saying.

"You are doubtlessly correct," said the doctor, "and we'll find that out soon. But the only way we will is by investigating more deeply. If you stop us from flying there, we'll have to take the bus. Or rent a car. The government relaxed the restrictions; they must feel it's not so dangerous anymore."

"A mistake, I tell you! That place is *very* bad. Terrorism *all* the time. Don't go, please?"

"I'm afraid we must. Unless you wish to arrest us."

"I cannot! I would if I could find *any* reason. Unfortunately, I cannot. Go then, but your blood is off my hands; I've done my job by warning you."

With that rather inauspicious beginning, we boarded our plane. The flight was full. Smoking restrictions had not yet found a foothold in India; strong tobacco fumes rose around us on all sides as soon as we were airborne. The officer had delayed us so long we had a hard time sitting together. With some haggling, I managed to sit by Sharon; Aphrodite and Steve had similar luck, but the doctor and Edg were separated from us. It hardly mattered; we Ascended through most of the flight.

The Punjab was a sea of wheat. Since the "green revolution" of the sixties, high-yield strains and chemical fertilizers have dramatically increased the state's yields. Whether the long-term effects of mono-culture, soil depletion and other technological byproducts soon take a catastrophic toll remains to be seen: India totters forever on the edge of disaster. With nearly a billion people, the subcontinent is never more than a flood or plague away from collapse.

Even though the Punjab has more than doubled in population in the last twenty years, the Immortal City Amritsar was significantly smaller than Delhi and therefore showed more of the inherent beauty of India and of the Indian people and less of the rampant problems. The brilliant red, purple, green, yellow and blue saris of the ladies contrasted sharply with the more muted blue, yellow and brown tones of the men. Turbans were everywhere; the last Guru of the Sikhs had enjoined all his male followers to wear them as a symbol of their faith.

Even at the airport, the military's presence was pronounced. There'd been a bus bombing just yesterday; the city was on edge, tight, moody, about to explode. Indian Army soldiers in their light brown uniforms and carrying automatic rifles were throughout the airport and on most street corners. They did not appear pleased to see Westerners. Nor, in fact, did the turbaned Sikhs. It felt like we'd landed in Belfast on a bad day.

Edg was looking worse and worse. He was coughing a lot; his breathing was hard and raspy. I didn't know if Ascending would help him, but the smoke-filled flight had definitely hurt him. He was weak and wobbly on his legs; his color was gray.

We secured two bicycle-driven rickshas and headed toward the private estate Alan had rented on the outskirts of town. Amritsar passed swiftly by; our driver knew not a word of English -- or at least none he would speak. The doctor, Sharon and I stared in wide-eyed wonder at this very different part of the world.

We passed a huge bazaar, in this late afternoon busily selling strange and familiar fruits, vegetables and nuts. Huge stacks of bananas, oranges, mangoes and pineapples alternated with spreads of enormous squash, beans, rice, peanuts, leafy greens and other vegetables we did not know.

Sharon was tempted to shop, but Edg had assured us there would be plenty of food waiting for us. Besides, I hadn't any idea how to communicate with our driver; we continued on through the cacophony that was the life of Amritsar. Horse and bicycle and buffalo carts, camels, elephants, buses, trucks, private cars, scooters, countless pedestrians, other rickshas -- all vied for space on the narrow roadway. Our vehicles, being rather small and unpretentious, were often jostled aside or had to run for cover from a shrieking behemoth of steel and glass or leather. We were separated by the masses of humanity from Edg and Aphrodite and Steve; I said a little prayer our driver had understood Edg's pain-fully dictated directions in Hindi.

Apparently he had -- as the city ended and we entered a garden-like suburb, our driver pulled into a gravel driveway; the others were already on the porch, talking to a pretty red-haired woman in a lovely white Indian sari we assumed must be Mira. We were just in time to see her cover her eyes and run back into the house, sobbing.

The house, built in the Victorian style, was old but still handsome. The British governor, staff and the top military once lived in this part of Amritsar -- it was *the* upscale neighborhood in the Punjab. The front yard, alive with color, was covered with sweet-smelling flowers and flowering trees, not one of which I could name. A cracked and broken fountain of a Greek nymph was at the heart of the circular drive; I felt that a proper symbol for the last remnants of foreign rule. Traces of British influence will be found throughout India until time rots all their houses, buildings and gardens.

"Don't tell me," rasped Edg to the doctor as we reached them. "Not a word. I'm going. See you tomorrow. Late. Mira said Lal and Hari made dinner. She may come out. Don't count on it. She took it hard. Didn't foresee it. 'Bye." He disappeared into the house to do major repair work on himself. He was beyond pale -- he had a gray pallor that looked one step removed from terminal.

"Damn fool," muttered Dave. "He should be hospitalized. Completely deteriorated."

"I can't imagine Indian hospitals are particularly tempting," I observed, putting our bags on the porch.

"I hope he'll be all right," commented Sharon without much hope in her tone.

"Oh, he will," Steve replied cheerfully. "He's got the entire Third *and* Fourth Spheres, you know."

He said that as though it should mean something to us; as it didn't mean a whole lot, I said, "Well, where's the promised meal? It is getting late; I'm *hungry."*

"Poor boy," murmured Sharon.

"Out back," suggested Aphrodite hopefully. "There's a dining porch, I suspect." We set our bags inside the front door then followed her along the wrap-around porch.

The two Indian cooks, Hari and Lal, met us as we approached their domain, smiling and bowing. They were both slight of build with short hair and neatly trimmed sparse mustaches; evidently they were particularly fond of light blue cotton shirts and pants. They gestured for us to follow them.

It was not a dinner, it was a feast spread before us on a huge table inside the screened-in porch. There were mounds of pineapples, oranges, mangoes and papayas; four different kinds of breads -- flat peppered tortilla-like papadams, fried chapattis, flaky puffs of puris and flat but soft parathas; seven kinds of chutneys; three different dahls -- red, blue and green; white basmati rice -- with and without saffron, onion and pineapple; curried potatoes with young spring peas; lassis; raita -- cucumbers and vinegar in yogurt; fried chick-peas; mashed potatoes; pakoras -- vegetables dipped in flour and fried; steamed cauliflower and broccoli; several dishes I had never seen before *and* sweet gulab jamuns and rice pudding for dessert. We ate on fine china left over from the British and felt like royalty.

The garden in the back of the house was equally incredible -- there were flowers everywhere, lilies, roses, trumpet vines, as well as mango, orange, plantain, date palm, and pecan trees. A strident brown and red monkey scolded us from atop a stone wall; several jackdaws flew by, cawing raucously; a dozen kinds of birds sang and warbled in the trees and bushes. This was an India I had not seen before but had hoped must still exist somewhere -- tropical glory shimmering yet through her long and painful twilight. I once read India was the greatest nation on the Earth, long, long ago; seeing this decaying garden inspired me to think perhaps it was so.

A troop of brownish-red monkeys came to join the one on the wall; they harangued us in a screeching chorus until Hari chased them away with a serving spoon, calling out, "Chalo! Chalo!" His companion cook Lal thought this enormously funny and laughed until the tears ran down his cheeks.

As we were finishing our last bites of dessert, Mira came slowly out of the house. Her eyes were red and moist, but she seemed in control of herself. She had braided her hair and put a black bow in it, but was still wearing her white sari. Mira appeared a year or two older than Lila had been, but was equally as pretty. Her emerald eyes, soft red hair and translucent skin gave her a look of aristocracy. She belonged well in a home such as this, but not now -- rather a hundred years ago, at the height of the British Empire.

Mira did not see Hari in the garden and asked Lal, "Wo kahaan hai?"

"Waheen!" he replied, laughing and pointing.

"Come here!" she called to him; after they were both hovering around her, she talked to them earnestly in Hindi for a few moments; they scurried off to fulfill her commands. She now turned to us, smiling a little crookedly, and sat at the table.

After we introduced ourselves, she said softly, emotion occasionally breaking her words, "Welcome to India. You have traveled far to pursue this ancient Teaching. I will do everything in my power to assist you. Even though it now seems there will be only one ceremony at the New Moon in Kulu on Saturday, I intend to honor in my life the memory of Lila and Balindra and the others.

"The guest is God in this country and should be so, everywhere in the world. Permit me to serve you in any way I can. I'm leaving for the Kulu Valley in Himachal Pradesh to join with Alan and Nanda on Thursday -- if you wish, you may accompany me. We had prepared for more... but of course you know that. You are welcome to come."

Speech was becoming too hard for her; I feared she was suffering greatly but could think of nothing to say except, "I didn't know your sister long, but I believe I knew her well. She will live in me forever, in the gratitude and praise of my heart, for she taught me how to Ascend. Never could I have deserved such a gift; she freely gave it to me. Whatever else she has done for the world, I hardly know; but I know she saved *my* life. I am eternally grateful."

Sharon squeezed my hand and said to Mira, "I loved Lila from the moment I met her. She gave me an invaluable boon in the Second Attitude. She is part of me forever, too, because of that -- her life is an inspiration to us all."

"To me especially," agreed Doctor Dave. "Because of her example, I am going to become a Novitiate."

"Excellent!" exclaimed Mira, almost looking pleased. "Thank you for your kind words. I've just met the three of you, but feel

I've known you for years. And Dite and Steve, it's so nice to have you here. I'm glad *you*... are all right.

"Here's what I propose. To honor my sister and the others... I wish to give you all your next technique tomorrow. If you would like."

We all agreed except Sharon, who said slowly, "Many thanks, Mira. How should I say this? I can't. In a few days. I've still some work to accomplish with the Second."

"You don't have to stop using the Second when you receive the Third, you know," she replied, taken aback.

"I know. But I need more time with the first two -- if that's all right."

"Well, of course it is, sweetheart. Just tell me whenever you're ready."

"Can you tell me more about the Twenty-seven?" I asked. I was curious, but my idea was to keep her mind moving. She was so terribly sad; I wanted to distract her, to give her a little time with a different focus so her subconscious could work the ideas longer.

"Yes!" agreed Sharon brightly, undoubtedly sharing my intent. "How do Twenty-seven Techniques divide into Seven Spheres? Are there different numbers of techniques in each Sphere?"

She recognized our game but agreed to play: smiling crookedly, she answered, "Well, the first five Spheres are similar: the first technique of each is a Praise Attitude, the second is a Gratitude Attitude and the third is a Love Attitude."

"How about the fourth?" asked the doctor, as enthusiastic as Sharon and I, certainly for the same reason.

"The fourth technique of each of the first five Spheres is called a Cognition Technique," she replied, looking at him warmly, apparently appreciating this respite. "Praise, Gratitude and Love move the awareness *vertically*. Cognition introduces a horizontal movement of awareness. The first three Attitudes of each Sphere are like mine-shafts, taking us down to the treasure, the Cognition Techniques are like tunnels to dig out the gold."

"So you're saying, without the vertical movement of Ascending, the horizontal motion would be pointless?" Dave asked.

"Exactly," she said, sounding precisely like Lila. "There is no value in staying on the surface of the mind. Cognition without the inward movement of Ascension first would be a waste of time."

"But *with* the vertical movement," I said, "the Cognition Techniques enable us to explore what's there at the deeper levels?"

"That's right. Isn't that your experience, Dite?"

"Oh yes, Mira, it is. I Ascend, then the Cognition Techniques allow me to stay locked in the Ascendant as long as I wish. I think of Ascension as climbing the stairs of my house; the Cognition Techniques turn on the lights after I've climbed. They are *very* powerful."

"They're the links that hold the chain of Ascension together," said Steve.

"That's an excellent analogy!" exclaimed Sharon. "So that is the structure of the first five Spheres -- three Ascension Attitudes and one Cognition Technique to stabilize them. That's why they're called Spheres, isn't it? Three dimensions and then motion?"

"That's one reason," agreed Mira. "And since each Sphere is subtler and more powerful than the one before, an Ascending spiral of light and energy, of joy and love is created. As the mind becomes more familiar with subtle experience, each additional technique paves the way for expansion to the next threshold of experience. It all unfolds gracefully and naturally."

"Edg said he'll heal himself with the Third Love Attitude," said Doctor Dave. "Do some of the techniques focus more on the body than others?"

"Sure, but not in any way you're likely to think. Each Ascension Attitude, in my experience, is immediately obvious as soon as you've learned it, all but impossible to discover before you're ready. That shows, I think, how aligned they are with the Nature of Creation. It demonstrates their Divine Origin."

"In an Ideal Age, then," asked Sharon, "if the world were not stressed, would everyone know how to Ascend? Naturally do it all the time?"

"I believe that would be so, yes. I think that's one reason John hid his monastery so far from civilization. There wasn't even a road into the Kulu Valley until the 1930's. It was about as isolated as any place could be on Earth -- until now, of course."

"Where's the Kulu Valley?" I asked.

"A couple of hundred kilometers Northeast of here, in Himachal Pradesh."

"That's not too far," I said, translating in my head to miles. "About a hundred and twenty miles, right? A couple of hours down the road?"

"Your math is right, but it's a hard, all day trip. This is India, remember? You'll find out Thursday..." She decided to end our game. She'd held out as long as she could. "If you'll excuse me, I've got a great deal to do tonight. Shall we meet at say, eleven? for your instructions? All right. Good night, then. Hari and Lal will show you your rooms. I've already told them. They understand English perfectly, but you'll probably never hear them speak any."

Sharon said, "May I see you, please? Alone?"

I looked at her, surprised. Was she having second thoughts about our engagement? Since she'd met another Novitiate?

Sharon glanced at me with a frown and dug her nails into my hand, as if to say, "Don't be silly." Did she ever miss anything?

Mira looked as if she intended to demure. But instead she shook herself, smiled sweetly and said, "Yes, of course, if you wish. Come then."

They stood and entered the house, arm-in-arm.

18
An Objective Attitude

My room was small but neat. A few ancient paintings, mostly of ducks and sunsets, graced the walls; the faded blue and yellow wallpaper must have come straight out of the forties. The bed was soft but not lumpy; the pillows were of down. I put my bag on the cane rattan chair, undressed and settled in for a long Ascension and sleep. The large ceiling fan, slowly turning overhead, gently stirred the air. It was hot, but the humidity is low in the Punjab at that time of year; it wasn't too uncomfortable. I lay on my back, Ascended and dreamed of Sharon.

I woke to some loud howling out back, beyond the garden wall. Had the monkeys returned? It didn't sound like them; it was more a cross between a coyote and human laugh. I had never heard anything like it. *Jackals,* I thought, *or perhaps hyenas -- what a terrifying sound.* I returned to a fitful sleep, more troubled than peaceful.

Morning began warm. I showered, dressed in loose whites and wandered out to the dining porch. Sharon was already there, peeling mangoes and slicing them on a large plate. She had prepared an enormous stack of them -- were they all for her?

I greeted her with a kiss and said, "Success last night with Mira?" I sat down and eyed the mangoes, wondering if she'd offer me any.

"I think so. Lila was her only sister. She had a brother, but he died from cancer a few years ago."

"Parents alive?" Sharon didn't seem to have any intention to share; with a sigh I picked up a sharp knife and began peeling my own.

"No. She's all alone now. Not even any cousins. Lila was her last."

"That makes it harder. Never married? Ow!" I haven't ever been too successful at peeling anything.

"Careful! Don't bleed on your fruit... They both were, but it didn't work out for either of them, in different ways. Lila was divorced, but Mira's husband was killed by terrorists in Ireland. He was a bodyguard for the British Governor. The IRA planted a bomb in his car."

"You're kidding! Two violent deaths, so close to her, so similar? That's weird." I abandoned peeling for the simpler technique of slicing the sweet fruit into manageable portions; I'd let my teeth do the work.

"Not kidding. She wonders if her family's been cursed. It gets even stranger: she says her father was a bomber pilot for the RAF in the Second World War."

"I expect to hear Twilight Zone music! How's she doing?" My stack was rapidly growing larger now, but was still way behind hers -- it looked as if she intended to build a mango mountain.

"Actually, well. She cried a long time, succeeded in letting a lot of it out. She's not holding anything back, at least nothing I can feel; she's not repressing it. She's done incredible work on herself with Ascending. I've never seen anyone move so quickly."

"How many Spheres does she have?" I decided I had to quit. This race was impossible to win. I wondered how long I would have to wait until she started eating.

"She said five. She's ahead of everyone except Alan and possibly Edg."

Doctor Dave joined us now; we had a three-way competition to see who could eat the most of the succulent fruit. Not surprisingly, Sharon won easily, by at least half a dozen.

Six of us -- everyone except Edg and Hari and Lal -- gathered in the living room at eleven. It was already blisteringly hot, but here there were three large ceiling fans and a giant floor model; the moving dry air made the heat bearable.

Aphrodite and Steve seemed to have spent another night without much sleep. I grinned to think of my early twenties and was a little grateful I was older now. I still had a strong and healthy interest in sex and was certain my fiancée did as well, but we were on a quest that was taking precedence -- at least now -- over activities we otherwise would be enjoying.

Mira looked much better. In fact, she looked completely in control. That is not accurate -- there was no visible effort in this, she was not straining to remain in a positive, Ascending mode. Rather the strength emanating from her was the natural byproduct of the clarity and depth of her inner experience.

"My habit in teaching Ascension," she explained, "is to allow everyone to hear again the technique explanations, if those being instructed have no objections. So, if it's all right with you two, I encourage Sharon and Dite and Steve to be here for this discussion of the First Gratitude Attitude."

"Fine with me," I said; the doctor readily agreed.

"Good! Now, opening more channels into the Ascendant charms the mind in new and different ways, thereby speeding up progress. The rate of our growth can be accelerated almost without limit. This is the primary reason for advanced Ascension Attitudes."

"We keep using the First Technique?" I asked.

"Sure. We use all the Attitudes in every Ascension so the mind becomes more familiar with all the angles we take into the Ascendant. The First Attitude is like a magical doorway through which wonderful changes pass. Adding more techniques is like having a wider doorway. More wonder and glory comes through it."

"I see the First Technique as being like an express train," said Aphrodite. "We are traveling on it fast, yet become used to our speed and naturally wish to move ahead faster. So we step aboard a plane. We arrive sooner at our destination; the ride is more comfortable. We notice the difficulty of the trip less; all the bumps and changes in the terrain are less significant."

"I think of it like this," said Sharon: "the nervous system is like a wonderful electrical circuit that can accommodate continually higher voltage. As the experiences in Ascending intensify, it starts developing faster and faster. More and more of the Ascendant is used in life; the whole mind turns toward the Ascendant at every moment of the day and night. Advanced techniques accelerate this growth to Perpetual Consciousness."

"Good analogies!" exclaimed Mira. "Now, the structure of the Second Ascension Attitude is similar to the First. In the Second Technique, we use Thankfulness instead of Appreciation: Gratitude is the driving force for our hearts, for our emotional right hemisphere."

"And for our rational sides," I asked, "for the left brain, we continue using our personal Ultimate Thought?"

"Exactly. That concept naturally draws the rational mind out of boundaries and toward the Ascendant. Uniting it with Gratitude opens the whole of the mind to the Ascendant along this new channel. Then we focus this Ascending energy back onto our individuality... What do you suppose the focus is for this new technique?"

"Another of our root stresses?" asked the doctor.

"Precisely! As with the First Attitude, we want to focus the power of Ascension onto one of our fundamental blocks. If we can remove the causes of our belief systems in suffering, all the subsidiary beliefs will dissolve. If you cut the taproot, the plant will die."

"The First Technique deals with the root stress in our *subjective* lives," Dave said thoughtfully. "So the second major stress must be in our *objective* lives, in our outer world. Right?"

"Right! Is there anyone who hasn't thought the world could be a friendlier place? For that matter, is there anyone who hasn't thought his or her body could be healthier or prettier or stronger? Please don't misunderstand! I'm not saying there's no room for improvement in the world or in our bodies. I'm saying it's our *belief* there's something wrong with the world and with our bodies that is the root of all our limiting beliefs and habits about the Universe."

"Does this belief also keep the mind out of the present moment?" I asked curiously. "Abstracted away from the experience of right Here and right Now?"

"Yes! And that keeps our future locked into unfortunate experiences, based on our limited beliefs in the present. The First Gratitude Attitude heals our future. Gratitude for the objective is the master key to straighten the kinks out of our path.

"So to heal our relationship with the world, turn our lives back to this instant of time and transform our future, we Ascend with the Second Attitude, putting our focus on the objective, on everything external -- the body, the world, the Universe. Everything outside the Self. This may sound complex, but the concept is simple, a single idea: everything physical outside the Self."

"We don't normally think of our bodies as external," said Aphrodite. "I think this is one reason we believe so firmly in death. If a body is sick, we say the person is sick. If a body dies, we say the person has died. I'm learning the Reality is quite other; I'm recognizing my body is external to me, and therefore I'm moving closer and closer to the understanding that everything -- my body, my world, even my mind and my emotions -- everything is external to my Self and my Self is the same as the Ascendant -- infinite, Unbounded, never changing, never dying, established in Eternity."

"I believe that's so," said Sharon. "The body as it's experienced in the waking state is a creation of the mind. The body is not a frozen, unchanging sculpture; it's in a constant state of flux with the environment. It's made of stardust, as is everything around us. We are the same, this world and our bodies; we're all part of Earth, of Gaia, all built of congealed magic."

"I agree completely!" exclaimed the doctor, greatly enthusiastic. "The body is interchanging at every moment with the environment. I've heard 98% of the atoms in our body weren't there a year ago! That's how fast we are transforming. It is as if we live in a miraculous building in which every stick is being replaced each year, but because of ignorance, we rebuild it exactly the same way, year after year after year. If the body is sick, we rebuild it sick. If we have a tumor, we recreate the tumor. If the body is old, we reform it old. So this Attitude cures us of these faulty uses of the body by re-acquainting us with the Master Builder, the Ascendant?"

"You're all exactly right!" exclaimed Mira. "And further: the body and the world are like two sides of the same coin, both simultaneously exist always. The world seems to begin where the body ends, but the reality is: the external world is a manifestation of the body, it results from the senses. When the senses don't operate, what becomes of the world? And the senses are a manifestation of the mind. By mastering this Attitude, the perception that the external Universe is a creation of the mind begins. When this is fully learned, mastery of the objective is inevitable."

"You're saying the Universe is a projection of our beliefs and judgments?" I asked. "My world is different from yours; Steve's is different from Dite's, everyone's is different from everyone else's?

They seem to share some features, but the reality is, my world, my Universe, is my creation, none other's?"

"Yes! This is the perspective from Unified Consciousness. This Attitude gives mastery of the objective world. It's also invaluable for anyone suffering from disease of any kind. Perfect health is the automatic byproduct of knowing the Truth of this technique. This is a priceless tool for removing all the stress from the physical nervous system."

The doctor commented: "In other words, this Attitude teaches that the subjective is primary and the objective is secondary. The old view of medicine and science claimed that the body alone was real; consciousness was a ghost in the body-machine. The Gratitude Attitude corrects all such faulty and superstitious beliefs by replacing them with the direct experience of Reality: the mind comes first, the body and the world are projections."

"Well said," Mira said warmly, smiling at him. Then she explained the exact structure of this new technique and continued, "So now, divide your program between the First and Second Techniques: about ten or fifteen minutes on Praise and then ten or fifteen minutes on Gratitude. It may be you prefer one or another on some days; it may be one or another of the techniques makes you uncomfortable from time to time. This doesn't matter. We don't Ascend for some feeling on the surface of the mind. It doesn't matter how we feel about it; we just do it.

"So, let's Ascend..."

At first this new Attitude felt a little rough for me, but soon I settled into it. Lots of judgments about my body and my world came up for my review, just as Mira implied they would; many memories flowed through I hadn't had in years. When she gently brought us out of it an hour later, I felt as if I'd hardly begun.

Sharon was right; this new Attitude was as great as the first, perhaps even greater.

19

A Prince, a Snake and a Well

Mira asked Sharon again if she'd like the Third Technique; again she declined. Doctor Dave went to his room to Ascend, but Sharon and I decided to explore the garden.

As we stepped off the porch, we frightened a pair of blue jays who flew away, chattering noisily. Their racket disturbed two rose-ringed parakeets in one of the mango trees; they flew around discussing this at great length for a few moments before settling down again to their arboreal perch.

We discovered a little cobblestone path through the garden, leading to an enormous banyan tree in the far back. Banyans are a kind of fig tree; they drop hundreds or even thousands of aerial roots, creating a forest from a single tree, spreading to an enormous size if left undisturbed. This one looked several hundred years old. There was a marble bench ornately carved with angels near the heart of its many trunks; we sat on it and stared into each other's eyes.

"The Buddha was supposed to have gained enlightenment, sitting under a Bo tree like this one," said Sharon.

"Really? How fitting... I'm so glad you're here with me, Sharon, or rather, I'm here with you, for you decided first."

"Only because I'd Ascended a couple of days longer! We're here together, that's what matters. That's why I didn't take the Love Technique yet, you know. I want to move through this Teaching step-by-step with you, grow into completion with you. This journey will be so much more enjoyable because of sharing it with you."

"That's true for me as well! I'm sure I'd enjoy Ascending if I'd never met you, but I'm also sure I'd feel something major was missing from my life. You may just be a projection of my mind, I may have out-pictured you from my own internal programming, but you are without doubt the best projection I've ever out-pictured. I'm glad you're a significant part of my objective Universe. I can't imagine life without you."

"So you're enjoying the Gratitude Attitude?"

"Oh yes. I partly understand now your experiences at Delphi. Is that still going on, by the way?"

"Not as strongly. I feel connected with everything, as if there is little or no line between me and the world; I feel everything is coming out of me, but it's not so dominant as it was there. In Delphi, every single thing in Creation was talking to me, singing back to me in love and joy. I guess it all grows in stages... Would you like to Ascend with me under this huge banyan tree? Maybe we'll be as lucky as Prince Siddhartha."

"Who was he?"

"He became the Buddha. But he was born a prince. Have you heard that story?"

"No, or if I have, I've forgotten it. Care to tell me?"

"Sure!"

There was once a wealthy Raja in India in what is now the Bihar state, west of Calcutta, near the Himalayas. Raja Suddhodana was good, wealthy and just, but he was childless. Finally he performed a great sacrifice, beseeching the gods to grant him an heir. The sacrifice was successful; the queen bore him a son. They named him Siddhartha -- "the Perfection of Wealth."

The day the prince was born, a Maharishi came to the court and told the Raja that Siddhartha would become the world's greatest Emperor -- or else a monk and a World Teacher.

The Raja looked at this as a mixed blessing: he wanted no spiritual leader as the son of a warrior. Deciding he could thwart the prophecy, he made three ironclad rules: Siddhartha must never leave the palace grounds; the sick, the infirm, the old and the dying must never be allowed inside the palace; his son must never be told anything of these conditions of planet Earth.

The boy grew quickly and strong; he was well trained in all branches of science and warfare. In these areas only was the lie maintained: Siddhartha saw no sick, he saw no aged, he saw no dying, he saw no dead, he was told nothing of these states. The Raja was wealthy enough and the palace grounds large enough to keep the illusion alive for twenty-nine years; Siddhartha married a beautiful princess and was as happy as a human can be.

But no lie can last forever: a lady of the court fell ill; the prince saw her before she could be hidden away. "What is wrong with that woman?" He asked his best friend.

"Alas, my prince, Jambuli is ill. She may even die."

"This could happen to me?"

"Sickness can strike any one, my Lord Siddhartha."

"This could happen to my unborn children?"

"Any man, woman or child can fall ill, my Lord."

"What is the cure for this? How can suffering be avoided?"

"My Lord! No one knows the cure for suffering."

Siddhartha stayed in the palace, but he was troubled by this new thing in an otherwise perfect world. More months passed; his wife the princess became pregnant; Siddhartha saw no more ill people, decided sickness was a rare thing indeed and decided to forget it. But the world had another need for the prince: one day an old, old man slipped past the guards and walked beneath Siddhartha's window.

"Who is that fellow? Why does he walk along using a stick? Why is his hair white? Why is he bent over? Why is his skin so wrinkled? Is he sick too?"

"Alas, no, my Lord. He is old. His body is worn out, he has lived so long."

"Will this happen to me?"

"Old age comes to all, my Lord Siddhartha."

"Even my father, the Raja? My mother? My wife, my unborn child?"

"Every man, woman and child will grow old, my Lord."

"What is the cure for this? How can suffering be avoided?"

"My Lord! No one knows the cure for suffering."

Siddhartha was shocked to the depth of his soul by old age. Was there truly no antidote to it? Why would the world be so poorly created? But soon his son was born; his worry was eclipsed in the joy of new life.

All might still have gone as the Raja willed, but the very next day, one of Siddhartha's closest attendants had a stroke and died before the prince. This was the final blow to Siddhartha's desire to remain in the palace. That night, he abandoned his home and family to seek the source of suffering and heal it for the good of all humanity.

"After six years of inner exploration, Prince Siddhartha realized enlightenment, at Bodh Gaya, sitting under a tree like this one. He became the Buddha, which means, 'One with an illumined intellect.'"

"That is a wonderful story!" I exclaimed. "Your knowledge goes far beyond physics!"

"Oh, I never used my degrees. Even before I finished graduate school, I realized there were whole universes I wished to explore. I've done a thousand different things and studied a hundred different fields since then. My search was never random, although it probably would have looked like it to any casual observer.

"But I'd gotten as far as I could when I arrived in Seattle. I hadn't found any answers as deep as I was looking; I still believed Truth must exist somewhere but had no idea where. So I kept my quest alive, hoping still but hardly believing I would ever succeed."

"Sharon, I read once: when the student is ready, the Teacher will appear. I guess that's what happened to you. And me. Although I don't know how ready I was to meet Ollie. I don't feel I've ever accomplished anything at all."

"I think God judges differently than we do," she answered me softly. "I think you must have been completely ready. Look how you've moved, in just ten days! You *were* ripe for the picking, you just couldn't see it. You matured from the inside, like a pear."

"I was ready for *something,*" I admitted. "My life was going nowhere. Fast. Maybe all the hard hits from Nature were designed to get me moving, to prepare me for change."

"That's what I think! The original meaning of the word 'bless' was 'to consecrate with blood' or 'to strike'. I think often our blessings come to us disguised as suffering, to cut away the deadwood in our lives and enable us to move in new directions. Pruning can be painful, but in the hands of a Master Gardener, great beauty is created."

"Maybe that's why our group has been cut down," I said. "From our side, it makes little sense. But we're not the Gardener of Earth. From Universal Perspective, their passing must have been perfect. If it's true all things work together for good in the world."

"I believe they do. Unfortunately, it's still more of a hopeful belief than a living experience. I'm still new at this."

"Me too... Shall we Ascend out here? With this gentle breeze, it's probably cooler than in the house."

"Yes, let's."

She wanted to lie down; I surrendered the bench and, sitting on a large root, leaned against a trunk of the tree.

I started with the Praise Attitude. As was my usual experience, after a few repetitions, I settled into deep rest; my mind was clear and still except for the gentle flowing movement of the Ascension Attitude. I often felt large inside when I Ascended; today, however, it was simply quiet and peaceful. Only a few other thoughts moved in me -- I was aware of the heat, of the chirping and cawing of the birds, of the sonorous buzzing of the insects, of the roughness of the trunk against my back and of the solid feel of the root beneath me -- but not much, not enough to distract me from my gentle, inward glide.

After half an hour or so of this deep peace, I introduced the Second Attitude. My awareness instantly split into three! Part of me was still sitting under the tree, Ascending; part of me floated about fifteen feet above, looking with perfect clarity down at my body, Sharon and the garden; and part of me floated out in space, above the Earth.

At the third level, I felt another presence beside me: it was a gloriously bright being, dressed in white with long auburn hair and beard, floating beside me, staring at the world below with love. He looked at me and smiled, but I thought I saw tears in his eyes. *Why?* I thought, and looked back at the Earth. It had changed: a gigantic serpent with glittering black and red scales was encircling it, crushing it in relentless coils of sanguine death.

Simultaneously, I saw an enormous cobra enter the garden and glide toward me where I sat under the tree! In shock, I stopped Ascending and opened my eyes. The three experiences melted back into one; I was again wholly under the tree, but not three feet in front of me was the giant serpent, erect, its hood expanded in rage!

The strike of the cobra is almost always fatal. Hundreds of Indians die every year from it. I didn't know if there was an antidote for it or not, but I did remember reading its venom was so virulent few live long enough to reach a hospital anyway.

As these thoughts flashed through my mind, the cobra hissed at me; its forked tongue flicked in and out; I stared into its unblinking snake eyes and wondered if the Earth adventure was about to end for me. Except for its flicking tongue, neither of us moved for what seemed hours.

Finally Sharon stirred on the bench, said, "Mm?" opened her eyes, looked at me and smiled.

The cobra shimmered, then disappeared with a small pop.

"Sharon!" I exclaimed, shaking all over and perspiring from head to foot. "Sharon, I -- I think I'm going to Ascend inside for awhile. Too hot out here for me. Want to come?"

"No, darling, but thank you. I think I'll stay out here for the rest of the afternoon. All the plants are singing to me."

"Fine," I said, standing a little shakily. I kissed her and said, "See you at dinner."

"OK," she purred, already slipping back inward.

I played with the idea of running away from Amritsar, India, Ascension, but knew I didn't mean it: I'd run my whole life and never gotten anywhere. Besides, there was Sharon. *No,* I resolved to myself, *I'm not doing that again. I may have demons in my garden, but I created them -- therefore, I can destroy them.* I lay down on my bed and started Ascending again.

Almost immediately, I split into three once more. Part of me knew I was lying on the bed, feeling the air gently moving from the fan. Another part was floating above the house -- Sharon was still in the garden on the bench, Ascending. I could see through the roof as if it were made of glass: Doctor Dave was in his room, furiously scribbling notes on his pad; Hari and Lal were cooking another feast in the kitchen; Edg was in a corner room, lying very, very still; Mira and Aphrodite and Steve were in the living room, Ascending together. And a third part of me floated again above the Earth, but this time I was alone. There was no beautiful white-robed being beside me; there was no serpent engulfing the Earth with its crushing coils.

Gently I re-introduced the Second Ascension Attitude; my mind split again: I lay on my bed, I floated above the house, I looked down on the Earth, but I was also standing outside the Golden Sphere I had experienced in the Grotto on Patmos. Inside it I could still see the seven spheres of fire as well as the entire Universe.

This time, however, there was the faintest silver thread connecting the various levels of experience. It expanded around me, revealing a fifth level of reality: inside the silver thread was another copy of the entire Universe -- and also, incredibly, Sharon.

Our language is linear. It is inadequate to describe experiences simultaneously ongoing on many levels at the same time. Each of these five levels of experience was coincident with every other level, and yet had independent reality of space and time.

Again I repeated the Second Attitude; as I did so, I became aware of yet another level of Reality, as far beyond the Golden Sphere that contained our Universe as that Reality was above my body lying on a bed back here on tiny, tiny Earth. That new Reality was filled with uncountable billions of Golden Spheres, each containing an entire Universe, each a complete and perfect Creation.

Once again the Ascension Attitude echoed through me; I split one final time -- at the deepest or subtlest or most expanded level, I merged into an infinite white light that was not light but was beyond all light, and yet contained within it all light and all color and all form and all sound and all time.

I knew I was That, I was nothing other than That. That limitless, infinite, Unbounded, Eternal Reality was nothing other than me. And it was the Ascendant. And so was I.

20

Punjab Tales

A gentle knocking on my door coalesced all the levels of size or space or time back into one. I was lying on my bed in my room in Amritsar.

I said, quietly, "Yes?"

The door opened and Sharon slipped in, radiant, beautifully dressed in yet another outfit I hadn't ever seen her wear. This one was a deep emerald green and covered with sequins and red stones. She looked like she was on her way to the most expensive restaurant in India.

"Dinnertime!" she announced cheerfully. "Time to get up, sleepy-head!"

"Dinner? So early? You're ravishing!"

"Thank you! But it's not early: it's eight o'clock. You've been in here for seven hours! I was beginning to think you were going to sleep forever."

"I don't think I was sleeping. Wow. What an Ascension."

"Me too. I'm glad I waited for the Third. Coming?"

The others were already enjoying another feast -- from every appearance, larger than yesterday's. I was amazed to see Edg there, sounding and appearing completely healed. He smiled at my astounded look, pointed his index finger at me, and said cheerfully, "Told ya."

I didn't feel like talking; rather mechanically, I filled my plate. Most of the others were done before Sharon and I really started; they chatted together about the heat and the coming trip and ate dessert: gulab jamuns and rice pudding.

A loud pounding on the front door sent Lal scurrying into the house and down the hallway. He returned via the porch, leading a white robed Sikh in his mid-thirties. He was tall and dark with a strong bearded face and a crooked nose, intense eyes, and very black hair.

"Kala! Welcome!" exclaimed Mira, rising to greet him. "Sat Sri Akal, Kala! Everyone, this is Kala, a Durga Novitiate and a dear friend."

Edg knew him also: he half-rose, half-bowed and said, "Sat Sri Akal, Kala-ji. Nice to see you again."

"Namaste to you, Ed Silver. It may be or it may not. Life moves on. May I sit at your table?"

"Of course," replied Mira. "Hungry? Lal and Hari will never learn to estimate amounts, as you can see."

"Sure," he replied, filling up a dish with the spiciest food as Mira introduced us all.

"'Practice makes permanent,' so master says," Kala said over his papadam, covered with rice and dahl. "Thus perseverance is its own reward. To that end, I will tell you a story my mother told me as a child. It was a Christian tale, but my mother was broad-minded. Fortunately! How else could I have embraced Ascension?"

Once, there was a small country, ruled by a wise and good king who had no heir. The king had a lovely wife and every good thing, save only a son to take over after he passed on. One day, as chance would have it, the Apostle John walked through this small kingdom, on his way to found his Ishaya monastery, and asked for shelter. The king perceived something of his greatness and received him, fed him and housed him.

As he was leaving, St. John asked him if he would like to learn about God. "No," answered the king, "I have no time to learn about God. I must rule my kingdom wisely and well. What I really need is a son to carry on after me."

John smiled in his heart to see the king so dedicated to his duty and said, "You have chosen, oh king. If you had asked of me God, you would have had God. Instead, you asked me for a son, and you will have a son. He will bring you joy and sorrow. But in the end, you will ask of me God."

John's prophecy was good; a son was born, but he was born with a deformed back. The child's mind was excellent, he easily learned whatever the teachers put before him, but the king's heart was not glad.

St. John passed through this kingdom a second time, seeking monks for his order; again the king received him well. Once more John asked him if he would like to know about God; once more the king replied, "Thank you, but no. I am busy, ensuring my people's happiness. I have no time for God. I must keep the thieves away from our borders. What I really need is for my young son to be healed, so he can take over when I'm gone."

John smiled in his heart to see the king so dedicated to his duty and replied, "You have chosen, oh king. Had you asked me of God, you would have had God. Instead, you asked me for health for your son, and you will have a healthy son. Tell him you will give him anything he asks for, then ask him what he wants; he will tell you what you need do. As for you, you will have sorrow and joy. But in the end, you will ask of me God."

The king sent for his son and asked him if there were anything he wanted, telling him he could have anything there was in the entire world.

"Why yes, father, thank you very much," the prince replied. "I want you to order a statue of me. Not like I look now, you under-stand, but the way I'll look when I'm fully grown, like you, father. Have them sculpt me strong and healthy and straight, not like I am now, but as I'll be then, when I'm all grown, please father? And then place it in my garden where I can look at it every day. All right, father?"

The king was surprised but did as his son requested; the statue of a handsome prince, tall, straight, strong, completely healed was sculpted and placed in the center of his son's garden.

The years passed; every day the prince saw the statue of himself as he would look when he was fully grown -- he saw it in the early morning light, standing erect to greet the dawn; he saw it in the brightness of noon, never wavering in the scorching heat; he saw it during the monsoon rains, standing straight and tall and proud through the thundering storms; he saw it at midnight in the moonlight, standing in all seasons and hours a perfect example of manliness, strength and health.

Every night as the prince slept, he stretched himself out a little bit more, to become more like the statue, imagining, willing himself into that perfect body. And do you know? By his twenty-first birthday, the prince was tall, straight, strong, completely healed.

Many more years passed; the queen and most of the king's life-long friends and counselors died from old age; the king ceded his kingdom to his fully matured and competent son and wandered off to seek St. John and learn about God.

"So you see," finished Kala, "the king fulfilled his worldly duties, *then* became a monk. the Apostle refused to teach him how to Ascend until he was ready to have his priorities aligned, to have God first in his life. Why should John share Ascension with those divided between God and the world? Let them fulfill their worldly desires, then teach them the Truth. That's the way we've always done it, for that's the only way that works. Our way is the only way. If you cast the pearls of Ascension before worldly people, they will trample them and gore you besides."

"The only goring going on around here," said Edg, "has been of our group. Are you aware of what's happened?"

"I? Ah, that is, I -- ah, well, unfortunately, yes. Regrettably, yes. This is one reason I've come tonight. Two of our new

Novitiates -- you've never met them -- did not, ah, *well* master their vows. They are also headstrong and wealthy, which illustrates my point once again. If they had been poor, all could have been avoided. A great tragedy, this whole thing."

"Tragedy!" cried Mira, fire flashing from her eyes. "Is that what you call murder?"

"I call it the insane acts of two who were unworthy of Ascension, Mira-ji. Durga has banned them from any further instruction. I can think of no more fitting punishment, can you? They are forbidden forever from learning the Secrets of the Seven Spheres. But if I may, you must see how this illustrates my point. If we who so carefully screen our recruits encounter such difficulties, how much greater will the problems be if you teach the highest wisdom to *householders.*" He practically choked on the word.

"I will tell you a story too," said Edg, fiercely. "Perhaps you might learn something yourself, Kala-ji."

"Should I listen to you? You with your five Spheres and no vows?"

"I believe in the five Novitiate vows and in the five Ishaya vows. I believe in them and I practice them. But I *don't* believe in making oaths about them. I don't want to be locked into anyone's religious observances."

"There is great and abiding value in formalizing the vows."

"For you perhaps! And for Mira, and undoubtedly for others too," Edg answered, glancing at the doctor. "But I don't believe in the value of mere words. If the heart is not in it, what use the words? Again, if the heart *is* there, what use the words? Look at your traitors. They took vows, did they not? And what did they make of them?"

"Unfortunately, little, that is true. Too often we Sikhs slip aside from the simple wisdom of our first Guru Nanak: *Ek Unkar,* 'There is One God,' and embrace instead that fool of a tenth Guru,

Govind Singh. His teachings have been a bane to my people. Very well, Ed Silver, let us hear your story. At the least, it will help me understand your confused minds more clearly."

"Thank you -- I think."

Once a merchant from the hill country traveled to the Ocean and saw white sand for the first time in his life. It was clean and silver and glorious and stretched as far as his eyes could see. "What beautiful sand!" he cried, deciding at once to sell it in his homeland. He built a fence around a few acres of it to protect it and started a business, packing it up and shipping it back to his native country.

One day, some robbers saw the fence and thought the sand inside the barriers must be special, else why would anyone build a fence? So they plotted to break in and steal the merchant's fine sand.

An informant told him what they were planning; the merchant built a stone wall around his sand, hired guards to protect his wall, then employed spies to keep track of the thieves.

The robbers, seeing how fiercely the merchant protected his sand, concluded it must be invaluable and enlisted the aid of a neighboring king to breach the walls.

The merchant's spies told him what forces were massing against him; in fear for his life he hired his own army to protect his sand.

Just as the two armies were gathering for battle, a small child came walking down the beach, carrying a toy shovel and a bucket of fine, white sand. For the first time in years, the merchant looked up from his private sand inside his walls and saw the sand stretching away endlessly in all directions. He dismissed his army and spies, tore down his walls and went home.

"If we defend Ascension, Kala, we will make a religion out of it. John was emphatic: this Teaching is a simple, mechanical process; it involves no beliefs of any kind to practice. This is why he always opened his doors to any who wished to learn the Truth, regardless of background. If we erect walls around Ascension and attempt to exclude the world, we will be destroyed.

"Maybe it was necessary in the first century, but even then, no -- the monastery's thick walls are not that old. One of the Maharishi Custodians decided it was necessary, probably because the local chieftains were growing more warlike: small, violent kingdoms were springing up throughout the Himalayas. Even then, I think it was a mistake; John would never have enclosed it so rigorously. They were there, those first monks, because of the hot spring caves. It was a later perversion to build the monastery."

"Yes," agreed Mira. "And do you see what could happen, Kala? If we keep Ascension isolated from the world, a single terrorist could erase this knowledge from the Earth. That almost happened during the war with Pakistan, remember? If not for the good fortune of Durga and Nanda being in Calcutta at the time, this Teaching would be dead! No, it has to spread, and now; we need hundreds or thousands of fully realized souls, possessing the complete knowledge of the Seven Spheres."

"I agree with that," said Kala, "but not by your methods. My point remains: this Teaching is too precious to give it to householders."

"We've had this conversation before," sighed Mira, "but I'm willing to have it as many times as you wish."

"This difference will never be resolved without an agreement between Durga and Nanda," said Edg. "Unless you intend to try to kill us all."

"That will *never* happen again! We are imposing a much stricter set of rules for those we teach. It is the only way to be safe."

"That is *not* what the world needs!" I exclaimed, discovering this argument had solidified my own belief. "You may not notice it here in the Punjab, but the Earth is teetering on the edge of destruction. World consciousness must rise. Ascension is needed desperately, and now. As people Ascend, they become more conscious; this changes their behavior patterns, makes them more Christ-like. It is backwards to think people should become better first. Your thinking is completely upside down. 'Be good' and deserve the Kingdom of Heaven -- that is what you're saying, once all the varnish is removed. This is the kind of belief that has emasculated Christianity and all the world's great religions. Ascension says, as John meant it, we all deserve the Kingdom of Heaven as our birthright -- we are all created in the image and likeness of God; therefore we are deserving. Our goodness follows our deserving. As we become increasingly clear because of Ascension, goodness naturally follows."

"That is an interesting point," said Kala sincerely. "I'd never thought in those terms before. Perhaps you could repeat it to my master this weekend at the monastery."

"You're going to be there!" exclaimed Mira.

"Yes, we're all coming -- three of us are ready to take our life vows: myself and Devi and Kriya. Durga-ji and Nanda have agreed to preside jointly over the Ceremony."

"I'm glad they're cooperating!"

"Oh, they always have about the continuance of the Ishaya monks. Their only area of disagreement is about revealing Ascension to the worldly...

"I'll be going now. I just stopped by to assure you, you are safe from any further violence. And also ask if I could ride up with you on Thursday."

"Sure," Mira answered coolly, "I guess so. Forgiveness and cooperation... We have the room. How many of you are here?"

"Only myself. Our other six left with Durga yesterday. Master is carrying a personal apology to Nanda; he asked me to stay behind to speak with you."

"So there are still only seven Durga Novitiates?" asked Edg.

"There are again only seven of us, yes. Our vows prove too hard, I fear. We tried a vigorous expansion program this last year, to meet the challenge you pose to us, but the new recruits... did not work out as we had expected. As I told you, Durga has released them."

"And how did they feel about that?" asked Edg with keen interest.

"They took it well, I think. They feel awful about what they've done. They were foolish, wrong. They were only trying to scare Ollie, at most damage him a little so he'd back off from teaching Ascension. They never meant to kill him."

"How about my sister?" asked Mira coldly. "And the others?"

"What others? What are you talking about?"

"You claim you don't know about the explosion at Patmos?"

"Mira, what? I swear I know nothing except of the accident in Seattle. What happened on Patmos? Is Balindra all right? Satya? Devindra?"

"Kala," said Edg heavily. "We are all that are left. The others died on a boat in Skala Harbor at Patmos. We thought your people were responsible for those deaths as well."

"That is horrible!" he cried, paling. "How can this be? Our two errant Novitiates flew home after the tragedy in Seattle. Are you sure it wasn't an accident?"

"No, we're not sure. It could have been. Or not. Who can say? Well, we'd best continue to be cautious. Perhaps we're all in danger, not just those following our interpretation of St. John's Teaching. Maybe there is someone else in the world who doesn't like the thought of Ascension leaving the monastery, in any form. I had wondered why your people would kill Novitiates. Now it's beginning to make more sense. You didn't."

"Then who did?" Steve asked, voicing everyone's surprise.

"I'm not quite sure," said Edg, "but I've been working on a couple of theories."

Something about his tone made me wonder what he was thinking. With a shudder, I realized I wasn't sure I wanted to know. Perhaps Edg could see the difference between ruthlessness and violence, but I was sure I couldn't. Something about him always reminded me of a feral animal -- a mountain lion, perhaps, or perhaps a darker creature, one of the night, a panther. A predator who would stop at nothing to destroy its prey.

Whatever he was and whatever he was planning, I was *very* glad he was on our side.

He was, wasn't he?

21

Immaculate Journey

Wednesday was quiet, the quietest day Sharon and I had experienced in a long time. We Ascended, we walked through the garden, we ate, we chatted with the others. It felt like order after chaos, peace after an epoch of war, heaven after hell. It had only been eleven days since I took the ferry to Bainbridge to see my high school friend, but it felt like eleven lifetimes. My world-view had been shaken to its roots and re-assembled, all but entirely new, all but completely different.

I knew now, if we could avoid destruction at the hands of the still unknown Opposition, the rest of my life might turn out well -- very well, indeed. Ascension was giving me a peace and a confidence I had never before known. My experiences with it Wednesday were not mystical at all, simply calm and still; but I felt the power of both my Ascension Attitudes working in me, re-writing my old beliefs and judgments about the nature of my life and my Universe.

These two techniques seemed complete. After a technique to heal my subjective stress and a technique to heal my objective stress, what more could there possibly be? They were all-inclusive. I couldn't imagine where the First Love Technique might take me, but I was sure it would only be somewhere even better. I believed now in the power of St. John's Ascension. Even if I never received another Attitude, the two I already knew had opened me to experiences unlike any I had ever known.

I still did not understand the philosophy underlying Ascension, but everything I had learned so far was consistent and logical. I particularly liked that belief was in no way required. This made perfect sense to me: since Ascension was so dramatic and powerful, it was only necessary to give it to people, let them experience it for themselves. There was no need for strict rules and regulations; the techniques stood on their own merit. All that was required was enough innocence to be willing to try something that looked new; then beliefs would naturally change, based on changing experiences of life. It was impossible anyone could long continue with the belief suffering was the supreme force in the Universe, for example, if one often (or even once) experienced the extraordinary power and unending light of the infinite. I did not know how long it would take to make such an experience permanent, but I knew I wanted it very much indeed.

The doctor spent most of the day with Mira; he seemed as drawn to her as he had been to Lila. Undoubtedly they were discussing the Novitiate vows and his desire to join their Order. My opinion of that was similar to Edg's -- it seemed a little superficial. But I supposed some found the guidelines imposed by such a life useful; they probably found it an inspiration to align with such an ancient order.

Whether Ascension had come from the Apostle John or not, I did not know and did not much care, for it was working wonderfully for me; at the least, the Ishaya monks represented a tradition that was hundreds of years old, its origins lost in remotest antiquity. If the doctor wished to dedicate his life to that, it must be right for him. I could almost understand this: a simple, life-long focus on growing into the Ascendant, free from all distractions. Viewing it like that, I could see its logic.

Not that Sharon could ever appear as a distraction to me! On the contrary, whenever we were together, our focus on the Ascendant only grew stronger.

Thursday began early. Hari and Lal drove two Calcutta-made cars called Hindustan Ambassadors into our drive. They looked like mini-tanks, squat, solid and ugly, but practically anyone in

India can fix them; spare parts are everywhere, even in the remotest villages. Edg, Kala (who arrived the previous night not to be late), Steve and Aphrodite piled into the one driven by Hari; Lal was behind our wheel, Mira sat beside him in the front, carefully placing a sheepskin under her white sari; the good doctor, Sharon (wearing a light cotton dress in blue with yellow daisies hand-stitched into it) and I lounged comfortably in the back of the enormous car.

Lal said, "Kya, apjaane waale hai?"

Mira replied, "Jaiye! Yes, let's go!"

"Off again!" beamed Sharon as we roared out of the drive.

"Another adventure begun," I agreed, hoping our peaceful days in Amritsar were not going to prove the eye of a hurricane.

Beyond the gate, we were back in the mainstream of India. Our garden walls had been the most temporary of shields. Floods of human beings were rushing by on vital errands known best only to themselves. The narrow roadway was clogged with animals, people and vehicles of every possible size, shape and description. We were again immersed in a sea of human chaos; all order was a dream of innocence past.

As we laboriously worked our way eastward, following the Beas River, the land slowly started climbing upwards into the Himalayan foothills; the plains of irrigated barley and wheat gave way gradually to orchards and forests of hardwood.

"Where are all the jungles I always think of when I hear of India?" I asked no one in particular.

"Very little is left forested," said the doctor. "I've read most of it has been cut for fuel and building supplies and to make fields for domestic animals and crops."

"You're kidding!" exclaimed Sharon. "What's become of the wild animals?"

"They're being squeezed into the 3% of the land that's been set aside for National Parks. Few of the parks are adequately patrolled, however; poachers kill many of the animals for hides, ivory or, in some cases, meat. And there are no corridors between the isolated tracts of land; the gene pool of many species is rapidly shrinking. The entire ecosystem of the Indian subcontinent is on the verge of catastrophic collapse -- too many people on too little land. The farmers have no choice but to plant their crops right up to the edge of the parks; therefore a certain number of villagers are eaten every year by the tigers. Many peasants feel the government cares more for the animals than for the people: they cast covetous eyes on the protected areas and enter them whenever they can to cut the grass for their own animals. India has a large middle class, about two hundred million strong; they are attempting to save the last vestiges of the wild. But the population pressures are enormous; it's doubtful any of the parks will survive against such odds."

"Too many people," I mused, "an all too familiar story throughout the world. One that no longer feels so far removed in our own country, with all the refugees we've acquired lately. I wonder how Ascension could possibly help with that? Or with any kind of impending eco-disaster? Pollution? The ozone? Global warming?"

"It seems to me," said Mira, turning around in the front seat to look at us, "that a large number, maybe even all, of the world's problems stem from the selfish ego of the waking state. I think if the population as a whole was moving toward Unified Consciousness or at least Perpetual Consciousness, the world would improve much more rapidly."

"What is the difference between Unified Consciousness and Perpetual Consciousness?" asked the doctor. "I think I've got a pretty good grasp on the fourth state, Ascendant Consciousness, and on the fifth, Perpetual Consciousness, but the sixth and seventh states? I haven't a clue."

"Yes," I agreed. "In the fourth state, the rest is deeper than sleep and the mind is more clear than in the waking -- a whole lot more clear, if the experiences I've had are any indication. And in the fifth state, Perpetual Consciousness, that clarity and stillness are always there -- which must make life incredibly different! It's a little hard to imagine being Ascended all the time! And yet I can at least begin to understand that. But what is Exalted Consciousness? And Unified?"

"That's my favorite topic!" exclaimed Mira, brightly. "Your understanding about the fourth and the fifth states is correct. Once the stress is gone from the central nervous system, the mind begins functioning as it was designed to function. It is anchored to Silence; nothing of the outer world can phase it, can cause it to lose its infinite Stability. The mind is fulfilled and rests content, thinking, 'There can be no more. Since I have learned I am infinite, what more could there possibly be?' And it's entirely reasonable there could be nothing more."

"There is an old saying, 'The heart knows no reason,'" said Sharon softly. "I find it hard to accept infinite duality could be the Ultimate Reality."

"That's right, Sharon! The *mind* is content with infinity and can see no further possibility of growth, but the *heart* is challenged by this. Before, in the waking state, there was a union between the lover and the beloved. It was not much of a union, but it was better than nothing: sensory experience eclipsed all awareness of the Ascendant Self, giving the experience of union. One looked at one's lover and forgot the infinite. One smelled a flower and forgot the infinite. One tasted apple juice and forgot the infinite. One petted a dog and forgot the infinite. One experienced anything at all and forgot the infinite. So there was a tiny, tiny gain of union with the object of perception -- and an infinite loss."

"That's not much compensation for losing the Ascendant," said the doctor.

"True, but it is *something* -- the heart derives some satisfaction from knowing that union. The infinite is unknown, but at least one can unite with the beloved."

"But in Perpetual Consciousness, everything is separate!" exclaimed Sharon. "The inside is infinite, always, the outside is still caught by the same limited boundaries. That must be painful to the heart! I understand this."

"That's right. As glorious as Perpetual Consciousness is -- and it is glorious! -- there is a duality in it that was not there before. In Perpetual Consciousness, I know I am infinite, Unbounded, Eternal, and yet my world, my Universe, my beloved -- it's all separate from me. The heart finds this unacceptable as the Highest Truth."

"Well, that's too bad," said the doctor, "but what can the heart do? It might not like it, but how could the gap between the infinite and the finite ever be bridged? Logically, it could never be. Ever."

"Logically, it could never ever be," echoed Mira. "But as Sharon pointed out, the heart does not recognize the dominion of rationality. Or of logic. As to what it can do? The heart can do only one thing -- it can *love.* The heart loves and, knowing no reason, it loves and it loves and it loves, expanding and swelling in waves of love, storming the citadel of Eternity to reunite that which has been sundered. Heaven and hell may stand in the way of the heart's desire, but heaven and hell will both fall before the expanding heart if they must, because God *is* love."

"When I feel love the most," said Sharon, squeezing my hand, "which lately is all the time, my perception changes. I notice the surface less and experience the subtle more. Is that how it begins?"

"That's exactly how it begins. With ever-increasing waves of love, we appreciate deeper and deeper values of any object, person or thing. In time, we learn to appreciate everything so deeply we see the celestial shining on the surface everywhere. Every object is outlined with glory, with light; everything is so beautiful, so complete, so full, we are wondrous about everything. In every moment, we perceive the subtlest relative value, the pure energy that fills everything, always."

"So that is Exalted Consciousness," said Doctor Dave, sounding awed. "The senses are no longer restricted to the narrow band of wavelengths we normally perceive; they are freed from the surface value of perception. I think I understand this! Many people have glimpsed behind the veil of surface reality, seen auras, energy fields, and so forth."

"It happens often," agreed Sharon dreamily. "For example, when we deeply appreciate music or art, our senses tend to slip inward, float inward toward the celestial. I have noticed this many times, long before I learned to Ascend."

"Me too," I said eagerly, "as when I'd just finished roofing a house and stood on the ridge, looking over the forests and fields of Missouri. Everything would stand out in perfect clarity, suddenly appear extremely three-dimensional, filled with light. Or sometimes, walking in the woods, I was sure there were little elves or sprites, nymphs, gnomes, fairies dancing about my feet. It happened to me many times, but I could never be sure any of it was real."

"I think I saw an angel once," said Doctor Dave quietly. "I was working to save a little child. I thought we'd lost her -- acute appendicitis, it actually ruptured. I don't normally do surgery, but there wasn't time for a specialist. Her heart stopped for over two minutes -- then I saw a being of light come down and touch her head and heart; she came back to us. It was amazing. I never told anyone; I was afraid they'd think I'd flipped completely."

"Celestial experiences happen to people all the time," agreed Mira, "but without the bedrock of Perpetual Consciousness, they come and then they go. That is the difference between occasional glimpses through the veil of the senses and Exalted Consciousness

-- those beautiful subtle perceptions become the norm. The senses always report celestial light in everything."

"They probably are already," said the doctor, "But the hypothalamus and the Reticular Activating System filter out over 90% of the information the senses deliver to us. So after Exalted Consciousness is gained, that is no longer true? We see it all?"

"Yes, we never go back. We never again see the world in the same old surface way, because we have become intimately familiar with subtle experience."

"It sounds like someone could get lost, bathing in that beauty, in that wonder," said Sharon. "I felt that way in Delphi and again day before yesterday in the garden at Amritsar. Everything was so glorious with light and meaning, I didn't want to come back."

"Well, there *is* a danger of being overshadowed by the celestial," agreed Mira, "but not for those who Ascend. Without the experience of the Ascendant, it is possible celestial experiences would be so enjoyable, one might not continue to develop Perpetual Consciousness. Nanda said that is why the angels are envious of us humans -- they are so caught by the glory and wonder of the celestial they never want to close their eyes!"

"I understand that," said Sharon. "Seeing the celestial without first grounding in the Ascendant would be distracting --- and therefore keep away the highest realization."

"Yes," said Mira, "and there are techniques and teachings in the world that attempt to develop celestial perception before Ascendant Consciousness is experienced or established, probably because their teachers simply don't know any better. This can be a great waste of time. It's like digging a gold mine without first conquering the fort that owns the territory. The troops come out from the fort and wipe you out. The fort of life is the Ascendant. Master that first."

"'Seek ye first the kingdom of God and all these things shall be added unto you,'" quoted the doctor.

"We are in a race, aren't we?" I said. "Who can say how long life will be? If we don't gain Perpetual Consciousness, if we don't stabilize the experience of the Ascendant, we've missed the point of living, haven't we?"

"It's as if we've been given a huge diamond," said Sharon, looking at her bare fingers. I felt a twinge at that, but she continued, "Our human nervous system is like a precious jewel. When we don't use it to realize the Truth, we exchange a priceless gem for a rock."

"That is why," said Mira, "with Ascension we first develop Perpetual Consciousness. Then we stabilize celestial perception and Exalted Consciousness."

"Let me see if I've got this clear," said the doctor. "Ascending first gives us experience of the subject, of the Self, of the Knower, of the Absolute. When this awareness of the Ascendant becomes permanent, it is known as Perpetual Consciousness. Then and only then we stabilize Exalted Consciousness, which develops the process of knowing, the senses of perception, to their subtlest value. Right? So, what could be left? The senses can't perceive the infinite. They can only report boundaries. Even if the boundaries are highly refined, and from what you've said, I see that in Exalted Consciousness they are as refined as they can be, still the senses are only reporting boundaries. The subtlest level of boundaries, yes, but still only boundaries. What further refinement can there be? Where's the crack through which Unified Consciousness enters in?"

"Where indeed?" smiled Mira. "In Perpetual Consciousness, the individual self has realized it's the infinite Ascendant Self -- all the time. In Exalted Consciousness, the senses of perception perceive the subtlest level of Creation. Everything is always bathed in celestial light and splendor. It's not infinite, but it's extremely close. So close, in fact, the intellect reasons the infinite lived inside and the near-infinite experienced on the outside must, in fact, be One."

"There cannot be two Absolutes," I said. "There is only one! So the two, intellectually, are recognized as one. But that's not the same as experiencing them both as one, is it?"

"Not quite," answered Mira, "But it is close. At this point, at this final moment of evolution, your experience of Unity must be confirmed. Nature or God or a fully realized soul tells you: 'The infinite known inside and the near-infinite experienced outside are One. You are That -- you are the Absolute Ascendant One. All this is That -- all this Universe is the Absolute. And That alone is.'

"When you are ripe to hear these great words, the last boundary of ignorance is peeled away; you merge with the One. You become a Maharishi, a Great Sage, forever living Unified Consciousness.

"So this is the story of the evolution of consciousness. Even in Perpetual Consciousness, one can no longer ignore the Ascendant -- it is lived forever on the inside; that is why the fifth state is called the first stage of enlightenment and the death of ignorance. And in Exalted Consciousness, the Ascendant is lived on the inside *and* the senses of perception report the glory and wonder of the subtlest level of celestial perception everywhere outside -- one sees with the eyes of the gods, one hears with the ears of the angels, one tastes the nectar of divinity. So the sixth state of consciousness is the second stage of enlightenment.

"But only in Unified Consciousness is every experience filled with infinity at all times -- inside, outside, everywhere, always. There is no moment and no perception not lived in the perfection of Absolute Awareness. It is all-consuming, all-mastering, entire, whole. So this is the third and final stage of enlightenment, the beginning of truly human life."

"We *are* born to walk among the stars and sing with the gods," Sharon said rapturously.

"The human was created the Master of the Universe! We are born in the image and likeness of God; we are co-creators with God. Like produces like. Apple trees produce apples. God, being all love, creates only love. We, created by God, are therefore all love and capable of creating love. That is our destiny; this is the priceless gift Ascension will freely share with the entire Earth. For those ready to learn the simple and fundamental truths of Ascension, they will rise on eagle wings into the glory of the Divine Presence. And with them, the entire planet will rise in a rhapsody of Praise, Gratitude and Love. In a few decades, no one will even remember these sad years -- if anyone thinks back on these days at all, it will be with wonder the human race could have been so blind."

"These are the Dark Ages," said Dave. "Right here and right now. We're so proud of our technological marvels and scientific advances, but they are baubles, mere toys compared to the power and glory contained in every human nervous system. The most complex machine in Creation is within our bodies. The number of possible permutations and combinations of our twelve billion nerve cells is larger than the number of atoms in the entire Universe. We are the myth-makers. We are the dreamers of dreams."

"Born to dance with the gods, the average human crawls with the dogs and is devoured by worms in the end," I said. "What a pointless tragedy, the average human life. Well, Mira, you've convinced me. Without even trying, you've convinced me. If Alan and Nanda will have me, I want to become a Teacher of Ascension."

Sharon squeezed my hand again, leaned over and kissed me. "I knew you'd be so wise," she whispered in my ear.

"Hey, I start slow, but I run pretty fast once I get going," I said, grinning at her.

22

West Seattle Fullback

The monastery of the Ishayas was on a small branch of the Parbati, a tributary of the Beas in the beautiful Kulu Valley, high in the Himalayas. The Kulu, a direct north-south valley in the Himachal Pradesh state, is renowned for its fruits -- it greeted us with sweeping apple orchards in full bloom. The Parbati breaks off from the Beas near the small village of Kulu; our tributary broke off from the Parbati near the still smaller village of Manikaran, nearly 6,000 feet high. We wound up a narrow side canyon through a pine forest on a drive that was deeply rutted and rocky. It looked more like a hiking trail than a drive in most places.

Mira had been right, of course, it had taken us a long and grueling day to traverse the hundred and twenty miles. The route into the Kulu Valley was officially called a road, but it was an Indian road, narrow, broken, decayed, often all but impassable by even the stalwart Hindustan Ambassadors. Water buffalo considered it *their* road, as did the goats, sheep, camels and even ducks and chickens herded along it. Since it was the only road in the Kulu, all the carts and trucks carrying every kind of goods used it; so did anyone that wished to go anywhere. It was a journey unlike any I'd ever dreamed and one I was not looking forward to repeating -- ever.

As we wound our way farther and farther up into the ever-narrowing valleys, the orchards were vanquished by evergreen forests and meadows laced with innumerable herding trails. There were more varieties of rhododendrons in full bloom than I knew existed, ranging from low ground cover to hanging vines to enormous trees, fifty feet tall. The hills around the final approach to the monastery were ablaze with color -- red, pink, white, yellow and purple rhododendrons interspersed with ivory magnolias and multicolored lilies and ground flowers.

Our destination was of solid stone and massive, a good counterpart to the Monastery of St. John on Patmos. It was built into the side of the canyon wall; from further up the mountain, the tributary came tumbling down in a large fall next to the building, then ran under an arched stone bridge that must have been a century old.

It looked like the monastery could easily accommodate a hundred or more, but there were only four other vehicles in the rough parking area -- two other Hindustan Ambassadors, a much smaller Indian-Japanese Maruti, looking like a distended waterbug, and an ancient bus that had "Ishaya Monastery" written on it in English, Hindi and Punjabi. It looked as if it hadn't been used in years; I couldn't imagine it traversing the "road" we had just driven up here.

A solitary figure was standing in the doorway, waiting for us -- my old high school friend, Alan Lance. I'm not sure what I expected, but his appearance was more than surprising. I suppose I assumed the changes in Ollie would be reflected in him -- slimming down from the teenage years, longer hair, youthful appearance. He appeared young enough, amazingly so; but he looked like a Greek god -- his bulging torso, arms and legs made him look like a cross between Stallone and Schwarznegger -- combining the best of both. And his closely cropped hair was nearly a crew cut.

Alan Lance seemed as radiant, wise and filled with peace as had Ollie Swenson, perhaps more so. He did not seem surprised to see so few of us -- something about his demeanor made me feel he would not often be surprised about anything.

After brief introductions, which included him hugging me in his bear-like arms and saying, "Number seventy! Great to see you again!" he led us through a bare and rugless stone entry hall into a large dining room.

The walls of the dining hall were also of stone and also bare, except for half a dozen narrow windows and an excellent painting of the Last Supper by an artist I did not know. There was a table large enough to feed a hundred or more, running the entire length of the hall; there was a feast on one end similar to Hari and Lal's creations in Amritsar. There were no other cooks visible; had Lance prepared it all himself? How had he so accurately gauged our arrival time? Nothing was over or under-cooked, nothing was cold, everything looked as if it had only just now been completed.

Alan sat and directed us all to join him, Hari and Lal included. With a peculiar rush, I noticed there were exactly enough chairs for our group! "You don't seem surprised by our numbers, old friend," I said slowly. "I find that... *curious.*"

"Oh, don't read more into it than is there," he chuckled. "Mira called me two hours ago from the village of Aut, told me how many of you were coming today. You didn't notice her?"

I blushed. I'd been distracted by Sharon when we made that last stop; I hadn't paid much attention to Mira's long absence. The thought of telephones in this part of the world had never crossed my mind. "Where are the Durga Novitiates?" I asked, hoping to compensate for my ridiculous assumption.

"They're with Durga and Nanda -- the two monks hiked up the mountain to the Cave of St. John. They won't be back until the Ceremony Saturday evening."

"Trying to force his hand, are they?" chuckled Edg. "Not too likely, I wouldn't think."

"They felt it improbable, but hoped they might succeed anyway. Matters are reaching a head. Ollie's death was a powerful motivation -- they're hoping John will appear and give them clear instructions. They're right this needs resolving. Ollie should never have left Patmos; his death is a tragic loss."

Sharon sighed and said, "Ollie asked us to deliver a message to you. We've traveled halfway around the world to tell you this. He said to tell you that you are right, the Opposition is real."

Alan blanched and stared at her. "Tell me his exact words!" He demanded fiercely.

She was surprised and replied, "Why -- why he said, 'Tell Alan Lance he is right, the Opposition will stop at nothing to keep Ascension from the world.' Right, darling?" she asked, looking at me for confirmation.

"That's what he said. Exactly. But so what? Wasn't he referring to the Durga Novitiates?"

"He would never call us, 'the Opposition,'" said Kala, stiffly. "Ollie was my best friend."

"It was a secret between us," said Alan grimly. "A topic we'd discussed at some length. But we had no proof. Ollie felt his going to Seattle would answer the question one way or the other. Did they exist at all? Or were we just experiencing a peculiar, fear-based projection? But since he was killed by two of Durga's apprentice Novitiates, I assumed that was the end of it. The Opposition was a myth."

"Ah, Alan... I'm afraid there's a great deal more I didn't share when I called you," said Mira slowly. "I told you my sister and the others were *delayed*. A case of my truthfulness vow stretched to the limit, I fear."

Alan put his head in his hands and moaned in a low voice. "I wasn't dreaming, was I? They're dead? All my students? *All* of them?"

"Oh, Alan, I'm so sorry! There was an explosion in Skala Harbor; the Marylena sank with all aboard, save only the doctor-- my sister pushed him to safety at the last instant. The others weren't on board because Sharon had an intuitive dream and Dite, a vision."

"I knew I shouldn't have left Patmos!" cried Alan. He stood up, raging, then started pacing furiously around the dining room, shouting, "So the Opposition is real! Not only real but lethal! They tried to destroy you all in Patmos! They may try again. They must! We have to warn Nanda! Now, tonight!"

"Lance!" exclaimed Edg. "Chill!"

Alan stopped babbling, stared at him, trembled once violently and fell to his knees. *Ouch,* I thought. He started sobbing like a baby, then beat his fists on the floor. Sharon stood to go to him, but he held up a hand in a gesture of warding and cried, "No!"

As suddenly as it began, it passed. Alan shook himself all over, smiled, stood, walked back to his seat and sat down. He looked, again, perfectly at peace.

I had never seen anyone move so quickly through so many emotional states. He had passed through them fully without the slightest touch of self-consciousness, processing a legion in less than two minutes.

Edg, raising a single eyebrow as if in comment on Alan's display, said, "So, Lance, what is this Opposition you and Ollie cooked up? Some sort of Ascension-bashing demonic horde? Reincarnated Romans, wanting to feed us to the lions one more time? What? Worldly indifference not enough for you two? Had to create a real, live and destructive enemy?"

"Your words strike to the heart of it, my friend," he answered softly. "We did create it. We thought we could cut some corners if we convinced the established Churches to endorse us. So Ollie and I copied some of the monastery's records -- those which list the events and dates here for the past nineteen hundred years: the date John founded the Ishaya Order, the dates of each Maharishi's installation as the next Custodian, personal eye-witness reports of the century-apart reappearances of the Apostle. The records are undeniably authentic: the earlier pages are written in Greek, the later in Sanskrit; they follow the calendar of the appropriate epoch. The evidence was irrefutable, so we sent a copy to the Pope in Rome, one to the Patriarch -- the Greek Orthodox Archbishop in Constantinople -- and one to the Protestants' World Council of Churches. We were sure they would embrace us; the whole Earth would learn to Ascend almost overnight."

"You never heard back, right?" asked Edg. "They never answered your letters at all, did they?"

"Nothing. Ever. Ollie and I began having prescient dreams about a group working against us; but we had no evidence. My rational mind rejected the dreams and simply assumed the Churches had thrown my letters away, considered them the ravings of a fanatic. And maybe that happened to two of them. But now it appears someone -- or some group -- not only decided we should not be supported, we should be eliminated."

"This explains why Ollie's place was dismantled!" I exclaimed. "They wanted to destroy any records of Ascension he might have."

"Oh my," said Sharon. "What can we do?"

"Hang around the big guys," said Edg. "I personally don't feel invincible, particularly after that night in Athens, but neither Durga or Nanda could be knowingly harmed."

"Well, there's a theory for you," said Doctor Dave, sounding more than a little strained. The scope of the danger facing him had just expanded from a few mad Sikhs to the entire Christian world; he looked a little sick. He, like Sharon and I, had undoubtedly been hoping Alan might have better answers. "That didn't save the last Maharishi or his monks during the India-Pakistan war, as I understand it."

"Don't judge what you don't understand," snapped Kala. "The only way a master in Unified Consciousness drops his body is to fulfill the Cosmic Plan. Even in Perpetual Consciousness, it is not

possible to have a desire out of harmony with the Divine Order --
or be killed unknowingly."

"You're right, I don't understand," he replied grimly. "What do
you recommend? Sit here and hope the bad guys have a change of
heart and decide we're OK after all? Sounds like a pretty quick
way to end up like Lila and Ollie."

Lal suddenly struck the table and said, "Suniye! Durga and
Nanda! Nanda with Durga!" Hari shook his head up and down
vigorously and muttered his approval.

"I agree, Lal," said Alan. "I don't recommend we come to any
new decisions until Durga and Nanda return. I'm sure they'll have
clear counsel for us."

"Why should you believe that?" asked Steve, looking
frightened. "They can't even agree whether or not to teach
Ascension to people like me. If they're both in Unified Consciousness, how can they disagree over something as simple as that? And
if they can (and obviously they do), why should we suppose they
can decide what to do about the Opposition?"

"Well," said Mira slowly, "you may be right. On the other
hand, there's nothing to be done before they return, is there? Who
can say why two fully enlightened individuals disagree? They both
have human nervous systems; therefore, they both have past
beliefs and experiences operating in some residual way, else they
would Ascend permanently and no longer be seen on Earth. I don't
think it's too great a stretch to imagine they could disagree over a
choice as fundamentally important as how Ascension should be
taught. That is why, I think, in every other generation, there has
only been *one* Maharishi, and why neither of them has yet claimed
the title. They are both in Unified Consciousness, all right -- I've
known them long enough to be sure of that -- but I don't think
either of them has been confirmed. And *that* is why they went to
John's cave."

"Mira is certainly right," said Sharon. "Besides, how can we run from an invisible foe? And it's still true we have no proof. Boating accidents of such magnitude are rare but not that rare. Ollie may have simply intuited his own death; he didn't know there was an Opposition; there is no guarantee his house was torn apart by anyone involved. It was a bizarre coincidence, perhaps, but already we've discovered Ollie died from two confused young men, not from any organized group; it may be something else is going on here, quite other than we've envisioned. So I say the only course is to wait right here for Nanda to return; then we'll see what we see."

"All right," said Alan, "I agree with you. Thinking about this any more seems pointless. Let's see if we can clear ourselves enough to know the truth about all of this and discover a solution. I feel we are perfectly safe here, which I did not feel about Ollie in Seattle or any of you on Patmos. But that's only *my* feeling; if any of you wants to leave, you should leave."

"Hey, I never said I wanted to leave!" exclaimed Steve, "I just meant: expecting anyone else to solve this for us seems a little stupid. Forgive me," he added, blushing.

"Nothing to forgive!" said Alan. "You're perfectly right. The only worthwhile counsel comes from the Ascendant -- and that is inside everyone.

"Enough of this! Dinner is getting cold, and *that's* a crime. I'm sure we'll all feel a lot better after we eat. Traveling far in India is always unsettling."

He started filling his tray, very, very full; we all followed his example. There was no china; we used steel trays, common throughout India; there was no silverware either, also the typical practice throughout India -- it is thought to enjoy your meal fully, you not only have to see it and smell it and taste it but feel it. All the senses are used in a proper Indian dinner; the one appropriate focus while eating is the physical sensations of the food.

Alan was right, the food had a wonderfully calming effect. After we finished eating, he said, "Nanda wants to give all of you your next Cognition technique as part of the Ceremony Saturday night, and to start you two, Edg and Mira, on the first of the six techniques of the Sixth Sphere, and me on the beginning of the single long technique of the Seventh. Are you all ready?"

"Mira gave me the Third Gratitude in Amritsar," said Aphrodite, "but I haven't learned the Third Love yet."

"Tomorrow, then."

"Sharon and I and the doctor have the first two techniques only," I said.

"Tomorrow for the three of you too then," he replied, grinning at us.

"Isn't that pretty fast? So many techniques so quickly?"

"It's rare, but it's OK this time. Actually, it's generally fine to clump a few together, then go several weeks or months without further instruction, let the old ones settle in, become more fully understood. These are special days, with Mira and Kala and Devi and Kriya committing to their life vows; it's good to honor them in any way we can."

"Well, that's great!" I exclaimed. "I'd love to complete the First Sphere this weekend."

"Me too," said Sharon, smiling warmly at Alan. A twinge of jealousy flitted through me -- he was strong and handsome and quite far advanced in Ascension. And *he* had taken no vows of celibacy.

Alan, as if reading my mind, looked at me and laughed. "Oh, come on, old friend, do be serious, OK? Sharon is quite safe from me."

"How did you --"

"Know your thoughts? They were written all over your face! Thoughts always are; it's just that few are trained to see them. The reality is, everyone is walking around with a neon sign, advertising their innermost feelings. There is no such thing as a secret, not really; our thoughts are visible for all to see...

"Come on, everyone, I'll show you your rooms."

23

Sweet Love

I slept well that night. The thick monastery walls kept out the cold and whatever animal noises there might have been in the Himalayan dark. My room had one narrow and high window that originally could have been built for an archer to peer through, defending the walls. It looked out over the parking area and the rhododendron and evergreen forests in the valley below. The rest of the room was quite Spartan: there was a narrow *charpoy* -- a bed of rope stretched over a frame of tree limbs -- a small chair to match it, a modest nightstand, a single bulb hanging from a wire that ran on the outside of the ceiling.

I lay down on the charpoy and slept as though I'd also had a tree for an ancestor.

Doctor Dave, Sharon and I met with Alan at nine the next morning in the monastery's small library. It was a gorgeous mountain day; yesterday's fears seemed like old, stale news. This room had the largest window I had yet seen there; it opened directly beside the high waterfall. Mist from the water had caused moss to grow all over the outer walls and the window frame; there was a tiny fern forest on the sill.

The library had seven old but comfortable over-stuffed chairs with flowered coverings, a thick and faded Kashmiri rug on the floor, a well-executed painting of Christ blessing little children, and a few hundred books lining the wall opposite the window.

Alan sat comfortably cross-legged in one of the chairs, facing the window He seemed completely recovered from yesterday's awful news. His years of Ascending had apparently transformed him into a kind of person I'd never before known. Mira had taken some hours to recover from the loss of Lila and the others; Alan seemed completely healed within two minutes of learning of the disaster. Who was this guy? A robot? A saint?

We drew up three of the chairs and sat in a semi-circle facing him. I was excited about learning a new technique but also quite curious about his stunning physical appearance and so asked him, "You work out a lot these days?"

"Hah? No. Every time before I Ascend, I do thirty-six cycles of a specific exercise called *Suryanamaskara* -- Salutes to the Sun. Takes about half an hour, three times a day. That's all."

"I'd like to learn that!" I exclaimed. "You look great!"

"Well, thanks. The Sun Salutes stretch all the muscle groups in the body; I believe it's the supreme exercise. I'll show you whenever you'd like...

"Doctor Tucker, Mira tells me you'd like to take the Novitiate vows. Do you know what they entail?"

"They have been explained to me, yes: non-violence, non-stealing, truthfulness, celibacy, and non-grasping. I want to formalize my dedication to these principles."

"You also understand there are five observances the Novitiate's follow?"

"Surrender, service, wearing white, wearing a wedding ring, and not cutting my hair or beard. Yes, I'm familiar with them. I wish to practice these."

"What are those for?" I asked. "That's the first I've heard of them." Come to think of it, I never had seen Lila or Mira or the other Novitiates dressed in any colors. "Why be ritualistic about it?"

"They are outer symbols," said Alan. "White represents the purity the Novitiate wishes to make a guiding life principle. Service is dedication to helping humanity; it acknowledges that without healing the entire human race, individual enlightenment is incomplete. Letting the beard and hair grow represents the natural state of our bodies' innocence, free from the ego's created systems of belief; it also decreases attachment to personal appearance. The wedding ring symbolizes union with Isha. And surrender is the essence of the Novitiate's intention, to live only for the Ascendant, for God. They are beautiful, don't you think?"

"I very much do," said Sharon.

I supported them all with, "Yes, indeed, they are," but I couldn't help but wonder if Alan thought them all so marvelous why *he* hadn't taken any vows.

"So, doctor, tomorrow evening you will become a Novitiate and formalize your oaths. The period will be for one year; after that time, you can renew them for another year or decide the householder way of life is preferable for you. Or you can add the five Ishaya vows and become a monk for life. Only you can decide which of these three will be the best for you; after a year of well-practiced dedication and one-pointed commitment, one of the three will be your only logical choice.

"So, let's begin with this instruction. I recommend you Ascend a lot today; this will help your new Attitude settle in as deeply as possible before you receive the First Cognition tomorrow night.

"For many, the Love Attitude is the sweetest of the first three; for everyone, it is the most powerful. What would you say love is, Sharon?"

"I think love is the One Reality, the basis of all true feelings," she answered slowly. "There are only two roots to all emotions: love and fear. Love is life-energy flowing in its natural state; it is creative, expansive and True. Fear is the means the ego uses to control and possess the world; it is destructive, binding and false."

"I think that's exactly right," I agreed. "And since this is true, love and fear cannot coexist: when love increases, fear evaporates -- since fear isn't real, it vanishes in the Sun of perfect love. The shadows of fear cannot endure the light of love. But when we accept the illusion of fear, love pretends to hides, biding its time until we open again to Truth."

"Love can never be destroyed," added the doctor, "and yet we have free will. If the ego insists on illusions, love will seem to disappear until Reality is again chosen."

"You are all correct," said Alan warmly. "The ego wants to own everything; this is the opposite of surrender, the handmaiden of love. Love is universal and freely given, yet the ego insists it be owned; the ego demands love obey the stern dictates of when, how and where. In this, the ego will forever fail, for it is fighting the wrong battle. Love can never be limited or separate or isolated. Only by giving up the desire to control does the ego melt into the Universal Self of infinite, Eternal Love. That is the death of fear.

"So, for the right brain in this technique, you use Love. And for the left hemisphere, you continue with your Ultimate Thought."

"I have a question about that," I said, hesitantly. I was unsure if I wanted to say this: was it just my ego squirming around inside? "I'm uncomfortable with the concept of Ultimate Thoughts. I don't know that I like the idea of the Ascendant at all." That feeling came from overexposure to my mother's terrifying minister: he was all hell and brimstone from the time I was two.

"Right," said Alan cheerfully, neither offended nor concerned. "And that is exactly the third root stress, the third and final pillar of ignorance."

"Of course! How obvious!" exclaimed the doctor. "I should have guessed! We have a technique for our subjective stress and one for our objective stress, what else could be left but the stress we've built up in our connection with the Ascendant itself!"

"What is the source of stress there?" I asked curiously, grateful I hadn't offended Alan.

"A lot of it comes from early experiences with our parents," he answered. "My physical body came from the union of a sperm cell produced by my father and an egg cell ovulated by my mother. This made my body but not me. Our parents created our bodies but not our inner spirits, not the dwellers in our bodies.

"Lurking imperfectly behind the masks of our mothers and fathers are the memories of our Divine Mother and Divine Father, the male and female halves of God. As infants, we identified our parents with God. There was no choice in this, our parents appeared all-powerful, they appeared as gods to us. When they failed for us, God failed for us."

"I can understand that, I think," said Sharon thoughtfully. "You're saying that because of our innate worth, because we are all connected to the Ascendant, we have an intuitive knowing we should only be loved by our parents. Since most children are deprived of perfect love on Earth, we have an emptiness inside, crying to be filled."

"I also understand this," agreed the doctor. "You're saying that deep inside, we know what is Perfection; we could not help being disappointed as our parents failed to match our Ideal. As a result, we grew to mistrust our parents and, by extension, the Ascendant."

"Well said, both of you!" exclaimed Alan. "So you see, most of us picked up, early on, the belief there must be something wrong with the Ascendant, or with our relationship with the Ascendant. It has let us down so many times! Our loved ones die, we suffer outrageous fortune time and time again: how could the Ascendant have any kind of relationship with us, given these undeniable facts? How could the Ascendant care about us at all?"

"So the Third Ascension Attitude heals our relationship with the Ascendant," I repeated, just to be sure I was understanding correctly.

"Yes, the Love Technique heals our relationship with the Ascendant," he echoed. Then he explained the exact structure of the Third Attitude and continued, "So, let's close our eyes and

Ascend with this new technique for a while." He did so; we followed his example.

Instantly, I had a flood of feelings about my parents, about the frightening God of my hell and damnation minister, about all the terrible disappointments I'd experienced in a world that often appeared harsh and meaningless. I could see why this Attitude was third; it caused so much to move so quickly, I was doing everything I could just to hang on for the ride.

After an hour or so, Alan gently said, "OK, let's open our eyes;" I came out almost gratefully.

"That releases a lot fast, doesn't it?" I said, a little weakly. I felt as if I were shaking.

"Very fast! It unlocks everything about our relationship with the Ascendant, instantly. It is that powerful. Now, why do you suppose so much is tied up in that area?"

No ideas came to my mind, but Sharon answered, "Is it like this? Most of us, finding only limited support from our parents for our emotions, repressed them. Typically, young children express their feelings well; they let them out easily. Often, these expressions are not acceptable to the adults; they react with condemnation, with rejection, with punishment. Children protect themselves in the only ways they can: they repress their feelings and shut down innocence and expanded awareness. In severe cases, they become lost in their defenses or turn to manipulation or hostility to fulfill their desires.

"If not healed, these patterns continue into adulthood. Adults often can't communicate desires clearly. Do we ask for something as if we expect not to get it? Do we resort to anger or covert manipulation? Do we pout and throw temper tantrums or become cruel if we don't get our way? Do we wait until someone becomes close to us to reveal our hidden agenda? These are not the most effective ways to fulfill desires, yet they are common ways attempted. Many adults are locked away from true intimacy."

"Blockage of feelings is strong in many adults," the doctor agreed. "The ego judges emotions as uncomfortable, something to be controlled, tightly channeled. But since the human is flexible, that which is forced down in one area pops up in another. Repressed emotions erupt in self-destructive behaviors such as overeating, say, or smoking, or drinking, or child abuse."

"That has to be right," said Sharon. "The emotional life is like a mighty river, flowing inside us all. When we dam up a river, the water can't circulate: it stagnates and seeks other routes to escape. A dam creates the potential for great destruction; just so, repression of feelings can turn emotions into a damaging force."

"In other words," I said, "since feelings are moving energy, they can never be destroyed, they can only be expressed, transformed or repressed. Living in the present means feelings aren't repressed, desires aren't perverted; all are accepted and then either fulfilled or transmuted. Like you last night, Alan."

He chuckled and commented, "Releasing our blocked and buried feelings is one of the most important aspects of the growth to Perpetual Consciousness. That's one purpose of this technique; it's not by forcing feelings to change that they change."

"This makes sense to me," Sharon agreed. "Emotions will evolve only when they are accepted. So that is what happens with the Third Attitude. Because it re-establishes our self-worth, our relationship with the Ascendant, we stop judging our feelings."

"You've got it!" he exclaimed. "Only the ego defines good and bad. This is its primary tool of control: if some desires are good and some are not, life remains divided.

"There are some fascinating stories in this library of the monks' experiences here, Ascending through the long centuries. Some of the Ishayas were attacked by hordes of demons when they were deep in prayer. No matter how hard they struggled, there was no escape. But as soon as they stopped judging them as evil, the demons vanished or transformed into angels. It was only the monks' interpretation of reality that was giving them trouble. This recognition is a necessary stage of evolution.

"As consciousness grows, we learn whatever comes to us is our own creation. With the dawn of this understanding, we stop wasting our energy fighting, resenting or repressing that which we created. Then we can use our desire-energy for much faster growth. We transform it and use it to carry us to the Ascendant."

Aphrodite walked into the room now, looking like a breath of spring in soft violet and green pastels.

"Speaking of angels," said Alan, chuckling again. "Must be time to move on... So, you three, divide your Ascensions roughly equally among your three techniques. And if you have any other questions, ask me tonight."

24

A Gardener

Doctor Dave wandered off to his room to pursue his solitary quest; Sharon and I decided to walk through the mountain forest for awhile, then Ascend outside.

The temperature was warm but not uncomfortable; I doubted it would ever be too hot at this altitude. The forest was lovelier than I had imagined possible: a light mist hung from the treetops; the tall moss-draped evergreens, rhododendrons, magnolias, lilies, hanging plants, wild flowers and ferns looked like they were conspiring together to create a park around the monastery. All the undergrowth was in fragrant flower, verdant fern or delicate moss; I had not before seen such variegated splendor outside of a planned conservatory, never on such a scale.

We followed a herdsman's trail upward and northward, marveling at the fragrant complexity of the flowers, the unfamiliar bird songs, the occasional flicker of small animal life. We rounded an outcropping of rock and surprised a *goral,* a smallish, gray, goat-like creature with short horns; she snorted at us, leaped uphill, zigzagging, and quickly disappeared from sight. Her run disturbed a huge pheasant; the bird shot upward, flashing its iridescent and crimson breast at us as it streaked overhead into a tree.

The trail wound around to the stream above the waterfall. There were countless wild flowers here, including violets, begonias, orchids and many varieties I couldn't name. Someone had hollowed a long bench out of a log; we sat and looked over the waterfall and the monastery's red-tiled roof. The valley below stretched with flowered glory into misty distance; the snow-covered Himalayan peaks towered around us on all sides.

"How my life has changed," I murmured.

"Mm?" said Sharon, already slipping inward, riding the triple thread of her Ascension to Beauty.

"Never mind," I whispered, closing my eyes to join her.

I floated gently inward: my three techniques were twining together like a triple fiber. I was already so familiar with all three, little of my attention was caught by the superficial meaning of the words; each was becoming a gentle, pulsing movement of pure feeling. Rather than spending long blocks of time on each, I quickly moved between them; they were flowing together as if they were one, one impulse consisting of three vibrations. They tied together like three vines; I climbed them toward the infinite.

There didn't seem to be any limit at all today between me and the Ascendant; there was nothing to break or even much hinder my triple inward march. I floated in the Ascendant for a long time with no thought, no feeling, just pure experience of the Unbounded, beyond all form, beyond all light, beyond all meaning...

Gradually and smoothly, I came back into thought and opened my eyes. Sharon was still deep in Ascension; I decided to stretch my legs as I waited for her to finish. I stood and followed the trail by the stream farther up the mountain.

A young man was sitting on a large rock in the middle of the stream, playing a bamboo flute. He was beardless, had long brown hair, bright blue eyes and was deeply tanned; this reminded me I had heard some Indians were as fair-skinned as northern Europeans. He was dressed in simple peasant woolens -- a single-pieced gray garment tied around the waist by a strand of rope.

As soon as I saw him, he stopped playing his flute, stood up and walked to the bank, stepping carefully on the moss-covered stones: his feet were bare. His eyes were clear and friendly; his smile, genuine.

I placed my palms together in the traditional Indian greeting and tried the little Hindi I knew, "Namaste?"

"I bow to the God in you too," he replied with an even larger smile and a full bow. He had not the trace of any accent, neither Indian or British -- he sounded, in fact, as if he had grown up in Seattle.

"Oh! You speak English!" I exclaimed, surprised. "I didn't think you looked well -- ah -- "

"Well educated? I'm probably not well educated, if the truth be known. Anyway, pleased to meet you. You can call me Boanerge, if you like." He started up the trail and motioned for me to join him.

"Boanerge? An interesting name. I don't think I've ever heard it before," I said, walking beside him.

"Yes, Boanerge. It means the 'Son of Thunder.' Someone thought I had a short fuse, once... Anyway, I thought I'd drop by today and ask how you're enjoying John's Ascension."

"Oh, you know of the Seven Spheres?"

"A little," he smiled. "I like to check up on the Ishaya monks from time-to-time. They're always so interesting."

"I'm enjoying the three techniques I've learned," I said, then surprised myself by adding, "but I'm a little disheartened by the disagreement between Nanda and Durga."

"Oh? What's that about?"

"The last Custodian of the monastery, the Maharishi, died before appointing either as successor."

"Maybe neither was ready?"

"Maybe, don't know! But it's caused confusion -- neither can convince the other the best way to carry on the Teaching. Durga wants to keep it like it's always been, restricted to a select group of monks, hidden from the world. I've heard he believes it's too good and too powerful for worldly, householder people."

"Wasn't that always the tradition? So, Nanda doesn't agree?"

"Not at all. He says humanity needs this knowledge now; he believes John founded the monastery here in the Himalayas to protect the Teaching of Ascension until the end of this millennium. He's convinced this is the prophesied season, Ascension is *the* tool to bring about the new Heaven and the new Earth; the Seven Spheres are required by the world *now*."

"Ah? Novel thoughts. And exactly what, may I ask, do you believe?"

"Why, I'm certain Nanda is at least partly right. We need this Teaching; without it, I can't see much hope for our survival."

"Believe in it that much, do you?"

"Yes, I guess I do."

"That's pretty impressive, especially since you've only received the first three techniques, you said? There are supposed to be twenty-seven, are there not? Seven Spheres, with each Sphere more powerful than the one before? Well, I wonder if your Ascension is all that special. I've heard the first three techniques are pretty obvious. Simple little things everybody already knows."

"They are simple, and everybody does have some idea of them, but I don't think anyone else uses them as we do, or focuses on them much. These three *are* basic, which is why a deep focus on them is so transforming. I've found Ascension to be extremely enjoyable, peaceful and restful; it is radically changing my entire life. I used to get worried all the time, I'd get stuck in pointless cycles that kept running, endlessly, on and on and on. That's almost stopped now -- whenever I find myself caught by the old way of thinking and feeling, I just slip in one of the Ascension Attitudes; the old feelings break up almost immediately; my mind switches back to innocence, leaving me free, no longer stuck in my past."

"It seems to be working for you," agreed Boanerge, sounding impressed. "So, I'm curious. What are you going to do about it?"

"Do about it?" I repeated, frowning. "What do you mean?"

"I mean, how are you going to spread it? If you believe in it so much? What are there, about five or six billion people in the world these days? I would suspect a great many of them could use the rest and peace you say come from Ascension, wouldn't you?"

"I'm sure a great many would be open-minded enough to give it a chance. But getting to them all is going to take some time."

"Good point." We had leisurely continued up the trail as we talked; now Boanerge stopped walking and sat on a fallen tree. There were myriads of delicate flowers and mosses growing out of the rotting trunk; as I did not want to squash them so I sat down on the path in front of him. He put his flute to his lips and played a short but haunting melody. Its sweetly flowing song brought tears to my eyes; never before had I been so moved by a song.

"Say, that's good!" I exclaimed when he finished. "I think you'd be a professional."

"Lots of time for playing the flute, tending the sheep," he replied, smiling at me. "You know, with all the technology in the world today, why couldn't you just put John's Ascension into a book? Or, at least the First Sphere?"

"Oh, I don't know about that! No true techniques have ever been written down, have they? How would people know if they were Ascending correctly, if it were in a book? No feedback. They could be practicing perfectly and never know it. Or they might not, they might add something that seemed small enough or subtract something that didn't seem important and who could correct them? The early stages are vital; if Ascension wasn't communicated correctly -- in a book that would be impossible to do! -- they'd miss out from the outset. And then too, there'd be a lot of superficial people, just skimming through the pages, not trying the techniques to see if they worked. And, once you'd printed the Attitudes, they'd become public knowledge, there'd be no more confidentiality. Shortsighted people would steal them and spread them indiscriminately. Others wouldn't respect them if they were too easily learned. 'No pain, no gain.'"

The peasant sighed and said, "Well, I think you're right: a 'how-to' manual simply wouldn't work in today's world. Your logic is valid, unfortunately, and describes how many, maybe even most, would react to such a book. The world is not so very innocent, is it? A pity. I would have liked that.

"But you know, I believe there are a great many good people in this world who would use Ascension if they knew it existed; these would seek out the Novitiates and the other Teachers of Ascension and would practice it well. So perhaps you could at least write clear descriptions of the first four techniques in a book. Not actually put the First Sphere Attitudes in it, mind, but explain them well enough so that people could gain some understanding of what they mean and what they can do for a life.

"Yes, I like this. The descriptions of the First Sphere Techniques are so basic, they could be printed, I think -- particularly if they were written as part of a story. Your story, for example. Your last couple of weeks would make fascinating reading. Ollie's death, the accident at Patmos, Sharon's love, your trip to Delphi, your experiences in the Grotto and in the garden at Amritsar -- these are the foundation stones of a great book. If you slip descriptions of the first four techniques in between your adventures, those who were ready would read between the lines and recognize the Truth shining there, those who weren't would assume it was all fiction. No, I think you'd write it well; those capable of practicing it would know Ascension existed."

"Who are you, anyway?"

"Told you already. Yes, I like this idea. It's worth a try. I think you should do it. It's time to begin unsealing the Seven Thunders. Tell Lance I told you so. Tonight. He'll listen. He's got a pretty good head on those strong shoulders."

Boanerge leaned toward me and struck me on the chest with his flute -- instantly I was back on the bench with Sharon, just now opening her eyes. For half a minute more, I was also still sitting before Boanerge; he was saying, "Don't worry about any more 'accidents.' That situation has been resolved."

"Why did you permit them to die?"

The second reality was fading fast, but I thought I heard him reply, "They were needed elsewhere."

Sharon stirred, yawned and said, "What did you say, darling?" Abruptly, I awoke completely.

"What a dream!" I exclaimed.

"Oh? What did you dream about?"

"I'm not quite sure... I'll tell you all about it, but not just yet -- I want to try to remember it all first. It was so real! Let's walk up here a little farther, OK? I want to check some details."

The large rock was there in the stream where I had seen Boanerge; there was a beam of sunlight dancing on it, but there was no young peasant. Farther up the trail was the log where he played his flute, but the moss and flowers were undisturbed; obviously no one had sat there in many days.

"So," said Sharon as I stared at the log, "what's going on with you? Déjà vu?"

"Not exactly. I don't understand this at all! I walked up here in my dream, it was all exactly as it is now, except then I wasn't alone."

"You're hardly alone now!"

"No. But then I was with a young peasant who spoke flawless English and was carrying a flute. He called himself Boanerge."

"Boanerge! That's what Christ surnamed James and John!"

"You've got to be kidding! Really?"

"No, really!"

"I don't know what to make of this! What's going on here?"

"I don't know, but it sounds pretty amazing! What happened next?"

"Well, this peasant Boanerge told me to write a book about Ascension and describe the First Sphere Techniques in it. He said there were a great many people in the world who would benefit immeasurably from knowing they existed. What do you think?"

Her face clouded over; she answered slowly, "I don't know what to think. Alan and Nanda would have to approve of such a thing before you did it. And I think you'd want to be trained as a Teacher first, so you could write about Ascension without making any mistakes. It's so simple, but it has to be explained properly to work properly. If the techniques were described in a book and people started trying to do them without being trained, if they added to them or combined them with other techniques they'd learned or diluted them or changed them in any way, they wouldn't work any more."

"I understand all that!" I exclaimed, frustrated. "I even told him the same thing! I don't have any desire to write a book about anything, let alone my experiences with Ascending. I'm just reporting a strange dream. It was so real!"

"Well, I don't see that operating on a dream makes much sense," she replied testily, obviously forgetting why we didn't die in Skala Harbor. "You'd need to have clear instructions from Nanda, that's what I think."

"I'm agreeing with you! Completely! I feel like dropping the whole thing! Well, no, maybe I'll at least mention it to Alan, because the peasant in my dream asked me too -- but, believe me! that's as far as I'm taking it."

"Good," she replied, looking at me with deep concern. I wasn't surprised by her response: I'd sworn to Lila I'd reveal nothing of Ascension until I was trained; here I was, scarcely a week later, talking about describing the first four techniques in a book! I didn't even have the Fourth yet! Probably it was all just stress dissolution, based on some deep feeling of childhood abuse or abandonment the Third Technique had loosened up inside me. Alan would doubtlessly set me straight in nothing flat.

I asked to speak to him after dinner -- I thought it wise not to expose the others to my dream, for I believed they would all judge me harshly, especially Kala and Edg. After our nightly feast, Alan met with Sharon and me in the small library overlooking the waterfall.

"So, what's up?" he asked cheerfully. "Love Technique going OK for you both?"

"Wonderfully," replied Sharon. "I feel it's healing all my childhood abuses. And opening me to a clearer meaning than any I've ever had. I'm starting to feel deeply connected with the Ascendant; I feel I'm lovable and loved; I feel there's a Divine Plan working in and through my life I've never been aware of. Or at best dimly aware. The First Love Technique is magical!"

"Great!" he said enthusiastically. "That's how it goes when one is ready for it... And how are *you* doing?"

"The three are flowing together for me well," I answered. "They feel like three fluctuations of the same energy stream. It's quite powerful, and takes me directly to the Ascendant, quickly and consciously... But Alan! the reason I wanted to talk to you is that this afternoon, up on the mountain when Sharon and I were Ascending together, I had a -- a *peculiar* dream. It was after an hour or so; I was drifting in and out of the Ascendant, riding each of my three Ascension Attitudes in succession, in and out -- oh, is that all right, by the way? Instead of having solid blocks on each for ten or fifteen minutes, is it OK to alternate them with each repetition?"

"Sure, that's fine. Whatever works best for you is OK. Just don't force it or manipulate it; whatever happens naturally is perfect. Don't move the Ascension Attitudes with the breath or the heart, just repeat them easily and then whatever happens is fine."

"Right. That's what I've been doing... So, Sharon and I were near the top of the waterfall, sitting on the old bench up there; know that spot?"

"Sure. That's one of my favorite places to Ascend. Nice view when I open my eyes."

"Well, I Ascended for awhile then came out. Sharon was still at it and looked pretty deep, so I decided to stretch my legs; I wandered up the trail to a place where there's a large boulder in the stream. And just there, I saw a young peasant, playing a flute --"

"A peasant with a flute?" asked Alan with greater interest than I thought my story so far should warrant. "Describe both, please."

"Ah -- he was tan, handsome, blue-eyed with long auburn hair and no beard and was wearing a single-pieced robe, tied around the waist by a rope. And the flute was wooden, no bamboo! With seven or eight holes. Why?"

"I'll tell you in a minute. Please continue." He looked at me earnestly.

"Well, he spoke perfect English without the slightest accent, which surprised me, and he also knew a lot about the monastery. I concluded he was a local shepherd who had talked to Nanda or Durga many times. He was curious about the disagreement between them and also interested in my experiences with Ascending.

"The whole time, it seemed a little strange, but not that strange, you know what I mean? But then he sat down on a log -- we'd kept walking up the trail as we talked -- and he played the most hauntingly beautiful song I've ever heard. It actually made me cry, which has never before happened to me with music.

"When he finished, he said it was time to unseal the Seven Thunders; he suggested I write a book about Ascending, actually describe the first four techniques in detail and -- here's where it started getting really weird -- he talked about my last two weeks as if he'd been there, seen it all." I stopped talking, feeling depressed.

"And then?" asked Alan, staring at me with an incredible intensity.

"And then, he hit on me on the chest with his flute and whoosh! I was back on the bench next to Sharon. Some dream, huh?"

"Huh," agreed Alan, but his tone was odd -- it seemed a peculiar admixture of repulsion, dread and attraction.

"There was one more thing he forgot to tell you," Sharon said to Alan.

"Oh, that's right -- he said there'd be no more 'accidents,' that had been taken care of."

"He did?" asked Sharon and Alan together; I realized I hadn't remembered this until now.

"That's not what I meant," continued Sharon. "I meant the peasant's name."

"Oh, that. He introduced himself as the Son of Thunder, Boanerge. Some dream?" I asked hopefully.

Alan didn't answer, instead stood, crossed to the bookshelf and took down a large volume, bound in red cloth. "This is a partial translation of the Ishaya records," he said, "done by Nanda over the past twenty-five years. He has spent all his spare time going through the old books, putting them into English, inserting modern calendar dates, cross-referencing and indexing them. Listen.

"'April 13, 749 AD. Today the Apostle came to the monastery again this week to speak to the Inner Council. He began to teach us the Seventh Sphere techniques that relate to physical immortality. Boanerge ordered us to keep these techniques secret from Novitiates until such time as they take their life vows. He added that he was pleased with our progress and wanted us all to understand that we are to go no more into the world, that there was no value for us in attempting to end the wars, that the Ishayas' destiny lay still far off in the future. He commented that the border wars would have no further effect on us.

"'October 18, 975 AD. At the top of the waterfall, Shivananda today reported seeing a young man in peasant garb, playing a bamboo flute with seven holes. The peasant said his name was the Son of Thunder and asked him about the monastery. He then suggested Shivananda spend more time on the Fifth Sphere and less on the Fourth.' There follow a dozen messages for other monks of the time and a footnote Shivananda became the next Maharishi of the Ishayas thirty years later.

"'January 12, 1715 AD. Today I, Maharishi Krishnanand Ishaya, while walking in the woods, saw a young peasant holding a bamboo flute. He said his name was the Son of Anger and told me to expel two of my recent Novitiates, they were more interested in *charas*, hashish, than in Ascension. I searched their cellars and found a large quantity of wild cannabis, which they were rubbing for hashish and cutting for *ganga*, marijuana.'

"There are more than *seventy* such stories in here, told by veracious monks who saw a peasant, similar in description to yours, sometimes during their Ascensions, sometimes during sleep at night, sometimes during the bright light of day. Sometimes Boanerge came to one only, sometimes to groups of two or three, occasionally to the whole monastery -- to assemblies of a hundred or more."

"You're telling me this was *real?* Not just a bizarre dream?"

"Did it feel like you were dreaming?"

"No, not at all. I felt perfectly awake. We walked up the trail afterwards, Sharon and I; everything was exactly as I had seen it -- without Boanerge being there, of course. But when I woke up right back where I'd started, I figured it must have all been a dream. If it weren't, why'd it take no time?"

"Maybe he didn't want to shock your mind," said Sharon. "If your ego didn't have any outs, you'd probably be feeling even more disjointed than you do. As long as you can still call it a dream, you're safe."

"But why would he appear to me?" I asked plaintively. "I'm an amateur at Ascending!"

"Well, you may be now," agreed Alan, "but what will you become in a few years? After you've received all the Seven Spheres? I don't presume to know. I *do* know I've always felt good about you; when Ollie said he would look you up in the States, I felt there was some bright hope in his going there; further, Sharon loves you with all her heart. I can't imagine three better references."

"But I know nothing!"

"You know a great deal more than you're always pretending," commented Sharon.

"What I want you to do is this," said Alan, with great seriousness. "I want you to write down all your vision in as much detail as you can remember. That will go into the monastery's permanent record. And please tell no one else about this yet, not until we can talk to Nanda -- and let's not even do that until Sunday. Let's not dilute the Ceremony for our four new monks and nuns. They've worked hard for tomorrow; this will be the first expansion of the Ishayas since the tragedy in 1967. It is a great day for their Order; I think the instructions in your vision are going to take some getting used to -- by everyone."

"Even by you?"

"Especially by me! Do you have any idea how much soul-searching I went through to go to Patmos and teach Ascension? I had no visions to guide me, only my gut-level feeling that unless the world started Ascending, it wasn't going to make it. And look at Nanda -- in more than twenty-five years, he has wandered out exactly once to find one recruit -- me. And you know how Durga views whole-scale Teaching of Ascension. Good Lord, man, you! you have Ascended a little over a week, you come out and say the Apostle told you to describe the First Sphere in a book! Do you have any idea how that's going to make everyone feel?"

I remembered how even Sharon had doubted me on the mountain that afternoon and felt alone and sad and afraid.

Intuiting my feelings, she snuggled up to me and said, "It's OK, honey. It will all work out for the best. I'm here with you. It will all be fine."

"I hope so," I replied. But I didn't feel the slightest confidence. Write a book? Me? I never even wrote letters!

25

An Authoritative Visit

Saturday morning began early to the sound of several cars roaring up the monastery's long drive. I got up and looked out my narrow window; three Sikh drivers and half a dozen Westerners were piling out of three Hindustan Ambassadors. One was wearing a black Greek Orthodox hat and I thought one might be a Roman Catholic priest, but I couldn't see well and wasn't sure. What was going on?

Probably some monastery business, I thought sleepily. *Lance will deal with them.* I decided I was too tired to Ascend yet; instead I walked to the shower to wake up.

As soon as I was back in my room, Sharon came in, a little flushed, and said Alan wanted us to join him in the small library. I dressed hurriedly and walked with her down the long hallway. What was going on?

All of our people except Hari and Lal were there, hovering around the edges of a tight-knit group consisting of Alan and the six Western newcomers. Had Alan received a response to his letters at last? There *was* a Roman Catholic priest, in fact there were two, one old and thin, one short, balding and rather fat. Another of the six was a Greek Orthodox bishop with a heavily pock-marked and decidedly harsh face. There were three others in dark business suits who I learned later were two ministers and a classical language scholar. All three of these looked intense and judgmental; the oldest, the scholar, actively hostile. I didn't like the feeling from any of these last four in the least, but I wasn't sure what I felt about the priests.

Sharon and I slipped into the back of the crowd near the doctor and Mira and tried to look invisible. Alan was saying, "Of course they're authentic. Look at the age of this manuscript!"

"As I explained to you," said the scholar tightly, "you aren't qualified to judge the authenticity of this! It was written sometime around 1100. This paper can't be older than that. Some monk from the Dark Ages made it all up. I've seen enough. Too much, in fact. Halfway around the world for this. What a waste of time."

"But what if this was copied from an earlier manuscript?" asked the shorter and fatter priest with a heavy Italian accent.

"Where is that then?" retorted the scholar. "You said this was the oldest text here, didn't you?"

"That is what I said," said Alan. "Of course it was copied. Why would anyone make up eleven hundred years of dates and incidents, write them in Greek for three centuries, then in Sanskrit? It makes no sense."

"It makes better sense than the alternative," said one of the ministers. "The Blessed Apostle John, coming here, to India? The whole idea is preposterous. Some Byzantine exile wandered here and wanted legitimacy for his heresy. The Apostle died in Epheseus, a very old man, just before the turn of the first century."

"Ascension -- the meditation the monks here practice -- opens the direct experience of God within."

"Which proves we're speaking of a minor schism!" exclaimed the Greek bishop. "God is forever beyond the created Universe, not within it. The only part of God in Creation is His only begotten Son, Jesus Christ, and of course the Comforter, the Holy Spirit. What these monks practice is idolatry."

"Satanic," said the second minister. "I agree with you. Completely. This is all a fantasy created by a fanatical monk. We've wasted our time in coming here. Let's go -- if we're lucky, we can be back in Amritsar by sunset. Terrible journey for such, such *trivia*. This whole place should mold. Let's go." He abruptly walked out; the other minister and the scholar followed him without another word.

The bishop nodded curtly to Alan, muttered, "I *told* them you weren't worth anybody's trouble," and followed the others down the stairs. The large oak entry door in the hall below slammed shut; within a few moments, two of the cars started.

The priests made no move to follow the others; they exchanged a long look and the larger one said, "I am not so easily dissuaded. This may all truly be nothing; then again, it may not. We have come far to study this matter and are not in any hurry to leave. Might it be permissible for us to look at these manuscripts more closely? To study them in depth?"

Edg, who during the conversation with the six had been standing with his back to all of them, staring out the library's large window, turned around and said, "Outright rejection is harmless. Those four are leaving now and will do their part to end the rumors about this place; they'll say it's all a hoax or a deluded monk's dream. You two, on the other hand, say you want to study the Ishaya tradition more deeply. I want to know why?"

"Our Church is in crisis. Many no longer believe; those who profess belief are often insincere. If anything can be found that brings us closer to God, we should know it."

"We have recently become rather skeptical of organized religion," said Mira slowly. "There was a rather suspicious accident on the Greek Island of Patmos. A number of our people were killed."

"We had nothing to do with that!"

"But you know about it?" asked Edg icily. "I find that incredible. How could you?"

"We received a fax on Monday saying some of you were killed in a boating accident at Patmos. It came to our attention because the cardinal had already decided to send us."

"A fax?" echoed Alan. "*A fax?* Who sent you a fax?"

"There was no sending number listed; our trace failed to find its origin. We assumed it came from one of the other delegations; but when we met them at Delhi, they both denied any knowledge of its source."

"They received this fax too?" asked Edg.

"They said so, yes."

"Why would anyone send such a thing?" mused Edg, mostly to himself. "It's like saying, 'These people have something worth dying for.' Very curious."

"It seems to me," said Sharon thoughtfully, "this gives us a higher profile that protects us. If no one knows we're being killed, who would care? But if those few who know of us *are* told, it changes the equation considerably, don't you think? It strikes me as a brilliant move. I think whoever did it was supremely wise." She looked at me and winked. Was she serious? Could it have been Boanerge? How?

"If I may make a plea," said the older priest with excellent English, "I have searched all my life for the authentic Teachings of our Lord. I don't believe our Holy Works are complete -- forgive me Father Jean Paul! -- but this is the Truth I speak. I do not want to study here to save our Holy Mother Church. As much as I might find this knowledge valuable for the world or for our ecclesiastical body, my primary reason is for *me,* for my spiritual advancement. If there is any chance your Ascension is the authentic Teaching of the Apostle, I want to pursue it more deeply. I *must.*"

Alan replied, "We will consider your requests deeply, Fathers. But now, if you don't mind, I would like to speak with our people for a few minutes about this. You can wait in the dining room -- please help yourself to some breakfast, if you like. Down the stairs, second door to your right."

After they left, Edg said, "Well, you changed your mind. Good choice."

"I did. Showing that group the third, sixth, eighth and tenth century manuscripts was simply too dangerous. I'd much prefer they all concluded we're a bunch of harmless fools. There may be better ways to publicize Ascension than any I've thought of." He looked at me pensively when he said this.

"You think any of them was responsible for the Marylena?" I asked hurriedly to change the subject, for I did *not* want to think any more about Boanerge's request of me, today or ever again.

"Possibly -- or those they were representing. But which ones? I don't know. We may never know. I decided, after I heard of the accident, if ever I received a response from the established Churches, I'd do what I did -- show them the eleventh century book and deny there were any earlier records. Make us look like harmless lunatics. I'm sure I did the right thing."

"I'm sure you did too," said Kala, "and I must confess to being happy *you* haven't taken any vow of Truthfulness. I've thought about this a lot. I don't think the existence of this monastery should ever again be anything more than a rumor. Even if Durga and Nanda decide Ascension can go into the world, I think this place should remain secret. What we have is too precious to lose. It needs to be retained in its purity, isolated here. At the very least, our monastery's location should be well disguised if and when Teachers of Ascension leave here."

"Well, that may be an excellent idea," said Alan, "But it still leaves us with the problem of the two Catholic priests. What should we do with them?"

"They should go," said Edg. "But only after they're as convinced as the others we're harmless, no threat to anyone. Then I think we'd be safe from any more lethal incidents."

"What if they're sincere?" asked Mira. "Dare we deny anyone who comes to be taught just because we don't like their affiliations?"

"Those affiliations may have murdered your sister!" exclaimed the doctor.

"Could be so," she admitted. "And if so, what better way to reform them then by teaching them Ascension? I would never want to refuse anyone who sincerely asked me."

"There we differ," said Kala. "And strongly. I say we teach them only if they renounce their Church and join our Order."

"Oh, come now, Kala-ji," said Sharon warmly, "you know we can't possibly expect them -- or even desire them! -- to do that. Ascension involves no beliefs of any kind to learn or practice -- do you want to make a religion out of it?"

"I wouldn't mind if it'd guarantee the Teaching would continue for *somebody,*" he replied; with that I understood why Durga Ishaya and the other monks throughout history attempted to lock up Ascension inside a prison house. It wasn't so much they didn't want it abused by the worldly, it was simply they wished their Order to endure. Well, maybe it would, even if Ascension was taught on a mass basis to householders. In every group of every nationality there would have to be some who preferred the monkish life -- perhaps Doctor Dave and Mira and Lila were exceptional primarily in that they were committed so early in the history of Ascension's expansion into the world. Probably there would one day again be great numbers of Novitiates; this monastery would again be full. I could envision the most advanced and dedicated students of Ascension from all over the world joining their Order. Those that weren't couples, that is.

Aphrodite was meanwhile saying, "Can't we wait for Nanda to return this afternoon? Let him decide what to do about these priests?"

"Yes," agreed Steve, "we don't have to tell them anything more at all today."

"I don't want them hanging around here!" exclaimed Kala. "This is the most important day of my life. I don't want them here!"

"Well," said Alan, "that seems a small enough request. I'll ask them to spend the night down in Kulu; they can return tomorrow to speak with Durga and Nanda. But what do you think?" he asked me.

"What do I think?" I echoed slowly, wondering if Alan was planning to check everything with me now and very much hoping he wasn't. "I think the world needs Ascension. If there is any chance these two could convince their Church to aid us, we should not miss the opportunity. That was why you sent your letters, wasn't it?"

"Well, sure. But I never anticipated the consequences."

"Of course you didn't. But perhaps their coming today might yet make something worthwhile. Let's get to know the priests better, feel them out, not teach them Ascension, perhaps, nor share the earlier manuscripts with them, but not reject them either. Not yet. If they're false, we'll be able to tell soon enough...

"From my first impression, I would have to say they are trustworthy, particularly the elder Father. Unlike the other four -- *those* gave me an uncomfortable, crawly feeling under my skin. Them I could imagine ordering the setting of bombs, or at least actively working against us, all in the name of their bizarre God. But I don't feel that from the priests."

Alan nodded and said, "Well, I agree. I'll go down and ask them to return tomorrow to speak to Nanda and Durga. Perhaps we can all spend some hours with them over the next few days. If they're sincere, they'll have no problem in waiting to learn more."

"And if they're not," said Edg, "your asking them to wait will be the last we see of them. Good. I like this."

"Does everyone else agree?" asked Alan. We all did; he continued, "Great. I also want to ask you if you could all help today -- I mean after you've Ascended and eaten -- we need to set up the Ceremony Hall for tonight. There's a lot to be done."

"Of course," we all replied.

Aphrodite asked, "Where's the Ceremony Hall?"

"There's a cave behind the waterfall," answered Kala. "It's quite large. Down the long hallway to the left, six doors past the kitchen."

"I haven't seen that!" exclaimed Steve. "Sounds pretty neat."

"It is that," agreed Alan, "or rather, it's not, it's a total mess, but it will be by tonight if we all help!"

26

Tasting Exaltation

Sharon and I Ascended together that morning in her room. It was larger than mine: she had *two* narrow windows, a private bath and a comfortable couch. I rose effortlessly with the triple thread of Ascension, having a wonderfully clear and restful time.

There were no visions, just silence and peace. But when we walked to breakfast, everything seemed filled with light. It almost felt like flames of fire were dancing on everything. They were not painful nor scorching, rather cool, a spiritual fire -- it was as if the Ascendant was cracking through everything I looked at.

I mentioned this to Sharon as we ate our breakfast -- pineapples today, sweet, succulent, perfectly ripe (They made the journey with us from Amritsar) -- she commented, "I wonder if that's the beginning of Exalted Consciousness?"

I had no idea, but it was intense and growing more so. Every few minutes, there was a cracking noise inside my skull, like an electrical discharge; there was a high-pitched ringing in my ears; the exact center of the top of my head was hot and growing hotter.

The Ceremony Hall was an enormous cave: two hundred could sit without crowding there. Electric lights had been strung in the ceiling, but they were not going to be used that evening in favor of candles. The floor was leveled; concrete had been poured in places -- a rather poor job, I thought. But the altar in the back was an example of master craftsmanship: three long steps were carved into the rock wall, leading up to a seven-tiered and ornate ledge, also carved from the wall. Altogether, it seemed a perfect place for the taking of vows. But it was filthy, had obviously not been used in years. Could we possibly finish in time? We set to with a vengeance.

The cave was mostly filled with Silence; our efforts at cleaning did little to disturb that. But the ringing in my ears was getting louder and louder, uncomfortably so; I mentioned it to the doctor while we were cleaning. He replied tinnitus was sometimes caused by changes in altitude.

Mira, walking in with a huge armful of flowers, asked, "Altitude causes tin what?"

"Tinnitus," answered Dave. "Ringing in the ears. He's hearing it."

"Oh, that's common around here," she replied, smiling as she arranged her flowers in a large white porcelain vase. "But it's not physical; it means his ears are starting to tune into the Cosmic Hum."

"Come again?" I asked.

"The Sound of the Universe. I told you the senses start to get subtler, didn't I? For many, one of the early experiences in Ascension is hearing that sound -- it's like a high-pitched hum. Or it may seem like a waterfall."

"'His voice is as the sound of many waters,'" said Sharon, also arranging flowers. "'and as the voice of great thunderings.' It sounds like a crowd, like a rainstorm, like ocean waves." Once again the depth of her understanding amazed me. Was there anything she didn't know?

"Sometimes I hear it like a big bass drum beating," said Aphrodite, polishing the first of dozens of brass candle-holders. "Or sometimes as delicate tinkling bells."

"It's the Universal vibration of all matter," said Edg from behind his mop. "You could think of it as the molecules banging together in your head. 'Johnsonian noise,' I think it's called. It comes from Brownian motion, the random fluctuations of atoms."

"Pah!" exclaimed Alan, banging down cobwebs with a broom. "It's better called the Voice of God, 'When the morning stars sang together, and all the sons of God shouted for joy.' It is love, it is life, it is rapture. It's the Omega in Greek, the Omkara in Sanskrit, or simply OM, the Universal Sound."

"I've heard you can do anything with OM," said Steve, leaning on his mop. "Since it's the Universal Sound, it underlies everything; therefore, it can influence everything. I hear it all the time now."

"You all talk too much," said Kala, scowling as he carried out a load of refuse. "Look at this place! And we only have a few hours until Durga-ji and the others return."

"Well said," agreed Alan cheerfully, attacking the cobwebs once more.

Sharon and I Ascended on her couch again that afternoon. The preparations were completed well before the others were expected back; we all went to Ascend and clean up before dinner.

The peculiar sensations had been increasing all afternoon. The humming had grown so intense I could hardly hear others' words; the light burning on and through everything was so brilliant, the boundaries of all objects were simply melting away. I'd feared I was going to be clumsy when we were cleaning, yet had dropped only one vase; it did not break.

This Ascension was quiet. I was tired and fell asleep for a few minutes. When I awoke, Sharon was in her shower. That seemed a good plan; as I stood up to go to my room, I glanced out her windows and saw the hikers returning. There were a dozen mules, carrying the camping equipment; three locals by their garb, guiding them; behind them walked the six Novitiates, all in white. I was surprised to see them -- I had assumed they would all be like Kala, that is, male, Punjabi and Sikh; but there were only two turbaned heads and three of the six were women! And two of these looked Western, as did the third male.

Far back up the mountain, walking arm-in-arm, were the two monks. Nanda was taller by a head; he wore saffron robes and had long white hair and beard. Durga wore white; his jet-black hair was so long it reached practically to the ground, but he was beardless.

As soon as I saw Nanda, the fire filling everything leaped upward in intensity as did the high-pitched sound of OM. The surface boundaries of everything became hard to distinguish. I felt his Awareness reach up and touch mine -- he caressed me with his mind, saw me with it, recognized me, was happy to know I had come and was pleased with everything about me. He did not raise his eyes to the window where I stood, watching him walk by; but I realized from this mental touch that he knew me utterly and approved of me to the depth of my spirit; he was looking forward to working with me as I mastered the Seven Spheres. This was unlike any experience I'd ever had before, this meeting of souls through the monastery walls, but it was perfect and genuine and true. I'd never felt better understood, accepted or loved. *I've just been grokked*, I thought, remembering Heinlein's *Stranger in a Strange Land.*

"That one knows me to the bottom of my toenails," I said to the bare walls as I walked back to my room to change my clothes. "How perfectly bizarre."

We met the other Durga Novitiates at dinner. They seemed a nice enough group, all similar to Kala in intensity, all completely dedicated to their Teacher. Mira sat with Kala and the other two soon-to-be Ishayas: another one of the Sikhs, Kriya, and one of the Western girls, Devi, an American. Kriya and Kala had abandoned their turbans -- they were leaving behind their family heritage to embrace their life vows. I was impressed by the beauty of their jet-black hair, hanging in languid curls half-way down their backs.

Alan was meeting with Durga and Nanda in a private dining room. The other Novitiates were scattered around the table, as were our people: Edg was talking to the other Sikh and the Indian girl; Steve and Aphrodite were sitting with one of their Westerners, a German by his accent. Doctor Dave was sitting across from Sharon and me, and on his left was the last Durga Novitiate -- a short, fiery Southern girl in her twenties named Parvi.

We greeted her warmly; Sharon inquired of their success on their long trek.

"We didn't have much," she replied in a voice as sweet as gardenia blossoms in the moonlight of an August Carolina night. "Durga-ji and Nanda hoped St. John would bless them, but he didn't come. We camped before his cave for three nights, Ascending and waiting. Some of us

thought we detected ethereal light inside the cave, but it was empty --
John was not there, or not visible to our eyes."

"Why is it called the Cave of St. John?" asked Sharon, fascinated by
this new friend.

"Because the entire Apocalypse is engraved on its walls -- in Greek."

"I'd like to see that!" Doctor Dave exclaimed.

"If you stay here long enough, you'll have the chance," she smiled at
him. "Both the monks go up there every few months, at least once in the
spring after the ice melts and once in the fall, before the snow gets too
deep. And often in the summer as well. I personally think they just enjoy
the trek, it's a stunning journey; I don't think they really expect to see
the Apostle there. The histories say John has more often been seen in
other places, rarely at that cave. In fact, as I recall, only twice -- in the
900's and again five hundred years later, in 1470 or something."

"Maybe their trekking up there isn't so strange," said the doctor, "it
sounds like a five hundred year cycle. Maybe he'll show up there again
soon."

"Why are only three of you taking your life vows?" I asked Parvi.
This discussion of John's rare appearances was making me quite
uncomfortable. "Aren't you all equally committed?"

"We're all completely committed," she replied seriously. "We're all
desirous of joining the Order permanently. But Durga feels none are
ready, save only Kriya, Devi, and Kala. I don't know, he may have felt it
only fair, to balance your three with only three of ours... I can't believe
they're gone. It's so awful. I remember how we used to talk, late into the
night, Lila and I. She was my second great inspiration, after Devi. Once,
after I'd just received the Third Cognition, so much was stirred up in me
I thought I wanted to leave Durga-ji. Lila listened to my feelings, all day
and all night, never judged them or condemned them, never tried to
convince me one way or the other. All she said was, 'Only you can know
in your heart what's best for you.'

"I loved her like a sister. And now to hear she's gone -- it seems so
senseless."

"Maybe she was needed elsewhere," I said, remembering Boanerge's
last words to me. As soon as I said that, the intensity of the celestial light

and sound, which had been tapering off since its peak when I saw Nanda coming down the mountain, returned and intensified. The entire room was ablaze with light; the Durga Novitiates and our own people stood out as brighter flames in a sea of fire.

"What's wrong, honey?" asked Sharon, leaning close into me.

I looked at her; the radiance was more brilliant in her than in anyone or anything else. It was almost as if she were the Source of all the unlimited light of the world.

"You are *She!*" I exclaimed.

"Pardon me?" she asked, more concerned.

"Ah... Sharon. No. No, it's OK. I'm just seeing a lot of fire -- in everyone, in you especially. It's kind of intense inside here just now."

"I felt the same way when I met Durga," said Parvi. "I could hardly see, it was so bright everywhere."

"You adjusted finally?" I asked her desperately.

"Oh, it went away after a few weeks -- for me anyway."

"That's encouraging," I said uncertainly.

"How did you happen to meet Durga?" asked Doctor Dave.

"Devi dragged me to India," she laughed at the memory. "We were college roommates, studying nursing in Charlotte. After graduation, she had a strong desire to come to India, meet some saints. She'd read Yogananda's *Autobiography of a Yogi*, had heard of Sai Baba, wanted to find out about enlightenment, if it was real. Durga discovered her in Delhi -- he was there with Kriya on business. Devi has been with him for four years now; she's into the Sixth Sphere; she's left only once, to bring me back with her.

"Did I give her a hard time! I kicked and screamed all the way to Amritsar, thought she'd completely lost it. But as soon as I met Durga, I knew why I'd come; my life was remade in that instant. One look at his face was enough."

"It almost sounds," said Sharon with a touch of a frown, "That you Durga Novitiates are more attached to your Teacher than to the Teaching. Could that be so?"

"Might could? No -- of course we are. Surely y'all are here because of Nanda? Or Alan Lance?"

Sharon looked at me and raised one eyebrow in an exquisite arch, speaking volumes in a single, graceful motion.

"Fascinating," I said, responding equally to her fluid gesture, Parvi's curious information and the supermundane fires burning through everything. The part of my mind still open to rational thought was not surprised by her words. This was one of the final pieces of the puzzle to explain these Durga Novitiates' interpretation of Ascension -- it showed clearly how they were different from us in their thinking, exactly where they had turned a mechanical technique into a personal belief system. With this one misunderstanding, placing the importance of a single person above the value and power of the techniques, it became easy to see how their zealots had crossed the line with Ollie.

There will always be those who prefer devotion to another over the inner search for Truth, I thought, but answered, "Actually, for us, Parvi, not. I like Alan, I think he's going to be a close friend; I'm looking forward to learning a great deal from both the Ishaya monks. But I'm not here -- and I think I can speak for all of us in this -- we're all here to study Ascension, not to follow some Teacher."

"I don't think Lila or Balindra felt that way," she said, looking confused. "Nor did anyone killed at Patmos, come to think of it. They were all perfectly devoted to Alan or Nanda."

"Interesting," I said, noting she may have been right. And that made Boanerge's "they were needed elsewhere," fly to a whole new level of meaning. Thoughts of gardeners pruning vines flashed through me; for an instant I thought I was back on the mountain, sitting before the log; the young peasant was still there, smiling broadly at me. A tragedy that for over a week had seemed senseless glimmered with hidden meaning. If this were correct or not, I had no idea; but it made sense now. With that, my heart relaxed slightly, began to see some hope of good even in death.

27

The New Moon Celebration

The doctor walked with Sharon and me to the Ceremony Hall; I asked him if Alan had told him his new name yet.

"No, I'll find out tonight, after I take my vows. I don't remember ever being more excited!"

He sounded it, but I couldn't help but poke his balloon a little, "Any last minute doubts?" Sharon kicked me, but I wasn't just being obnoxious, I really was curious.

"Actually, not a one. I'm a little surprised myself. I've waited my whole life for this -- now, finally, I've come home. I never felt comfortable with the householder role -- my big house on Clyde Hill always felt about twenty sizes too large. It was always a burden to me, never an enjoyment; it felt as if I were *supposed* to have it, as if it were one of the requirements of the job. I'm sure -- at least tonight! -- what my decision will be next year. I want to devote my life, heart and soul, to St. John's Ascension and to the Ascendant. I know of no better way to serve humanity.

"Underlying my decision to be a doctor was the desire to heal. It got shrouded; so many of the trappings simply fed my ego. People didn't come for healing, they came to pretend to be healed so they could go on with their dreams and their lies. I want to be a true Healer! A Healer of Souls. That's why I'm doing this -- from what I've experienced so far with Ascension, I believe I'm going to become such a person."

"I think you already are," said Sharon. "I think you are a Healer -- and not far beneath the surface, either. I suspect you'll quickly manifest that energy."

"Thank you," he replied warmly. "I hope to -- I think becoming a Novitiate will speed this up for me. I believe genetic recreation is going to be replaced among at least some of humanity by conscious co-creation with God. This is the shortest path I can see to reach that goal."

"Probably it will be," I agreed. "Tell me, if you can, one thing that confuses me."

"Sure, anything."

"How is it Alan Lance makes Novitiates? He's not a monk of the Ishayas. How does that work?"

"Nanda gave him a special job. He's called a 'Novitiator,' I think Mira said. Alan can accept Novitiates into the Ishaya order without himself being a monk. But he doesn't feel qualified to supervise the transition from Novitiates into life-long monks or nuns. That's why we're here now, so Mira can take her life-vows in the presence of Nanda."

"Why do you suppose he hasn't taken any vows himself?" I asked.

"I don't have any idea. Why don't you ask him?"

"I think I will," I replied pensively.

Just then we reached the Ceremony Hall. Even though I had helped create it today, it had a powerful impact. The light of one hundred and eight candles -- Aphrodite and Steve were just lighting the last of them -- gave the cave an aura of mystery. The girls had practically filled it with flowers -- it was like a cascading garden, leading up to the seven levels of the ledge. On each side of the altar were soft chairs for Durga and Nanda; there were five cushions on the highest step for those taking vows tonight. On Nanda's side were six chairs, spread in a semi-circle around his seat; on Durga's side were four chairs for his other Novitiates.

In the exact center of the highest ledge was a huge painting of Isha, Christ, standing in the clouds, wearing white robes. It was the most beautiful painting of Jesus I had ever seen. Whoever painted it was a master of the craft -- and yet it was not oil, it was water-color. It captured the light of the candles in a unique way that made it stand out from the wall, seem to live.

Alan had said a picture of Isha was used whenever Cognition was taught: there was a brief Ceremony of Gratitude in Sanskrit. I had asked him what would happen if someone might be offended by a picture, call it idolatry; he smiled and replied, "Wouldn't matter. If people don't like it, we replace it with a cross or a Star of David, or a single candle flame, or whatever they do feel comfortable with. It's only a symbol, after all."

"And if there are those who are uncomfortable with any symbol at all?" I asked perversely.

"Why then," he chuckled, "we don't use any symbol at all! We strip the altar bare, by our act representing the Ascendant, beyond all forms and qualities. From our side, it makes not the slightest difference. I prefer to use the picture of Isha -- I'm naturally drawn to that representation of Divinity and like to give credit where credit is due. This teaching is from Isha through John, why not acknowledge it plainly?

"But the point is not what the symbol is but what the Teacher and the prospective student are feeling. This Ceremony gently reminds the student this is a big deal, a highly significant event: the five Cognition Techniques are the heart of the first five Spheres. Since that is so, each of them is capable of transforming a life completely. Equally important, the Ceremony helps the Teacher align with Isha when Cognition is taught. I often feel as if He's directing my hands, speaking through me; the entire procedure becomes automatic, refined, beautiful. You're going to love it."

"I hope you're right," I'd said, but wasn't sure.

The celestial light filling everything, which decreased slightly on the walk over here after dinner, started intensifying again as soon as we entered the Ceremony Hall. I sat on the chair farthest from the altar and wondered how one could function in the world when everything was so gloriously beautiful all the time. Sharon settled down gracefully beside me and said, "Everything still burning up?"

"I'll say -- and, speaking of burning up, feel the top of my head!"

"Wow! You really *are* on fire, aren't you? Hey, I'm impressed."

"I hope I'm going to survive this," I mumbled without conviction.

"Don't you worry, darling! I'll protect you from nasty old Exalted Consciousness," she smiled, putting her arm around me.

Aphrodite finished lighting the candles and sat beside Sharon, saying, "Pretty exciting, huh?"

"Sure is," agreed Steve, sitting beside Aphrodite and holding her hand. That seemed like a pretty good idea, so I took Sharon's left hand and tried to hold onto the Universe as she held onto me.

Edg came in with the four Durga Novitiates who were not taking vows; the end of their conversation made me think he'd been arguing with them. He sat next to Steve while they took their places and muttered, "Stubborn fools."

Doctor Dave looked pretty lonely, sitting on his cushion on the top step of the altar all by himself, but just now Mira and Devi and Kala and Kriya came in and sat beside him. All were here now, except only Durga and Nanda and Alan. How long would we have to wait?

Mira, looking at the picture of Isha, said, "I think it would be a good idea if we Ascended while we wait for the Ishayas."

That seemed like the best plan; we all closed our eyes. My Ascension was pretty rough; I didn't seem to go anywhere. Either the food in my stomach or the excitement of the evening was keeping me pretty much on the surface -- and yet, whenever I cracked open my eyes and looked around the room, the intensity of celestial light had not decreased. And the humming of OM was as loud as ever with eyes opened or closed. *The hazards of an evolving soul*, I thought wryly and wondered when or if I would ever feel normal again. Or even again know what normal was.

Durga and Nanda and Alan made their appearance within half an hour. Everyone stood to greet them, saying "Sat Sri Akal" to Durga and "Namaste" to Nanda. They bowed to us in return and took their seats. Up close, Durga looked like he was about twenty-five. He had a strongly muscled body (*Salutes to the Sun?* I wondered); there was not a trace of gray in his incredibly long hair; his skin was smooth, completely unwrinkled. And yet I'd heard he was in his seventies!

Nanda's hair and beard were white, but his skin also looked like that of a baby. He gave me an enormous smile, filled with love, when he walked by me; that had the effect of softening the harshness of the light in everything, transforming it to a dance of pure joy, to the Ascendant's laughing Song, singing through everything, shining equally in all Creation.

Alan turned his chair to face us and said, "I'm pleased to tell you all: Durga and Nanda have reached an agreement. The accidents in Seattle and Patmos have proved a powerful motivation; they have decided we must expand the Teaching of Ascension in a united way. They are going to work together now and are asking us to do the same. For this reason, I'm not returning to Patmos, I'm going to stay here to finish the Seven Spheres. I'm requesting those of you who study with me to stay here as well. And Durga desires his Novitiates to remain here also, not return to Amritsar.

"Their second joint decision is this: the requirement for anyone wishing to teach Ascension is mastery of the first three Spheres and a minimum of six months in-residence training."

"Does this mean *more* householders are going to learn to Ascend?" asked Kala coldly, icily inflecting the word "more."

"Not necessarily. On that point, there has been no final agreement. There hasn't been time; there is a little more I wish to report to them before we come to any other decisions." He glanced at me as he said this; I squirmed in my seat and wished I could go home. "I think it will help if we all sit together and try to reconcile our differences. We all practice the same techniques; we all want the world to be healed. I think we'll find our common ground. Our differences are, after all, small, compared to our similarities. I think if we put our heads together, we'll come up with something."

Edg looked as if he were restraining himself from commenting only with great difficulty. I wondered how such opposed viewpoints could find resolution and was afraid Alan was relying on my vision as the solution. That did not sit well with me; I hoped Boanerge would either pick someone else to visit or Durga and Nanda would simply make up their own minds. They were the experts on Ascension: they had been working with all the Seven Spheres for more than a quarter century. What did I know? Nothing.

Durga stirred and coughed; Alan stopped speaking at once and turned his chair around. With a rather heavy accent, Durga said, "Alan Lance is right. That which stands between us has a hair's breadth, it is hardly visible. There is nothing to it at all, it is so tiny. I have always believed Ascension would one day become available to all in the world; the only questions I've had are, 'Is this the right time?' and, 'Dare we act without John's approval?' So you see, there is no separation between Nanda and me. Never has been. It has never been the case that I or any of the Ishayas throughout history thought Ascension was too good for the world. No. That is a gross misinterpretation of our position. That is a misunderstanding of our policy. We wished only to hold Ascension intact for the human race, until the human race was ready for it. Just as a loving parent saves the best present for the last, we have kept the Supreme Teaching secreted away from the world, lest the children not appreciate it.

"The human race is maturing now, perhaps because there is no longer an alternative. Soon, humanity will be developed enough. Because this is so, I am convinced the Apostle will appear to us again before much longer; it has been nearly a hundred years; our current crisis is, I think, exactly the catalyst to precipitate our Founder back out of the Ascendant."

"I agree," said Nanda, with a softer accent. "If there is any similarity between St. John's past appearances, it has always been when the Ishayas could almost but not quite see the way ahead. I concur with Durga-ji absolutely; we need only wait. And yet we must not wait passively, we must be prepared -- all of you need to be trained to Teach Ascension. I personally believe the call will come quite soon."

"We stand on the threshold of a new era," said Durga. "The day of the New Jerusalem is at hand. Evolution has progressed in discrete, non-continuous leaps since the day the Universe was born. There was nothing; a fraction of a second later -- from nothing! -- came this enormous Cosmos, with its thousand billion galaxies, exploding in the Big Bang, so the physicists have told me."

"Again there was nothing," said Nanda, "no life, only lifeless matter, hydrogen and helium and, in the furnaces of supernovas, heavier atoms forming, but no self-replicating life. And again, somehow, miraculously, from nothing, life sprang. Another non-continuous leap ahead. Self-replicating and eternal, single-celled life was born."

"Once again there was a jump," continued Durga. "One fine spring day, a group of cells got together and said, 'Let's work to-gether!' Multicellular life burst forth into the pages of Eternity. Sex and its handmaiden death were born in that moment. Multicellular life learned to expand its evolutionary potential much more quickly; the price paid was killing off the older generation. This was a radical jump, truly as great as the jump from nothing to a thousand billion galaxies, no less a radical shift than the leap from inert matter to life."

"Think of these jumps!" exclaimed Nanda. "Imagine being nothing, then suddenly becoming something. It is a leap of stupendous proportions. Three times this happened in the long history of our Universe; the stage was again set in preparation for something. But for what? Who could guess? Only the Master Builder. Again Creation leaped ahead -- the human being incarnated on the physical. Now the ability to manipulate matter consciously even on the most surface level was born."

"One more shift in the history of the Universe has there been," said Durga; "this is ongoing even as we speak. It has been foreshadowed throughout history, by every civilization on the Earth. A few in the past have moved into this next, Ascended phase, in which the human aligns so perfectly with the Ascendant, there is no difference between Divinity and humanity. This is the next and last leap matter is going to make and it is coming soon to all the world."

"The Apostle John established our order to help bring about this global shift in consciousness," said Nanda, "What Christ and John accomplished in mastery of death is going to be repeated throughout all of humanity. The life that ends in death, begun when life shifted to multicellular existence, is going to be Ascended; instead of remaining stuck in inherited beliefs and habit patterns, we are going to rise into our destiny as co-creators with God."

"The potential of the human," continued Durga, "is restricted only by false and limiting beliefs. As we Ascend and experience the infinite inside, we learn there are no limits to our lives, no restrictions to our potential, no blocks to our abilities to live and to Heal. This is our destiny; the sooner we master the Seven Spheres, remove all the stress from our nervous systems and become permanently established in Unified Consciousness, the sooner we will be able to fulfill our destiny as World Teachers; the sooner we will be capable of assisting in the Healing of the Earth."

"Whether our part in this is large or small," added Nanda, "is not the point. We have a wonderful Teaching -- in my experience, the most powerful on the Earth. What does matter is this: each of us must master this knowledge. Then, from the platform of Unified Consciousness, our actions will naturally be correct, naturally in tune with the Cosmic Plan. From that level, it will not matter whether we personally choose to teach only the monks and nuns or open ourselves to everyone on the Earth. Nor will it matter whether the whole Earth responds to us, or only a select few.

"From this perspective, Durga and I have no disagreement. If we have seemed to differ, it was all part of the Cosmic Dance and had necessary reasons for each of you to see it. The need for that is ending now; when it has ended completely, you will find -- as do we! -- there is no disagreement between us ever, nor even the potential for disagreement. There is only harmony and co-creation with each other and with God.

"Enough for now. Durga and I are going to meet with you every evening, after dinner. We want you to spend most of your daytime hours Ascending. For the first week or so, also come together every afternoon, all of you, and talk through your differences. We would like to see you reconciled within a fortnight.

"Those of you who are new will also need to learn the Sun Salutations and the other exercises we recommend between Ascensions. Perhaps Alan and Devi could teach you tomorrow morning, say at eleven? Good. So, Durga, are we ready to begin?"

"Indeed, Nanda, we are."

"Very good!" He stood; we all followed his example. Everyone turned to face the painting of Isha. "Speak your vows," Nanda said to the doctor.

Dave cleared his throat and said, "Lord Isha, Christ, I pledge myself to your service. To honor this pledge, I vow for the next year to observe: non-violence, non-stealing, truthfulness, celibacy, and non-grasping." Alan leaned toward him and whispered his new name in his ear. The doctor looked surprised but then immediately pleased.

The four others, one by one, proclaimed their intent to follow the ten Ishaya vows for the rest of their lives; when they finished, Durga said, "Now we sing." Everyone who knew the words (which was everyone but the doctor, Sharon and me) sang the Ceremony of Thanksgiving. Alan was right, it *was* a beautiful song. For the second time in two days, music brought tears to my eyes. Had John written this too?

After the ceremony, Alan said, "Everyone! Allow me to introduce to you: Mira Ishaya, Devi Ishaya, Kala Ishaya and Kriya Ishaya. And our newest Novitiate, Deva." The five, flushed, excited, turned toward us and bowed; we all bowed back to them.

"And now for the Teaching," said Nanda. "One at a time, come here to me or to Durga; we will give you your next tool."

The instructions went quickly, hardly five minutes for each. As the others walked forward, received their next technique, then returned to their seats to Ascend, Sharon and I held each other's hands and wondered if it would be all right to go up together. Aphrodite and Steve did not -- but then, they were receiving different techniques.

"What should we do?" I whispered to her.

She shrugged and replied, "Don't know. I want to learn it with you, though, I know that much. Guess I'll ask him."

But the decision was made for us: Nanda motioned for us to come up together. We sat beside him on the floor as he smiled deeply at us. He had the warmest brown eyes I had ever seen: completely clear, flawless; a perfect complement to Sharon's deep azures.

"I'm so glad you've come," he said quietly to us. "You are great hopes for the world. With two such as you, I feel confident the next generation will be in good hands. It is often the case, the four-footed move more quickly on the journey than those with only two. Congratulations and blessings on your togetherness... Do you have any questions about Ascension?"

Sharon did not, but I wanted to know about my current sensations and said, "All day I've been experiencing an intense light on or about everything and a loud humming sound."

"Yes? This is good. Are they steady?"

"They come and they go. It feels as if the Ascendant is trying to burn through everything, like everything I've ever seen or known is only an eggshell; Reality is about to break out from the inside."

"Well said! Growth of consciousness, radical leaps ahead, are like birth experiences. It can be painful, but does not have to be. Talk about this more tomorrow evening, all right?"

"All right."

"Good... So, the First Cognition Technique is designed to hold the awareness in the Ascendant, it is not designed to take you to the Ascendant. Therefore the Ascension Attitudes need to be done first, at least a little.

"There are three different ways you can use this Cognition Technique. You can use it after you've used all the first three Ascension Attitudes, that is, at the end of your Ascension, for ten minutes or so. Or, you can use Cognition after each of the techniques -- after you've completed a block on Praise, do five minutes or so of Cognition; after Gratitude, five minutes of Cognition; after Love, five minutes of Cognition. Like that."

"I find all three alternate rapidly for me," I commented. "I rarely stay a long time on each Attitude."

"That's fine. So for you, the third way will probably be the best: use Cognition after each repetition of each of the Attitudes. Praise Attitude, Cognition; Praise Attitude, Cognition; Praise Attitude, Cognition. Then Gratitude, Cognition; Gratitude, Cognition; Gratitude, Cognition. Then Love, Cognition; Love, Cognition; Love, Cognition. Like that. Feel free to experiment with these three ways. One or the other will settle in quickly for you as your preferred method.

"Now, the First Cognition technique has three parts -- a part in the old, pre-verbal language, a part in English, and a direction to move the awareness. The part in the old language is... " He told us the first two parts and added, "When you think these two together, I want you to put your awareness just here." He gestured with his hand to a particular space.

"I'm not sure what putting my awareness there means," I said.

"It means your attention. If I say, 'Think of your big toe,' your attention, your awareness naturally goes to your big toe. There is nothing complicated or difficult about it. So, with this First Cognition Technique, when you effortlessly Ascend with it, let your attention drift to that area."

"And if it doesn't go there effortlessly?" asked Sharon.

"Then don't force it! Let it slip as far as it will go easily -- while remembering the ideal location."

"Why exactly there?" I asked.

"With the first two Attitudes, we are learning to Ascend, or rise beyond, our old way of thinking, and discover the Ascendant hiding inside. This causes energy to rise upwards. The third Ascension Attitude opens us to the energy descending down, as it were, from the Ascendant itself. We don't want either of these movements to get bottled up! The First Cognition Technique is designed to allow the energy to continue on through us, to connect us with the rest of humanity. This is the essence of true compassion."

"May I say this?" asked Sharon. "Put it in my own words? The First Ascension Attitude heals our subjective stress, it re-aligns our life with Universality and establishes for all time the best activity for the human in relationship with the Ascendant. This is an upward spiral. The Second Ascension Attitude extends this to everything in the world. All of Creation Ascends into the Divine Presence with Gratitude. The Third Attitude gently reminds us the Ascendant also has a personal interest in each of us -- without each and every one of us, the Ascendant is as if incomplete. Then with Cognition, we give our energy back to the world. We give away our Praise, we give away our Gratitude, we give away our Love -- back to those who need it. Correct?"

"Exactly correct," agreed Nanda warmly. "This technique allows us to pass the Ascending energy through us into the rest of Creation. It doesn't get stuck anywhere; it doesn't get blocked or locked up anywhere. And the more we give it away, the more we have of it. Love is magical. It increases as it is given away. That is the soul of compassion.

"So, now, go and Ascend with all your first four techniques. I think you'll find a new level of experience opening up very quickly."

We thanked him and half-bowed; he laughed gently and gave us two red roses from the vase at his left hand.

The room was by now still -- everyone was deep in Ascension. We tiptoed back to our chairs and closed our eyes.

The triple fiber of Ascension led me gently and quickly upward. With little transition, I found myself again floating in space. The stars were all around me, through me, part of me. I gently introduced the Cognition Technique; instantly the Earth appeared before me.

As I alternated the Ascension Attitudes with the Cognition Technique, I felt a rush of energy and light moving up and through me with Praise, expanding outward with Gratitude, returning down through me from above with Love, then outward with Cognition. The last movement flowed into the Earth floating before me, spreading light and hope and joy and love to all the humans and all the creatures of our beautiful azure sphere.

The celestial being I had seen while I was Ascending in the garden in Amritsar gradually materialized beside me -- he had the exact appearance of Christ from the painting in the Cave! He smiled at me and said, "You are learning, my son. Well done."

He raised his right hand in blessing, then floated toward me and into me; at once I was again sitting before the peasant Boanerge on the log where he was playing his flute. He took it from his lips, smiled at me and said, "So, do you see what's been happening on the Earth? It could easily have been destroyed: human beings come into technology so painfully. Seventeen of us saw this potential for annihilation some five thousand years ago and have been working to change that which seemed inevitable, to divorce humanity from competition and savagery so the underlying Love and Light could be revealed and resume their rightful place.

"It all goes in stages, you see. And each stage takes about a thousand years. All of the great leaders, Krishna, Buddha, Shankara, Mohammed, they were all of the seventeen of us, of Christ and his Teacher, the Baptist John, who was Elijah before and Moses before that. We've all worked very hard with a stubborn people, our human race.

"Two thousand years ago in the West, we broke through the veil. Punched it out completely. Love re-entered the Earth fully for the first time in more than three thousand years. Starting with the smallest handful of dedicated workers, we expanded the breach, forced chaos into form, isolated and imprisoned the destructive tendencies of humanity into ever more rigid boundaries. This forced, after a thousand years, the dominion of the anti-Christ. His reign began the year the Pope excommunicated the Patriarch and the Patriarch the Pope. Christ's Church was fragmented; this split has been continuing and accelerating for a thousand years. You have to draw the arrow back for it to fly ahead, you see?

"I saw this coming, this war between selfishness and Love, saw it as soon as I met Paul; we all did; therefore I established the Ishaya Order for this moment in history, for the dawn of the next millennium. Do you understand? Now begins the new and final cycle, the new Heaven, the new Earth, the new Jerusalem; all flesh shall be raised incorruptible, humans will no more die, there will be a global Ascension. What I have done, all can do. There is no more death when you discover you created death yourself by your belief in separation and isolation."

"Why me?" I choked.

He laughed and replied, "You and the others long ago chose yourselves to help bring this about. Now will the spirit quicken; the first Adam was born of the dust of the Earth, but now are we born of spirit -- in the image and likeness of God, co-creators of Immortality and Heaven on Earth. The entire human race is going to rise on Chariots of Fire into the Heart of God.

"I'll stop by and see you and the others from time-to-time, check up on your progress with my Seven Thunders. Tell Nanda and Durga they should continue as they are, they need to work together always now. Combined, they make one pretty good Maharishi. Maharishi Durgananda Ishaya," he chuckled. "Yes, I like that. And tell the others, it's all going to work out OK, particularly tell Edg and Kala, they worry so much. And Sharon -- just love her. She is greater than you've even begun to dream.

"And tell all the others of the Earth, all the good and sincere people of all nations, Ascension is *real*, Praise and Gratitude and Love and Compassion are the four feet of the First Thunder, the four syllables of the first Word of God. Ask them to experience

Ascension for themselves, then learn to share the knowledge of these four with everyone they know, with everyone who is ready for them. A new Sun will dawn for those who flow with these four in each and every moment; these are the master keys to unlock all the mysteries of Creation. To those who can board the swiftly-moving ship of Ascension, they will be carried into the full glory of Heaven. We will rejoice together again under the new Sun of love and manifest splendor.

Tell them -- the future will be beyond imagining in glory and wonder. Ask each of them to do what he or she can to share this information. Never underestimate the importance of this Teaching; never miss an opportunity to help spread it. Tell them! Tell them all!"

He reached forward and struck me on the chest again; I expanded upward and outward, beyond the Universe, beyond the Ocean of Universes, into the infinite, Eternal Presence of the One Unchanging. Meaning fell away, time fell away, all separation was gone forever. As I stood in the Ascendant and knew it, I understood to the furthest reaches of my being one thing more -- Boanerge was right -- *and* it was going to be glorious.

> *"Never doubt that a small group of thoughtful,*
> *committed citizens can change the world.*
> *Indeed, it's the only thing that ever has."*
> *-- Margaret Mead*

Dedicated on Maha Shivaratri, 1995
-- MSI

The history of the Seven Spheres will continue in

Second Thunder
Seeking the Black Ishayas

Afterword

Some names and events of *First Thunder* have been changed and compressed. This was done to protect the location of the Ishayas, and to enable those who prefer to believe this book is just a novel to be able to do so easily.

Ollie (whose last name is not Swenson) is alive and well. He is happily married to a beautiful and brilliant girl I introduced him to and has four lovely children.

Lila and the others did not die in Greece; there was no explosion in Skala Harbor.

The Ishaya monastery is not in the Kulu Valley.

None of the Ishayas died in the war between India and Pakistan. All one hundred and eight of them live in perfect peace in the secluded valley where the Ishayas have for nearly two thousand years kept Christ's original Teachings alive.

The Opposition is real and exists inside every human heart as the voice for fear, doubt, anger, greed, hatred and the ego. Those who actively serve the Opposition in this world promote these; their typical perception of life is, "We alone are right; all else are wrong." They have murdered throughout history to defend their beliefs, but their ability to continue doing so is ending.

Jai Isham Ishvaram

-- MSI